TRIAD deals in every form of vice and obeys no law except its own. It is invisible, and completely invincible, because whoever can't be bought, can be killed.

FROM PEKING TO PARIS
TRIAD
IS THE WORLD'S DEADLIEST
SYNDICATE.

Clive Hunter is the man bred from birth to inherit Triad's mantle of evil . . .

Diana Hunter is the beautiful socialite swathed in money and pleasure . . .

Macdonald is the only man on earth who knows their secret . . .

All three are part of
THE TRIAD CONSPIRACY
THE SPELLBINDING NEW SHOCKER
BY ALISTAIR McCOLL MacKAY

THE
TRIAD
CONSPIRACY

Alistair McColl MacKay

BANTAM BOOKS · TORONTO · NEW YORK · LONDON

THE TRIAD CONSPIRACY
A Bantam Book / January 1978

ISBN 0–553–11036–5

Published simultaneously in the United States and Canada

Bantam Books are published by Bantam Books, Inc. Its trade-
mark, consisting of the words "Bantam Books" and the por-
trayal of a bantam, is registered in the United States Patent
Office and in other countries. Marca Registrada. Bantam
Books, Inc., 666 Fifth Avenue, New York, New York 10019.

PRINTED IN THE UNITED STATES OF AMERICA

To Betty, who believed it would fly
and Judie, who got it off the ground . . .

999

After drinking the red flower-wine you will
        live for ninety-nine years,

When nine is added to this number you will
        live for one hundred and eight years.

Yenan
Shensi Province
China—1945

In 1935, in Yenan, Mao's epic 5,000-mile Long March ended. Of the thousands who had left South China with him, only one person in five had survived. The straggling column had passed through twelve provinces, crossed eighteen mountain ranges and twenty-four rivers, fought ten armies of local warlords, and had engaged in constant rearguard actions against pursuing government forces. Some 20,000 arrived at the mountain fastness, where safe dwellings were created from converted hillside caves.

Events proved Mao's choice of Yenan wise. When on July 7, 1937 the Japanese used the incident at Marco Polo bridge outside Peking as an excuse to declare war, the Chinese Communist party was well established in its new headquarters. Yenan, accessible only by air or a tortuous six-day journey on horseback, defied Japanese attempts at invasion as easily as it had the efforts of Chiang Kai-shek.

Here, in Yenan, the new China began.

Secured by brackets, oil lamps threw pools of light on rough cavern walls, but the vaulted ceiling was in shadow. Other lamps, spaced at intervals on the black lacquered surface, clearly illuminated the long table. The chair at the head of the table was unoccupied, though in the nine others—four on either side and one at the foot—men dressed in cotton robes and headdresses sat in contemplative silence. From their attire and bearing they might well have belonged to a religious sect. Indeed, the robes the men wore derived from those of Buddhist monks; yet the embroidered insignia on the shoulders and the spiderweb formation worked into the cloth above the waist had no meaning to the followers of Buddha. No student, searching ancient Buddhist records, would ever relate the cere-

1

monial robes of this assembly to the *Buddha-Dhamma,*
the teachings of Buddha.

Before each man lay a sheaf of virgin paper and a
newly filled pen. Three carafes of water with attendant
glasses and six spotless ashtrays were placed in a pattern whose symmetry suggested extreme discipline.
Each of the nine men wore a peaceful expression, and
though none conversed with his neighbors, all nine
appeared to be at ease with one another. Though deep
in the hillside, the cave was dry and comfortably warm,
and a faint aroma of incense perfumed the air with
spices and gums.

A slight draft caused the light from the wall lamps
to dance and was a signal for the nine men to rise
and face the vacant chair. The stout entrance door
closed soundlessly, the guttering flames steadied, and a
man, dressed like the others but with a different cen-
terpiece on the spiderweb embroidery, proceeded to
the head of the table. He stopped when he reached
the empty chair, took up a position on its right facing
the table, and placed his left hand on his chest. His
palm touched the robe, the thumb was raised, and
the index finger and the third finger were folded inward. All nine men acknowledged this salute by placing their left hands, thumb and little finger proud, and
the three other fingers folded, just above the embroidered web pattern on their robes.

The Leader inclined his head to the men on his left
and right, bowed deeply to the Incense Master on his
immediate right, and even more deeply still to the
Deputy Leader at the far end of the table. The nine returned a bow and the Leader assumed his place in the
chair at the head of the table. Seven men bowed as one
to the Deputy Leader and the Incense Master and
when these two were seated the others also sat.

The Leader was in no hurry to open the meeting.
Dark eyes subjected each member of the council to
prolonged appraisal. He placed his elbows carefully
on the table and laced his fingers so that the thumbs
supported his chin. Eyes closed, the fingers formed a
steeple and many moments passed as he sat in this
attitude of prayer. At length he sat upright. A slight
smile showed at the edges of his mouth as he picked up

the pen in front of him and tapped the blunt end of it lightly on the sheaf of paper. All eyes fixed on him as he said, "Welcome!"

The word acted as a sign to the others. They exchanged greetings, lit cigarettes, and the austere atmosphere of the chamber was broken by the hum of conversation. By custom the Leader did not join with the others and, similarly, the Deputy Leader and the Incense Master exchanged greetings but did not converse. After a few moments, the Leader brought the meeting to order with a second tap of his pen, and then began his address. His voice was soft, but absolute in authority. "Time, in itself, has little threat to an organization like ours. Already we have centuries of tradition behind us, and the structure of the organization assures its continuation. No power on earth is strong enough to interfere with our activities. As Leader it is my responsibility to ensure that our place in the world is maintained and that we prosper. And at the appropriate time it will be my sacred duty to appoint my successor." He paused and his eyes dwelt for a moment on the Deputy Leader, "If I die before a new Leader is appointed, our worthy Deputy will assume regency until my eldest son is capable of taking my place. In the event my son proves to be unworthy, you are aware of the procedure for electing a new Leader." He leaned forward and emphasized his next words by pounding the table with the flat of his palm. "The Society is larger than any one man. The Society must be the first consideration in the actions of all its members."

Though the nine nodded agreement as custom demanded, each waited to hear why the Leader had chosen to commence his address by reminding them of a procedure that they were all sworn to uphold. Each had chosen to devote his life to the Society and each had sworn categorical loyalty to the Leader. Any member who deviated from his oath would die. However, none feared death itself. It was the unimaginable agony of torture before death that none wished to experience as the price of failure or betrayal. Such was the code of Triad.

The Leader, upright in his chair but with hands

folded in a relaxed manner in front of him, resumed, "We have reached a significant point in the history of the world and a crucial point in the future of the Society. The war that has involved most of the nations of the world is over. Though it has been a very profitable war for the Society, there has been, nevertheless, a disruptive effect on the organization. I have conferred with each of you privately and sought your opinions in areas in which you are qualified. I have considered these opinions carefully and added the opinions of others who are on the Inner Council. I have reached several conclusions and come to some hard decisions. The most important of these decisions will seem strange for it will appear to contradict the first principle of the Society." He paused, then said, "I propose to enlist a Caucasian and by degrees raise him in the Society until he ultimately becomes a member of this very council."

A ripple of reaction came from around the table, but discipline was so great that no one uttered a complete sentence. The Leader raised his hand, then said, "Under normal circumstances, I would expect absolute acceptance of my decision and would offer no explanation. This decision is, however, without parallel, and I propose to explain why I have decided to break our oldest tradition." He again placed both elbows on the table and laced his fingers.

"Success of military operations is governed by espionage. Our race, like the Japanese, is at a disadvantage in the West because of our so-called 'Oriental' features. We are forced, for this reason, to rely on intelligence supplied by traitors in the camps of our opponents. Yet if a man betrays his own country and race, how can we rely on his loyalty to us? How much better to have intelligence supplied by men who are dedicated to our own cause! We of the Triad Society are fortunate in that all of our members are dedicated to the cause. How many times will a man pray for death if we suspect him of even harboring a thought of betraying our Society?" A hard smile played around his mouth and his eyes glinted as they searched those of his audience. They knew of the penalties imposed on the rare occasion that greed overcame loyalty. Betrayal was beyond price, and the higher the rank of the traitor the more terrible the agonies that preceded death. Theirs—the highest rank of all—had never included a traitor.

The Leader gestured toward one of the water carafes, and the man on his left poured a glassful and placed it before him. He sipped slowly, then proceeded, "As a result of the war the balance of world power will shift significantly. The British empire will dissolve, and the United States of America will assume the role Britain formerly played. Russia will take advantage of the disruption in Europe to gain power over the nations of Eastern Europe. The Western Allies will ensure that Germany no longer presents a military threat to them. However, in the long run, Germany must emerge as an economic threat to all major powers. France will lose her empire and will become a minor power. Japan will devote the same energy to peacetime production as she did to weapons of war, and, with American help, will remain a powerful force in world events." He took another sip of water. "The activities of the Triad Society will be governed by these conclusions and we will exert pressures where necessary to ensure that power is distributed as I have outlined. As for our own country, Chiang Kai-shek will be unable to prevent the Communists from establishing a government. Our activities will support Mao Tse-tung and, in exchange, we will be in a position to maintain our power here in China."

The Leader noted that from time to time one or another of the men nodded agreement as a specific point was made. Though nothing could change his decisions, he preferred they implement them with conviction rather than from blind adherence. "Our branches in the Far East have been disrupted but the work of reorganizing is well advanced. Singapore and Hong Kong will continue as the principal centers for our activities. For the reasons I have stated, Japan will grow into an important profit center. We must, therefore, strengthen our position in Japan and use the facilities we gain there for further penetration of America and Australia. We can rely on the Middle East as sources of supply for drugs, but the revenue from that

5

part of the world is unlikely ever to reach a significant level. As you are aware, we have met with the Mafia and the *Union Corse* and agreements for spheres of operation have been amended. Each will respect the activities of the others, but the change in balance of world power will affect these spheres of operation. *Union Corse* will continue to regard France as their exclusive territory, but after the French colonies gain independence, these areas may prove less lucrative to them than in former times. The Corsicans must therefore be permitted to extend their sphere. The *Unione Siciliano* will naturally have Italy and exclusive rights in the areas they controlled before the war. In the United States, the Cosa Nostra will continue to have exclusive rights to their traditional activities but will accept our right to further Triad interests in the traffic of drugs. We will, of course, take preventive measures against the possibility of either the Mafia or *Union Corse* invading Triad international interests."

He allowed the nine a moment to contemplate. Warfare between the three most powerful criminal elements in the world was unlikely but the possibility could not be disregarded. At various levels, "families" within the organizations might choose to squabble, but the all-powerful ruling bodies had met and agreed that each organization would ensure that these disputes were quickly and effectively settled. The Leader went on, "It is in the United States, Great Britain, and Europe generally that we are restricted because of our racial characteristics. My decision that a Caucasian will join us in the Inner Council will ensure that we can protect our international interests. We will, in fact, recruit ten Caucasians."

All but the Deputy Leader were shocked at the Leader's bombshell. One non-Chinese in the higher echelons of the Triad Society was an extraordinary departure from tradition. The possibility of ten was quite impossible to imagine.

The Leader moved quickly to put an end to their anxiety. "Ten is the number," he repeated. He glanced quickly around the assembly in search of challenge, then continued, "As always, we of the Triad Society maximize opportunities for success and minimize risk of failure. By recruiting ten for this important position, we will find the right man. Of the remaining nine, some will be integrated where they prove appropriate. The others"—he paused—"will be attended to."

His words dispelled the last vestiges of tension. Everyone at the table had absolute trust in the Leader's abilities. He had demonstrated these qualities with as much intelligence, efficiency, and ruthlessness as any Leader in a long history of absolute rule.

And so it was in keeping that the Leader deliberately allowed several minutes to elapse before continuing. It was a period of censure, a time for self-examination and recovery of "face." At length he bowed deeply in a manner that embraced the entire group after which he accepted a bow in return from each in order of rank.

Custom observed, the Leader resumed, "The Recruiting Officer will of course discharge this responsibility. He will search for twenty-five male children with a Chinese mother and a Caucasian father. After the recent war this will present no difficulty. These children will be about four years of age and each will be allocated a "guardian." When the time comes, all of the children will be educated either in England or the United States. Of the twenty-five, we will select ten whose features are Caucasian. These ten will, to all intents and purposes, be "orphans." They will be educated to university level without knowledge of their origins. At the proper time they will be advised of their obligations and responsibilities to us. When the education of the ten has been completed, they will be initiated into the Society. Some will be American citizens and the remainder British. We will be in a very strong position at that time to assess the potential of our recruits." He poured more water and sipped slowly from his glass. "These seedlings will not bear fruit before the year 1971, but after that, we will have a number of men capable of assuming their places in the Triad leadership."

7

I
Hong Kong
1967

1

It had been a long, hard day but a rewarding one. Inspector James Maxwell of the Hong Kong police was conscious of the wide patches of perspiration beneath the arms and on the back of his uniform jacket. He was looking forward to standing under the shower for a long time when he got home.

He reread for the third time the report he had written. Not that he could change one word of the precise record of facts it contained. Observe, analyze, put it in writing. No opinions and certainly no suggestions on paper. Present the facts and pass them upward. Decision, in this instance, would be made by his superior officer. Maxwell threw the pen he was holding on to the desk; there could be only one decision. All his painstaking efforts of the past weeks were set forth in the short police-style sentences, but the real action to come would be denied him. Though he seldom used the word "unfair"—since he knew the only guarantee in this world was that nobody got out alive—still it sure as hell was unfair that he had to pass on the information he had just dug up rather than act on it.

Unfolding the map, he stared at the colored lines that defined areas of jurisdiction. Two blocks—a mere hundred yards or so—and he could have gone ahead with a raid. Failure to report to his superior would be frowned on, but he could have used the excuse that time did not allow. The success of the raid would make his failure to report irrelevant, for the higher-ups would overlook it and so his immediate superior would have to live with it. The first time in three years he had come up with something big, and there was no way he could take advantage of it.

8

Disgustedly, he shoved the chair away from the desk and rose to his feet. He folded up the map and stuffed it into one of the pockets of his jacket. He carefully locked the top copy of the report in the desk drawer and placed the other two copies in his pocket with the map. His next step was to try to work something out with Frank Towers.

Outside, the shadows had lengthened, and it had become much cooler. Soon the tropic night would fall, and more subtle sounds and smells would replace the bustle and street-cries of the hawkers. Maxwell drove home through the crowded streets with one hand almost constantly pressed on the horn. Not that it really mattered; Hong Kong's inhabitants were maddeningly casual in the face of his blaring horn.

Maxwell parked his car in a space beneath his apartment building and climbed the stairs to the flat he shared with Frank Towers. It was an arrangement that suited both men. Each had a separate bedroom and they shared the rest. Splitting the costs meant that they could both enjoy a standard of living neither could afford alone. When Maxwell entered, he found Towers stretched out on the living-room sofa. The other man was wearing a Chinese silk robe and had a drink in his hand. He glanced up at Maxwell and said with a grin, "I'm impressed by your dedication, but I have to tell you it's a waste. I've been home for the past two hours."

Maxwell threw his cap and belt on a chair and began peeling off his soiled jacket. Without a word of greeting, he poured himself a drink and took a long pull from it. "I have news that might just change your attitude toward overtime."

"Balls!" Towers snorted, "If Her Majesty's police would pay me for my overtime, I'd be happy to give up my salary. I've lost count of the extra hours I've put in this month."

Maxwell flopped in a chair, "Don't feel bad, you might just get to be a hero. Underpaid and overworked . . . but a hero. Might even get a gold star toward promotion."

"What the hell are you talking about?" Towers drained his glass and refilled it.

Maxwell extended his own now-empty glass, "Fill that up again and I'll explain in simple one-syllable words." After the other man finished pouring, he went on, "As you know, I've been following up on a large consignment of drugs that were landed from mainland China last Tuesday."

"Jesus!" Towers returned to his former position on the sofa, "I told you to drop it. The tip was shit. You looked like a fool after you searched the boat and all the cargo was legit. . . ."

"The bloody stuff was there!" Maxwell broke in. "It was there all the time and I didn't find it!"

"Clever, the Chinese." Towers's voice took on a singsong intonation, "You lookee . . . no findee . . . look like prickee!"

"The bastards had it in the cases of peaches." Maxwell spat out the words. "Middle layer of cans in each case were dummies!"

"But you checked the cases, surely?"

"Of course I did—but the top cases were genuine. I checked out a few random cases after that but tested only top and bottom cans. Live and bloody-well learn!" Maxwell got to his feet and paced the room, "Seven hundred and fifty cases of fucking peaches! I was busy checking out the rest of the cargo. Figure it out for yourself." He stopped pacing and his voice rose as he said, "Let's say fifty cases were genuine—that leaves 700. Forty-eight cans to the case—sixteen of these are filled with dope. Seven hundred by sixteen equals 11,200, and each can holds a pound of dope." He threw his hands up in disgust, "Jesus Christ! That's more than five tons of the stuff!" His voice broke with emotion, "Five tons of the bloody stuff and I'm standing looking at it! Inspector Maxwell strikes again!"

Towers turned to face Maxwell. "It was tough luck. You got the tip-off and you checked out the cargo. It could happen to anyone."

"Just my luck!" Maxwell said. "Three years here, and at last a break. After pissing around with the routine stuff, I get a tip for the biggie and I blow it. The slant-eyed bastards must have laughed their cocks off." His voice took a new note, "But I'm going to laugh longer—I know where the stuff is now."

"You're kidding!" Towers almost spilled his drink in excitement.

"Kidding, hell! I know exactly where it is and where it has been for the past two days." Maxwell refilled his glass. "Same source that told me about the consignment told me how they got it and where it was delivered."

"Fantastic! Did you make the raid?"

"No." Maxwell eyed him steadily for a moment. "I didn't make the raid because it's outside my jurisdiction. The place where they are holding the stuff is in your area."

"Jesus!" Towers exclaimed, jumping to his feet, "Have you reported it? Whereabouts on my patch is it? Is Watson setting up a raid?"

"Hold it—one question at a time." Maxwell paused, "I made out a report—but I haven't filed it. To be honest with you, I almost decided to ignore the boundary and make the raid myself." His voice was bitter, "I love you dearly, but so-help-me, I grudge giving you a present of this one."

"Don't feel bad—I'd feel the same if our situations were reversed."

Maxwell looked at his friend for a few moments. "So," he said, "how would you like to make a joint effort of it?"

Towers's reaction was instantaneous, "Fine by me— it's your party, after all. What do you suggest?"

"First I get a shower and change of clothes. We go to see Watson at home—you call him while I get ready. We'll go to the office on the way to Watson's place so I can pick up the top copy of the report. I doubt if he'll do anything about it tonight, but no reason why we can't get everything tied up for the raid first thing in the morning."

"Earlier the better," Towers said. "Have you got somebody watching the place?"

"No," Maxwell shook his head. "No way we could keep a watch there without blowing it. You know what it's like in that quarter. A white face, and everyone shies off. Where do I find a Chinese I can trust to watch without passing on the good word to the Triad?"

Towers lit a cigarette as he asked, "Which particular

11

quarter are we talking about? Let's have a few details."

"Sorry." Maxwell retrieved his jacket and took the papers and map from the pocket, "shows how I hate to part with this one." He handed them to Towers. "You'll find all the details in the report, and I've ringed the location on the map. Read these and phone Watson while I get ready."

2

If Superintendent Watson was annoyed at the incursion on his off-duty time, his affable manner belied it when he greeted the two younger men. He served them drinks and joined in their small talk with Mrs. Watson before getting down to the reason for the visit. His wife, versed in the ways of the police service, excused herself when the conversation changed to matters that did not concern her. The superintendent took a long time filling and lighting his pipe. "Well now, what is so urgent that it can't wait until morning?"

Maxwell started to quickly outline the situation but after a few sentences, his superior interrupted, "Hold on, lad, let's observe procedure. Let's have your report." His eyebrows came together to form one line. "You do have a proper report all filled out, don't you?"

"Of course." Watson's sergeant-major attitude always infuriated Maxwell, but he controlled himself, "Just wanted to give you the outline first, sir."

"No need, lad." Watson took the proffered papers, "If the report's been filled out properly, all the information should be there." He puffed vigorously on his pipe, "Time for talk when I'm acquainted with all the facts." He opened up the report and began reading.

The two younger men exchanged amused glances while Watson had his eyes fixed on the typewritten pages, but they were careful to appear attentive when he finished and looked up at them.

Watson unfolded the map and examined it briefly before placing it on the floor at the side of his chair. He looked at both young men, then addressed Maxwell,

"Good report, got all the facts." He removed the pipe from his mouth, "Well, nearly all the facts. Who is your informer?"

Maxwell hesitated, "I'd prefer to keep that to myself, sir. I promised the man."

"Don't be daft, lad. We all belong to the same police force." Watson chuckled, "I've known more informers in my time than you've had hot dinners."

"I know that, sir, but I promised the man." Maxwell's tone was dogged.

"Promise, my arse!" The superintendent jabbed his pipe at the younger man. "I'm asking you for the last time—or do I have to make it an order?"

There was no option. He could invent a name, but Watson would check it out anyway. Maxwell, tight-lipped, said, "Hup Wah Kee—he has a clothing shop at Temple Pavement."

"Good," Watson smiled. "Now why would he tell you about the consignment coming into Hong Kong —even more important, why would he tell you where the stuff is when you blew the ship raid?"

Maxwell squirmed inwardly; he could have spat in his superior's eye. Instead, he shrugged, "He owed me a couple of favors. Is it all that important, sir?"

Surprisingly, Watson shook his head and smiled again, "No, I don't have to know everything, lad. If you say he's reliable, I'll take your word for it." His smile widened as he went on, "I suppose he is afraid of the Triad."

"Exactly, sir." Maxwell's voice was deadly serious, "They would kill him for sure—if not all his family!"

The older man glared at him as he said, "You and your bloody Triad! You have a bloody phobia about them!" He turned to Towers, "Has he got you on that kick as well?" Not waiting for a reply, he said to Maxwell, "Talk about Reds under the bed! Every time you give a parking ticket it's the bloody Triad! I've been on this police force for twenty years, lad. Twenty years of dealing with the Chinese and I'm *telling* you that most of the crime in this place is committed by gangs. Call them 'tongs'—or anything else you bloody well like—but they *are* gangs!" He rose to his feet and moved a few paces. "The Triad thing is a myth. It's a bogeyman thing that springs from the old days. We have more than our share of villains in Hong Kong and Kowloon but most of them are small-time crooks scraping a living. There *are* gangs and they *have* their own territories but that is the end of it. All this bloody nonsense about a central organization is just that—sheer bloody nonsense!" He resumed his seat, "Now, let's get on with this thing but we'll treat it as a gang operation."

Maxwell had kept silent during Watson's lecture. Now he said, "We are talking about five *tons* of drugs, if my calculations are correct. That's a fortune. I find it hard to believe that just a gang could organize a haul on that scale."

The superintendent shook his head sadly, and when he spoke it was in the manner of a schoolteacher to a backward pupil. "I grant you it is probably the largest quantity of drugs we have had a chance to nail in years. But take an old hand's word for it, son. The people behind it are probably a group of 'respectable' merchants. They put up the money and recruit some gang or other to actually bring the stuff in and distribute it. It *is* a big operation, and for that reason I'm going to take charge of it personally." Maxwell started to speak, but Watson held up his hand. "You've done a creditable job of police work, Maxwell. You've reported to me, and that is the proper procedure. Now the proper procedure is for me to fill out a report and pass it up. As to our course of action, it is my decision that we raid the warehouse first thing in the morning. No point in stumbling about in the dark." He applied a match to his pipe, then puffed experimentally until he was satisfied it was lit. "As for the glory, there'll be enough for everybody if the raid is successful. Not that I, personally, give a damn for any glory. Six more months and I'll be on my way home for good. All I'm interested in is getting a little place in the country and enjoying the pension I've sweated my guts out for in this bloody place for the best part of twenty years."

Towers, who so far hadn't spoken, looked at Maxwell, then said to his superior, "Maxwell and I will be involved though?"

"Of course you will!" Watson knelt down on the floor and spread the map, "Each of you will clock-in in the morning as usual. You will take ten men each and approach the warehouse from different directions. I'll come in with a further ten men from here." He indicated a road on the map, "This will bring me in at the front of the building." He pointed to another road, "You, Towers, will arrive by this route and cover the back of the place. Maxwell will join me at the front. He and I will burst straight in with fifteen men. We will leave five in the street at the front as a backup and you, Towers, will cover the rear and side street with your ten men." He spread his hands and shrugged his shoulders, "Thirty-three of us, armed. It will be as easy as falling off a log." He got to his feet and took the map to a table, "Right, let's make sketches. We brief the men on the way to the raid so there will be no chance of a leak. The time for the rendezvous will be"—he consulted his watch as though, by some magical means, it could offer confirmation—"9:00 on the dot."

When the raiding party left headquarters, the streets were jammed with people and vehicles of all kinds, ranging from overladen buses to gaudily painted tri-shaws. A generous amount of time had been allowed to cope with traffic delays and all three open trucks converged on the warehouse at exactly 9:00.

Towers's task was a simple one. Half a mile from their destination, he instructed his driver to stop. In a few brief sentences, he outlined the operation to the men and made sure that each one understood the position he was to take up at the warehouse. When they arrived, everything went according to instructions, and both the rear and street side of the building were completely sealed by 9:02.

Watson and Maxwell also stopped for a briefing and arrived within a few seconds of one another. As the vehicles came to a halt, the men leaped out with rifles at the ready. The two senior officers had automatic pistols drawn. Without ceremony, Watson moved directly through the offices and out to the main storage area. Maxwell followed while his men rounded up the office staff to join the others in the warehouse. Ignoring all protests, the superintendent wasted no time in getting all the Chinese together at one end of the building. Maxwell signalled to two of his men, and they broke away from the main party. In a matter of minutes, they located the cases of peaches piled high in three stacks of neat layers reaching almost to the roof. Maxwell reported back to Watson.

The Chinese were standing, arms raised, with several rifles trained on them. When Maxwell stated that the suspect cases had been located, Watson pointed at a well-dressed Chinese at the front of the prisoners, "You! Come here!"

The man, his face impassive, advanced a few steps. Then, allowing his arms to sag a little, he said, "I trust you have a good reason for upsetting my place of business and my employees." His voice was low, but it carried clearly. There was no trace of fear or alarm in his manner.

"You'll find out soon enough." Watson indicated that the man was free to drop his hands, as he said, "You own this place?"

"That is correct. I am Yat Soong. I ask again why you have intruded here."

"I have reason to believe that a large quantity of contraband drugs is on these premises. My men are about to conduct a search. You will instruct your employees to remain where they are. After they have been individually searched, they may put their hands at their sides. I don't want them making any sudden moves while this warehouse is being searched. If everyone cooperates, there will be no accidents."

"Very good." Without turning around, the Chinese issued a string of instructions, then addressed the British officer, "You have a search warrant?"

Watson took a piece of paper from his pocket and waved it at the man. To four of the policeman he said, "Get on with searching the staff."

As the personal searches were being conducted, the Chinese businessman spoke again in a firm, but deferential voice. "May I see your warrant?" When the superintendent handed it to him, he glanced at it briefly. His eyes betrayed nothing, but there was a slight indication of a smile around his mouth as he said, "It appears to be in order. I regard this intrusion as irregular, but we will let it pass for now." Watson snatched the paper from the outstretched hand, "You'll see just how irregular this is when we find what we came for, laddie." He turned to Maxwell, "Okay, get on with it!"

Maxwell led his men to the stacks of cases. The attitude adopted by the Chinese businessman bothered him. No fear, no panic, almost no surprise. The raid had been carried out swiftly but some reaction should have been visible once the staff had been herded into the warehouse. Despite the fact that they were Chinese and supposed to be inscrutable, his experience told him that there should have been some high-pitched chatter among the women and the men should have been cowed. Instead there had been almost no protest. It was out of keeping with his expectations, and he didn't like it.

The searchers scaled the stacks of cases and heaved and strained to lower the topmost ones to the arms of their companions on the ground. Maxwell calculated swiftly. Seven cases lengthwise and three crosswise in each layer . . . that made ten. His eyes traveled upward and his lips moved slowly . . . twenty-five layers . . . that made 250 to the stack. A quick, unnecessary, glance assured him there were three stacks . . . 750 cases in all. . . . The full consignment was here.

His confidence restored, Maxwell watched impatiently as the men cut the fiber bands around the cases and pried open the wooden slats. The contents were removed carefully, layer by layer, and random cans were opened. As the can openers cut the metal away to expose the contents of the first cans, Maxwell found his excitement mounting. But each can he looked into for the heroin, seemed to mock him with its contents: half-peaches in heavy syrup.

One hour, 620 cases, and slightly over 2,000 cans of peaches later, the search had yielded nothing. As the stacks of cases were reduced, Maxwell's hopes faded. The litter of opened cans had grown and the heap of debris piled higher and higher. After the first negative reports, Watson joined Maxwell and brought

Towers and his men into the warehouse to help speed up the search.

The superintendent and the inspector exchanged fewer and fewer words as the stacks of cases diminished. Maxwell was frustrated and angry, but he was even more aware of his superior's anger than his own. When it became apparent that the drugs were not in the cases of peaches, Maxwell turned to Watson, "Shall I search the rest of the place?"

Watson looked the younger man up and down slowly, then took him aside. Out of earshot of the still-sweating policemen opening the cases of fruit, Watson said, "You want to open up all the other stuff in here?"

"Yes, sir, it's obvious that they've moved the heroin."

"How right you are, laddie." The superintendent's face was turning red as he struggled to control himself, "I can see a bright future for you in the police. You've got brains, you have." His voice rose slightly, "You want to add to the damage already done in here? You're about as smart as my wife's fucking poodle!" He swung around and walked a few paces, then swung back. "If I lose my pension in six months because of this fuck-up, I'll cut your balls off!"

3

The next day was hell to pay when the owner of the warehouse arrived at headquarters, lawyer in tow. Grudging compensation was agreed and paid. The police force had once again been made to look like fools. Maxwell had appeared before the chief of police and had been taken apart. He had no doubt that one more mistake would mean his return to England on a one-way ticket. Watson also had been on the carpet. The issue in his case was the moral one. If the raid had been successful, the fact that policemen had laid hands on the female employees during the course of the search would have been overlooked. Because of the failure of the operation and the loud protests of the Chinese businessman—not to mention his threats to give the story to the newspapers—there had been angry words directed at the superintendent in charge of the raid.

For a time, peaches were the stock practical joke around the police station. Maxwell knew Superintendent Watson wasn't amused by the joke because he made a point of telling him so. It was rare that the superintendent spoke at all to Maxwell after the raid, and both looked forward to the day Watson would finish his service and leave for England.

Maxwell was also concerned with something more important. He knew somebody had leaked the raid to the Chinese. He had sense enough to keep his mouth shut about his suspicion. But he brooded on it. Only three men could have been the source of the leak: Towers, Watson, or the justice of the peace who signed the search-warrant. As it happened, the J.P. was a titled, independently wealthy, retired naval officer. The field was therefore narrowed down to two.

As closely as he watched Superintendent Watson, there was no evidence his superior was other than what he appeared to be: a long-service professional who wanted to get back to England, buy a modest cottage, and take life easy.

However, Maxwell found himself noticing little things about his friend, Towers, which he had formerly ignored, like the way his flat-mate spent money on women, drinks and entertainment while complaining about never having any. Continuing to share the apartment with Towers became increasingly difficult. Following the raid, a barrier grew between them. If Towers realized that Maxwell suspected him of leaking information, he did not raise the subject. Towers had to be aware that *somebody* had given the tip-off, yet he never once discussed it. Maxwell drew his own conclusions and, after a time, each man looked for a place of his own,

There was another thing that concerned Maxwell. A week or so after the raid he had discovered that his informer, Hup Wah Kee, had moved and the clothing store in Temple Pavement had a new tenant. He could find no trace, and he hoped that the man had gone to ground. He decided to forget him and hoped he had escaped, one way or the other. Above all, the abortive raid had strengthened Maxwell's belief that a central criminal organization of Triad *did* still exist, but he knew it wasn't a good time for him to pursue the subject and he had no access to files and records at headquarters. Nonetheless, he determined to keep on probing when opportunity to do so presented itself.

On the eve of Superintendent Watson's departure for England, six months after the raid, he threw a party. Surprisingly, Maxwell found himself invited. The party was held at the Officers' Club and it followed a long-established pattern of colonial farewells. Though informal, a code of behavior going back to the days of Queen Victoria ensured that the gentlemen behaved themselves while in the company of ladies. The supper was buffet-style, and when everyone had finished eating, there were a few short speeches and a toast to the queen, followed by a further toast wishing the departing couple health, wealth, and happiness back in the Old Country.

After a time, the older men bonded together at the bar to talk about the "good old days" when men were men and discipline the key to organized society. The older women formed a group at two tables placed together close to the bar. They chatted happily among themselves and kept an eye on their spouses. A five-piece band played dance music for the younger people. Maxwell had not brought a partner. He was involved with a Chinese girl who served his sexual needs adequately but would not be acceptable to the assembled company. He had refrained from asking an English girl for the simple reason that gossip was the life's blood of the Officers' Club.

Since Maxwell did not feel comfortable in the Officers' Club, his intention was to have a few drinks, wait a decent length of time and leave. Shortly after ten, he went over to Mrs. Watson and wished her a happy retirement in England. He chatted with her for a few minutes and then went over to the older men at the bar. Superintendent Watson saw him approach. He had been drinking fairly heavily, and his speech was slightly slurred when he said, "Well, young Maxwell, found any Triads under your bed lately?" Laughter greeted this sally, so he went on, "How about peaches—still your favorite canned fruit?"

Maxwell forced himself to grin, "I think I'm more of an expert on 'lemons' after my last two efforts."

"Never mind, lad. We all learn by our mistakes." Watson took a gulp from his glass, "It's other people's mistakes that can be costly ones."

"Sorry about that, sir." Maxwell held out his right hand, "I'm glad it all worked out for you and I'd like to wish you all the best."

"Thank you!" Watson took the proffered hand. "You'll have a drink with me."

"Okay, sir, I'll have a scotch and water."

"Drinks around and a scotch and water for our friend here." Watson addressed the steward and then returned to Maxwell, "I'm glad you've kept your nose clean these past few months. None of your bloody Triad nonsense. It's like I told you before— bogey man stuff to frighten kids. All a fairy tale from the old days. The Fu Manchu and Charlie Chan stuff you used to see on the films. I tell you, lad, crooks are crooks the world over. There's them and us. The cops and the robbers—remember that and you won't go far wrong."

Maxwell picked up his drink. "I'll try to, sir." He raised his glass, "Good luck in your retirement." When the older man nodded his thanks, Maxwell emptied his glass, shook hands with Watson again, and left. He was inwardly angry, and the last drink had made him a little high.

In the parking lot Maxwell struggled with his key before finally unlocking the door. When the courtesy light came on, he saw an object on the driver's seat. It was a can of peaches—same brand as the ones in the abortive raid. Another practical joke at his expense! About to throw it away in anger, he realized there was something peculiar about it. It was the weight. The contents, packed in syrup, should have been sluggish as their weight shifted, and it should have been around a pound. This can weighed only about half-a-pound, and the liquid sloshed around in it. Then he saw a typewritten message taped to the top of the can:

"This served you once but never again." Maxwell placed the can on the passenger seat and quickly drove home.

When he got to his apartment, he went right to the kitchen and opened the can. Removing the jagged lid a strange smell rose out of the can. It was vaguely familiar, like the cloying apple-sweet smell of chloroform in a hospital. The can was three-quarters filled with liquid and a brownish-pink rolled-up object gently floated in it. He took a clear mixing-bowl from a kitchen cupboard and emptied the contents of the can into it. The empty can fell from his fingers and Maxwell's stomach rolled over several times as he stared at what he had found. It was a human tongue.

It was a moment or two before he recovered sufficiently to pour himself a stiff drink. Hup Wah Kee had gone to ground all right—six feet under—but the Triad had removed his tongue first. Maxwell emptied his glass and threw it across the room, as he shouted aloud, "Goddamn you, Watson! Triad is a fairy tale, eh? Tell that to the poor bastard who had his tongue pulled out by the roots!" He pounded his fists in frustration on the countertop, "Lousy stinking bastards!" Then he was chilled at the thought that they had kept in it embalming fluid for six months and delivered it on the night Watson retired.

Maxwell got a fresh glass and poured himself another drink. There was no doubt in his mind that the man's tongue had been removed within hours of his having told Watson and Towers the identity of his informant. Which one had tipped off the Triad and what the hell could *he* do about it anyway? Report the incident at headquarters and produce the can and its contents as evidence? What good was a human tongue floating around in embalming fluid? He couldn't prove whose tongue it was without the man's body. He could *say* that Watson and Towers were the only two people who knew Hup Wah Kee was his source of information, but he had no proof that either man was in the pay of Triad. He laughed aloud mirthlessly. Triad! Back to Reds under the bed! There had to be somebody at headquarters who was on the ball and realized that the Triad *did* exist. Somebody, but who? Common sense dictated he carry on with his mouth shut until he had something to say. Continue to keep an eye on Towers and wait.

In the months that followed, Maxwell settled down to a routine. He did his job and mixed with his fellow officers at work. The man who replaced Watson was younger and more flexible. Maxwell had known him casually before his promotion and they got along. On the social side, Maxwell avoided his colleagues as much as possible. His Chinese girlfriend was all the company he needed or wanted. He kept his eyes and ears open for any hint of Triad activity but did not allow himself to be unduly preoccupied with them.

In many ways, Maxwell considered himself to be lucky. He knew his escape from his beginnings were due to his own efforts, but he conceded that luck was an element which he couldn't ignore. To *want* to do something or other was one thing, to succeed in attaining a goal—no matter how much one strived—required timing and circumstances. Having been around the Chinese during his army service and the three years in the Hong Kong police, he understood the fatalistic approach they had to events in their lives. He knew he could only wait for a break to provide him with some answers about Triad. He was to experience a convergence of critical paths where circumstances beyond his control would combine with fate, luck—call it what you like— to clarify the situation. It would have a profound effect on the rest of his life.

Some months later, Maxwell had completed his paperwork and reached the end of another routine day. He had dismissed his men, and all he had to do was tidy the papers on his desk and go home. He took one last look at the mess of unfinished work, then gathered it all together and placed it in the drawer. It could wait until morning. His priority right now was to get home, change, and get over to his Chinese mistress. It was her birthday, and they were having a quiet celebration at her small apartment. Drinks, dinner for two, a few more drinks, and bed. He stretched luxuriously, not a bad way to go if you had to go. Die in bed with a girl at your side and an empty bottle on the floor.

He put on his cap and belt and was about to go when the door was pulled open by the superintendent in charge of the oncoming shift. He glanced around at the empty desks, looked at Maxwell, and said, "Sorry, but it looks as if you're elected."

"Elected for what?"

"Minor riot at the docks—we need a backup."

"For Christ's sake, I just got finished!" Maxwell thought of his girlfriend waiting to start their party, "Surely you have somebody on your own shift."

"Two off sick," the superintendent said. "That's show business, Maxwell. Let's go!"

Having no option, Maxwell followed the other man to the main office.

Some twenty Chinese constables in the charge of a sergeant were already assembled. The superintendent handed a sheet of paper to Maxwell. "Trucks are ready outside. Smith is coping with things at the docks, but I want the situation squared away fast. You know how things can get out of hand in this bloody place. The sooner we can restore order, the better." His voice took on an edge, "You've seen it all before, Maxwell. Now, get going!"

Having no option, Maxwell saluted the other man, "Very good, sir." He turned to the sergeant, "Okay, get them on the trucks!"

Maxwell was furious, but there was nothing he could do. The riot could be over in half an hour, or it could take all night. (He had heard the crap about somebody "coping with the situation" before. On each occasion it had meant chaos reigned while the man in charge was fighting a losing battle to contain the rioters.) Arrival of reinforcements to restore law and order either demoralized the rioters or inflamed the situation. Whichever, he was going to be delayed by at least two hours.

The constables were all aboard the trucks and Maxwell was about to take his place beside the driver of the leading vehicle when he saw Towers's familiar sports car move head toward the main gate. He jumped from the truck and ran forward to flag down the car. As it came to a halt, Towers's head emerged and he asked, "Where's the fire?"

"Never mind that—the bastards collared me for extra duty. A riot at the docks."

"Tough luck," Towers's tone was sympathetic.

"Tough luck my arse!" Maxwell exploded. "Where the hell were you? I had an important date tonight."

"Car wouldn't start. Took ages to get it going—plugs, I think."

"I could kick myself for still being around." Maxwell glanced at the trucks, then said, "Look, I've got to get going. Will you do me a favor?"

"Sure, name it."

"On your way home, stop at my girlfriend's—she doesn't have a phone. Tell her I've got extra duty, but I'll be over as soon as I can." He scribbled down the name and address and handed it to the other man. "I'll do the same for you one day."

"My pleasure." Towers laughed and pointed to the trucks, "There, but for the grace of God, go I. Keep your head down, son!" Maxwell was already running back to the lead truck.

The situation at the scene of the riot was nasty. Maxwell took it in quickly as the trucks swung into the docks. Six policemen—plus an inspector—were penned in where two walls came together. It was obvious they had been in retreat, backing off yard by yard. Some of them had managed to find lids from trash cans or pieces of board to use as shields against the shower of bricks and debris being hurled at them by the screaming, slogan-chanting demonstrators. The inspector and one policeman were unprotected, and both had blood running from head wounds. The leaders of the riot were spurring people on. The initial target of the angry demonstrators had been forgotten, and the police were taking the brunt of the mob's fury.

There was only one course of action to take. Maxwell told the driver to stop some fifty yards from the fringe of the crowd and tersely reported to headquarters by radio that he was going to initiate Moran Three. Within minutes of Maxwell's orders the three trucks pulled in to face the crowd of demonstrators. Two men on each truck, protected by the cab, used the roof to position a Bren gun. The rest of the men dispersed and took kneeling positions with rifles aimed to cover the rioters.

Maxwell fired three shots into the air. The mob was suddenly quiet, and Maxwell ordered the Chinese sergeant to speak to the crowd through the microphone. The man's voice, speaking in rapid Cantonese, reverberated from the surrounding buildings. "Whatever your grievances are, they will be listened to by the proper authorities. At this moment you are disturbing the peace. If you disperse, nobody will be hurt and nobody will be arrested. If you continue to disturb the peace, we will take whatever action is necessary to restore law and order. You have exactly two minutes! After that, we will take action!"

Isolated jeers and catcalls from the mob had punctuated the delivery of the ultimatum. But when the voice from the microphone ceased, a general muttering swelled until it became an angry roar. A few rocks were thrown in the direction of the reinforcements. There was a lot of shuffling of feet and shaking of sticks, but no real advance.

Maxwell had no illusions—they *would* advance. At that point, his men would be ordered to fire over their heads. According to plan, the men behind the crowd should, a split second later, also fire over the heads of the crowd. Hopefully, nothing would go wrong and no stray shots find their way into the crowd. But in the excitement of the moment, one of the Chinese constables might just panic and allow the muzzle of his rifle to drop. If that happened, it would put an end to the demonstration, but it would sure as hell have repercussions he could well do without.

Suddenly a hail of rocks and debris came from the crowd and they moved forward. Maxwell shouted, "Take aim!" Fourteen rifles were leveled, and the barrels of the three Bren guns swung to cover the advancing mob. It was all for effect, and the demonstrators hesitated. Those in front stopped and checked the progress of those following. Maxwell knew that the professional agitators would not be impressed. A few voices rose up from the crowd haranguing them

26

to move forward. He dropped his arm as a signal. "Fire!"

As the chatter of the Brens mingled with the rifle fire, the crowd broke to left and right. When the firing stopped, the people paused but kept on going when the second burst of fire came from the rear. Only the agitators remained and they, too, took to their heels when they saw the rout was complete.

The disturbance was over.

4

Despite the cooling temperature as darkness crept over the now-almost-deserted dock area, Maxwell was conscious of the perspiration trickling down his body. It had been a close call. If the balance had shifted, he and his men would now be in an explosive situation. Since his men *had* opened fire on the demonstrators, they would have had to continue doing so. The police would either have been overwhelmed by the mob or been forced to shoot them down like animals. Casualties on both sides could have been high. He shuddered at the thought of the consequences *that* would have had.

He glanced to check that Inspector Smith and his men were safe, then he turned to his men and said, "Great job! You handled it beautifully—I'm really proud of you!" They were glad for his praise, but he knew that they, too, were mainly relieved it was over without casualties.

When Smith and the others joined them, Maxwell asked for a report. "No serious injuries," Inspector Smith said, dabbing at a minor wound on his forehead, "A few bumps and bruises but nothing serious. Before you arrived, it looked as though we were in for some real fun and games."

Maxwell smiled without humor, "It certainly didn't look like you were winning!" He glanced at his watch, "Anyway, that didn't take long to sort out. I'll leave Sergeant Ting with ten men to patrol the area, but I'd better report to Headquarters right now." As he turned away, he asked, "Where is your truck?"

Smith gestured, "Around the corner—turned over. You might ask them to send a tow truck for it. We'll come back with you."

Headquarters was pleased with Maxwell's report. His instructions were to get back and complete the inevitable paperwork. Now that the danger had passed, it was business as usual. They would probably even forget he had been off duty when he was sent out. His thoughts turned to his girlfriend. He was going to be a couple of hours late, but it could have been a whole lot worse. It was 8:00 when Maxwell finally left headquarters. He had taken longer over the report than he intended and decided to go directly to her tiny apartment. She had waited long enough. A wash in the men's room had freshened him up, and though his clothes were drenched with sweat, he did not intend to have them on for very long.

He drove the short distance with total disregard for the speed limit. Having parked his car in the main street, he walked to the narrow alley where his girl lived. In the alley, his car could be stripped down to the chassis by the time he returned to it. Maxwell was not afraid of the alley itself. He had been down it many times before in the dark, and if the threat of his pistol wasn't enough, he was perfectly prepared to use it.

The narrow, unlit stairway creaked with his weight as he climbed to the second floor. There was a chink of light beneath her door. With pleasurable anticipation he turned the handle and entered the small flat. Hot food, drinks, and a willing woman awaited him. The rigors of the day were fast fading to the back of his mind. Closing the door behind him, he turned around, expecting a deliciously fragrant body to melt into his arms. Nothing happened. The only illumination was from the bedside lamp. The bed itself was in shadow, but he could make out a large form beneath the covers. Too large to be just his mistress. There had to be *two* people in there! He moved forward, anger exploding in his head, and dragged the light blanket off in one sweep. Still clutching the bedclothes his stomach heaved.

His girl lay naked, a large bullet hole beneath her left breast. His policeman's mind noted the hole was

28

jagged and the area around the hole was black with powder burns. She had been shot at close range. Beside her lay Towers. He too was naked. Nerveless fingers loosely held his service revolver. The tip of the pistol barrel was still in his mouth. The top of his head was blown away.

Maxwell's mind raced. In a building like this, a rabbit warren inhabited by scores of Chinese, the double explosion of the service revolver must have sounded like a bombardment! Why had nothing happened? No alarm raised and everyone going about their business just as if nothing had happened. Death was no stranger to this district but it usually came with the silent thrust of a knife or a cord slipped around an unsuspecting throat. He could hear the sound of several radios, an occasional burst of laughter, and here and there voices raised in heated argument over the clatter of *mah jongg* tiles.

Looking at the bodies again, Maxwell took a few faltering steps backward, and the bedclothes fell silently from his hand to the floor. What the hell had happened here? *His* girl and Towers naked together. Had Towers forced her into bed to submit to him? Then what? Blown his head off after he had taken the girl? Balls!

Maxwell took a deep breath and tried to pull his thoughts together. The sight was gruesome, but he had seen worse. His eyes darted around the small room and took in every detail. The remains of a meal for two were on the table with an empty wine bottle and two dirty glasses. At the side of the bed, on the table where the lamp burned, were two more glasses, both partially filled with wine. On the only armchair in the room were Towers's uniform jacket and pants, neatly folded. His cap and belt, holster empty, were beside his shoes and socks beneath the chair. His underpants were on the floor at the side of the bed, beside a second empty wine bottle. *Die in bed with a girl at your side and an empty bottle on the floor*—Maxwell's fantasy flashed through his mind.

On the floor at the other side of the bed was a heap of pink silk. Maxwell recognized it as the robe his girl wore sometimes. A robe and nothing else. There never was anything else when she knew they had planned to stay home all night. Only one explanation was possible for him: If one Chinese looked like another to a European, it was a certainty that one uniformed police inspector looked like another to a couple of Chinese thugs. This pantomime had been staged as *his* swan song! Towers—poor bastard—had mounted the stairs and walked along the dim corridor. A chop to the back of his neck and he was out cold. The meal must have been already prepared; it was easy enough to make things look as if two people had eaten. Probably the cold-blooded sons-of-bitches ate the food and drank the wine before they left. Maybe the girl had been part of it! Maxwell felt slightly disloyal at the thought, but one never knew. Certainly she hadn't expected to end up as dead as Towers.

Towers's car? There had been some cars parked in the main street, but he hadn't noticed the familiar sports car. Hell, his mind had been on other things. What difference did it make—the car would be in the vicinity. Had to be the Triad. Who else could commit a double murder using a gun, knowing nobody would come to see what the shooting was about? The bastards were taking their revenge for the warehouse and got their inspectors mixed up. One thing for damned sure—it exonerated Towers from having Triad connections. That left good old Watson! Sanctimonious son-of-a-bitch! Back in England growing roses. Needed his pension like a dog needs fleas.

Suddenly Maxwell needed a drink. He knew that watchful eyes had seen him coming here, followed him up the stairs, along the passage, and into the room. His movements were undoubtedly already being reported by Triad informers. His jaws clenched; he didn't give a shit! He released the safety catch of his pistol—first slant-eyed face that came through the door would get it between the eyes! Moving to the cupboard where the whiskey was, he grabbed the bottle and drank greedily. The fiery liquid coursed through his body, and his hands stopped shaking. He thought of his fingerprints on the bottle, then laughed out loud; his fingerprints were all over the room from previous visits. The place wouldn't even be dusted when some dummy saw the evidence. Two bodies on the bed—one with a hole in her chest, and the other with the top of his head missing. Murder and suicide! A British police officer in bed with a Chinese slut! They would be so busy covering up that there would be no time for a routine investigation. Somebody—somewhere—was in for a hard time whitewashing this one!

It was time to go. Maxwell tilted the neck of the bottle toward Towers and whispered, "Sorry it happened this way, old friend. I promise you I'll pay them back someday." He took a long pull at the whiskey. "I don't know when it will be—but I'll get a crack at Triad someday. And they sure won't knock me off now. They couldn't afford an epidemic of police 'suicides,' and I can tell you I'm going to keep well out of their way for a while." He put the bottle back in the cupboard. "I'll fix Watson's wagon the next time I'm in England on leave. I'll fix him for you *and for me*— put him where the birds won't ever shit on him!" Maxwell glanced around the room once more, then left.

Unfortunately—or perhaps fortunately—ex-superintendent Watson died of natural causes long before Inspector Maxwell found himself on leave in England. Still, Maxwell was to find Triad very much alive in England.

II
England
1960

5

Eton, the largest and most famous of English public schools, since 1440, together with Harrow and Rugby, has produced the statesmen and soldiers who built the British empire. The Duke of Wellington said that the battles of England were won on its playing fields and he, the victor at Waterloo, was an old Etonian. If Napoleon held an opinion of the products of Eton, it was hardly likely to have been flattering.

A cricket match was in progress. The thoughts of the young students clad in immaculate whites were concentrated on the bowlers and the batsmen. If the outcome of this game were to have a profound effect in some future battle, it was of no importance to them. What was important was winning this particular game. After the annual clash with Harrow at Lords, it was the most important match of the season. Winning or losing was the difference between being in the position to hurl condescending insults or having to be the squirming recipient of them for a full year.

The player at the wicket shifted his feet to take up his stance. His eyes were on the ball as it was polished in the crotch of the bowler's pants. Time was now meaningless to him. It was just he and the bowler. Three more deliveries remaining in the over, and three chances for him to get the four runs necessary to win. Either to be the hero of the hour or have to be content with commiseration and remarks of "tough luck" back in the dressing room. He abhorred sympathy. Something in his makeup cringed from being the object of pity. Though it was only a game and he was just one player on the team, he was the focus of attention. To be a hero was important, but to have to walk away in defeat was unthinkable. He *had* to get the four runs. He *would* get them!

It was difficult to force his tense muscles to relax in order to make best contact with the ball, but he succeeded. As he watched the bowler commence his run, he noted with satisfaction that the palms of his hands, which should have been perspiring, were dry.

The bowler's arm swung, and the ball flew with savage speed. Instinctively, Clive Hunter knew this wasn't the one. Even so, as the ball sailed past him, he felt his whole body contract. He dreaded having to wait for the retrieval of the ball and the ritual of the polishing prior to the next delivery, but somehow he was certain the next one was his and he would make no mistake.

When the blade of his bat made contact with the leather ball, Clive put every ounce of his strong frame behind it and, with savage satisfaction, followed the course of the ball past the fielders, past the boundary line, for four runs. The rules demanded that the third delivery be made, but the bowler merely went through the motions. Clive simply pushed the ball a few yards along the grass.

On the field, the opponents exchanged restrained congratulations and commiserations. Once at the sidelines, Clive Hunter's back was pummeled by his teammates and a horde of delirious spectators descended on him. He was lifted from the ground and carried shoulder-high to the pavilion in triumph.

As he slowly dressed after showering, the excited chatter of his teammates prompted a wave of nostalgia to flood over Clive. In a few short weeks, this school, the traditions of it, the fellowship, and the disciplines, would be memories. Although he was looking forward eagerly to Cambridge, it would be a wrench to leave. To him, more than the others who had parents at home, this *was* home. Holidays with his grandfather, occasional parcels, birthday cards and presents had punctuated the years he had spent at Eton, but it wasn't the same as having parents. To him the school had been almost his whole existence. More so these past two years since Amy, his grandfather's housekeeper, had died. He deeply missed the love and affection she had given him. Since her death, a woman from the village had come in on a day-to-day basis while Chin, his grandfather's Chinese manservant, attended to all the other duties.

Thinking of Chin, he was a trifle disturbed to recall that they had been close when he was a small boy, but in the past few years, a barrier had risen between them. He had speculated that it was caused by a resentment on the part of Chin against the British public-school system. Eton developed discipline and self-sufficiency in its students in order to produce young men destined to be leaders. The students were encouraged to develop a keen sense of class and privilege. He could understand Chin—or anyone else less privileged—harboring resentment, but every effort he had made to recapture rapport with Chin had been rejected. Not that Chin rejected his efforts outright, but the man had never, apart from when he was looking after Clive as a small boy, revealed any strong feelings for him. He was the inscrutable Oriental of popular fiction.

Clive thrust thoughts of home and Chin aside to join in the friendly banter of his teammates. Theirs was the victory, and it was fun to rub the noses of the other team in the ashes of their defeat. After a spirited exchange of jeers and retorts, the losers decided that the hero of the winning side should be rewarded with a second shower, fully clothed. The Eton players sprang to the defense of their man, and a good-natured brawl ensued. Being used as a human rope in a tug-of-war, with eleven athletic young men on one side determined to dunk him and ten athletes on the other equally determined that he should not be, kept Clive fully occupied. As the balance shifted, he was pulled and hauled back and forth, but at the height of the battle, he was reprieved.

A younger boy, somewhat out of breath, entered the dressing room and called out "Hunter, Mr. Blytheswood wants to see you. He said it's very urgent."

Clive, fighting to hold off the opposing factions for a second, said, "Right! Where is he?"

"In his study."

"Fine, you run along—I'll be there in a moment."

As he hurried to the school buildings, Hunter speculated as to the reason for the summons. To the best of his knowledge, he wasn't guilty of an infraction of the many rules governing behavior. Over the years one became adroit at dodging them. It was highly unlikely that Blytheswood wanted to congratulate him on the part he had played in winning the cricket match. Protocol ruled that communication between masters and pupils precluded direct reference to such matters. Recognition of his success would come in class in the form of some sarcastic witticism. He increased his pace slightly—the reason had to be of some urgency.

Mr. Blytheswood wasted no time when Hunter stood before his desk. "I had a call from your grandfather's manservant—Chin, isn't it? . . . He said your grandfather is very ill and that his doctor suggested you go home at once."

Clive nodded. "Yes, sir."

"I suggest you get off immediately. Have you enough ready cash, or shall I arrange for some?"

"Thank you, sir, I have enough." The news had not really surprised Clive. His grandfather was close to eighty and in recent years had taken to sitting about the house more and more. Nonetheless, it was his one blood relative and a feeling of anxiety gripped him. If grandfather died, he would be alone in the world at the age of seventeen. He thrust the thought aside, then asked, "May I go now, sir?"

The master nodded vigorously, "By all means. Pack the things you will need and I'll arrange to have you taken to the station."

When Clive emerged from Brighton station, Chin, inscrutable as ever, came forward and took his bag. There was no exchange of words until the Rolls-Royce glided into traffic.

Clive broke the silence. "Who is with grandfather now?"

"A nurse."

"When did you call in the doctor?"

"This morning."

"What did he say?"

"He will tell you."

Chin leaned forward over the steering wheel as

though concentrating on the traffic. Clive knew better. He was being frozen out, and while he would normally accept this from Chin, this was *not* a normal time. There was an edge in his voice as he said, *"You* tell me!"

"Doctor, he fix people—I drive car!" Chin kept his eyes on the road.

Exasperated, Clive spoke sharply, "I know you speak English as well as I do, so don't hand *me* that 'Chinee no understand' nonsense! I asked you a question!"

Chin turned his head for a brief moment, and hard brown eyes bored into the boy's. When his eyes were back on the road, he said, "Your grandfather is now an old man. He is very sick. The doctor told me only that I should telephone Eton and have you come home."

"That was all?"

"All!" The finality of the word convinced Clive that it would be a waste of time to pursue the interrogation. Containing his impatience, he settled back in his seat.

At the house, he leaped from the car as soon as it came to a halt. He turned the handle of the front door, only to find it locked. Swinging around, his exasperation was increased by the sight of Chin slowly advancing up the steps with the door key in his hand. Using more force than necessary, he grabbed the key, inserted it in the lock, and pulled the door open. He was tempted to slam the door in Chin's face but, instead, he hurried through the hallway and ran lightly up the staircase.

He tapped softly on his grandfather's door. There was no response. When a second rapping yielded the same result, he turned the handle gently and entered the room. It was empty.

Familiar pieces of furniture stood mutely. Only the ticking of the carriage clock on the mantel shelf disturbed the silence. The neatly made bed mocked him. Disbelief was replaced by seething anger as he ran from the room and back down the stairs.

Chin stood in the hallway like a graven image. He looked straight ahead as Clive descended, and it was only when the young man advanced angrily toward him that he raised an arm and said, "In the study."

Restraining himself with some difficulty, Clive moved toward the study. At the door he turned around to glare at Chin before entering.

6

Anger was replaced by confusion as Clive took in what confronted him. Here, in the study of an English country house, where he had expected to find his grandfather in some kind of a makeshift bed with a nurse in attendance, were two Chinese men perfectly at ease. One was seated behind the desk; the other, his legs crossed comfortably, was occupying an armchair. Both men were wearing what could only be described as benign expressions, and neither man reacted with surprise at his sudden entrance.

Clive advanced into the room, "What is going on here? Who are you and what do you want?"

The man behind the desk eyed him for a moment, then said in a soft voice, "We want to talk to you."

"What for—and where is my grandfather?" He was aware that his voice had risen in pitch and resolved to control it lest these men detect his mounting fear.

"At this precise moment, I cannot tell you what your grandfather is doing." The spokesman smiled slightly. "I can assure you, however, he is alive and well—enjoying life as well as a man can who has reached his great age."

Clive took a moment to digest this information before saying, "This is ridiculous, I'm going to call the police!" He turned to leave the room only to find Chin standing in front of the door. From his attitude, there was no doubt that nothing short of physical violence would move him.

Clive turned again to the man behind the desk. "I demand an explanation! Who are you and what game are you playing?"

The man's face hardened as he said, *"Games* we do not play. That we leave to the British. Play up, play up and play the game—that's what they teach you at Eton, isn't it? Better to lose with honor than resort to ungentlemanly behavior and win—that is the code, isn't it?" He smiled with a cruelty that reached his eyes. "We find no honor in losing—and we regard games as nothing more than a means of recreation." He indicated a chair, "Sit, be comfortable. What we have to discuss will take some time."

Haughtily, Clive replied, "I can think of nothing in this world that I would want to discuss with you. On second thought"—he paused to give his words effect—"there is nothing I would *care* to discuss with you!"

His attempt at bravado was rewarded by a slight smile from the man in the armchair who had not yet spoken. Turning to the first man he said, "It would appear that the efforts of the English public-school system have done our work well for us!"

"Just so, but much more is required." The spokesman turned to Clive and after a moment said, "I will ask you to sit just once again. You are seventeen years of age. In two weeks you will be eighteen. How would you *care* to die before you had the opportunity to celebrate that milestone in your life?"

Instinct warned Clive that the man's words were not to be taken lightly. He did not trust his voice to reply but merely shrugged his shoulders in what he hoped was indifference, and sat down.

"Now that you have decided to be sensible, we can proceed." The spokesman settled back in his chair. "For the purposes of this meeting, you may address me as Mr. Sung. My colleague you may address as Mr. Lee, and we shall call you Clive. You will appreciate that these are not our real names, but they will do for now." He opened his arms expansively. "We want you to be completely open with us and everything will be conducted satisfactorily. But before we begin, would you care for some refreshment?"

Despite his inner tension Clive couldn't help smiling. Something about the situation appealed to his sense of humor. "Yes, please—I'll have some tea."

"Excellent, the traditional British fortifier in times of stress!" He addressed Chin, "You will attend to that—

for three!" Turning back to Clive, he asked, "What did you find amusing?".

Clive considered the question for a moment, then answered, "Here I am in my family home, confronted by two strangers who appear to have taken possession of the place. You threaten my life one moment—presume to call me by my Christian name the next—and then offer me refreshments as though I were the vicar who has dropped in unexpectedly! It is a little incongruous, don't you agree?"

"As you say," the man called Sung replied. "However, although we are strangers to you, you are no stranger to us. We have known you almost all of your life. Take today—you were quite a hero on the cricket field, were you not?"

"Yes, I suppose so."

"Last Wednesday you went into Windsor and purchased several books that will be necessary for your studies at university. You withdrew fifteen pounds from your bank account and you flirted with a young lady in a teashop."

"Yes, it was Wednesday I went into Windsor—but how—"

"You also purchased a number of magazines that would hardly be classified as approved reading for young men at a British public school. Were these to be shared with your friends or purely for your own pleasure?"

Clive's face reddened, then he stammered, "Whoever gets to go into town usually buys them—just for fun, really—we all laugh and make jokes about them."

"Indeed," Mr. Sung was smiling, "I should have thought healthy young men would have wanted them for other reasons."

Clive was saved further embarrassment by the arrival of the tea tray. He used the time it took Chin to serve them to recover his composure. He was intrigued by the Chinese in spite of the strangeness of the situation. Intrigued, and curious as to why they had bothered to follow his movements so closely, he found himself eager to know the answers. Mr. Sung sipped from his cup for a few moments and then resumed speaking. "It may come as a surprise to you, young man, but there is very little that has happened in your lifetime that has escaped our attention." He dismissed Chin, and when the man had left the room he went on, "A great deal of time and effort—not to mention money—has been invested in you."

Completely puzzled, Clive asked, "What do you mean? What money?"

"Money is the least of it." Mr. Sung finished his tea and carefully placed the empty cup and saucer to one side, "We will start at the beginning, and everything you need to know will be made clear to you. I ask that you refrain from asking too many questions. As we go along, you may interrupt for clarification but no unnecessary questions. You understand me?"

Clive nodded, "I understand."

Mr. Sung nodded in return, "Good. The man you know as 'grandfather' is not a blood relative of yours. He is a guardian appointed by the organization Mr. Lee and I represent. Chin, known to you as your grandfather's manservant, was also appointed to you by my people. It was intended that Chin should tutor you during the important early years of your life. To teach you when your mind was receptive. What is learned as a young child remains with a person forever—provided it is not allowed to wither and die."

Completely confused, Clive could not stop himself from speaking. "My grandfather is not my grandfather? Who is he then? Why should I believe what you are telling me?" The questions were pouring out. "If *he* isn't my grandfather—who am I? What is Chin supposed to—"

Sung held up an admonishing hand, "I realize that what I have said has come as a shock to you. As to why you should believe me—it will become clear as we progress. All I ask in the meantime is that you listen without interruption." He leaned forward and, speaking in Cantonese, asked, "Can you do that?"

"Yes, if you will explain—" Clive broke off as he realized he was answering in the same language.

Sung smiled in triumph, "You see, Chin did his work well. How many of your school friends understand and speak Chinese?"

Clive answered with surprise, "None. Chin taught me when I was a child. We spoke nothing else, and my grandfather encouraged it."

"Exactly! Your grandfather also encouraged you to take an interest in Oriental studies, didn't he? Chin helped you in your studies, and this early interest prompted you to select Oriental studies when you go to Cambridge later this year."

"Yes," the logic could not be denied.

"Good. Let us go back to the beginning. I said the man you know as your grandfather is no blood relative to you. Your actual father was not *his* son. It is true that his own son was a prisoner of war in the hands of the Japanese. It is also true that his *wife* gave birth to a male child. Furthermore, the mother and father of that child died in captivity. The child survived, but *you* are not that child!" He leaned forward, "Do you understand what I have just told you?"

"I—I think so."

"Excellent! Now, *your* actual father was a British officer who stayed on in the jungles of Malaya to organize guerrilla resistance against the Japanese invaders. He came from an excellent family and he attended Cambridge. What his name was is of little importance. All you need to know is that he died in the jungle. Who your mother was is of little importance beyond that she was Chinese and of a good family. She was a solace to your father and gave birth to his child." He leaned forward again, "Are you adult enough to understand *that?*"

Clive nodded. It *was* confusing, and something of a shock to find that the man and woman whose photographs he had seen many times were not really his parents; that some unknown soldier had used a Chinese girl and *he* was the result. That Chin, friend and companion of childhood, had really been employed by some "organization" to brainwash him. It was all a shock and very confusing. But it was also fascinating, exciting, and exhilarating! He found himself leaning forward.

The Chinese exchanged meaningful glances, Sung continued, "For reasons that you will learn in the future, our organization substituted you for the child born as Clive Hunter. To all intents and purposes, you *are* Clive Hunter. You have been brought up in the manner to which the grandson of Sir Gerald Hunter was entitled. You have been educated at the school where the Hunter family has been educated for generations. You will be attending the university your 'father' and 'grandfather' attended. As heir, you will inherit this house and the nonexistent wealth when your grandfather dies." Sung smiled. "I use the term 'nonexistent' because our organization provides the money to maintain Sir Gerald in the manner to which he is accustomed!"

Clive nodded with dawning understanding, "Is it because of the money he took me? Or does he even know that I'm not his real grandson?"

"He knows that you are not his grandson but, beyond that, he knows nothing of the circumstances of your birth."

"So it was for the money?" The young man's voice carried bitterness.

"Unfortunately, it is worse than that. When Sir Gerald held a very high post in the Foreign Office, he was posted to Hong Kong. While he was there he was—I think the best term is 'indiscreet.' He maintained a household other than that occupied by his wife and spent more money gambling in Macao than he could afford. The organization to which I belong very generously helped Sir Gerald out of his difficulties, for which he was very grateful. So when the time was— shall we say—opportune, we presented Sir Gerald's debt for payment."

There was no mistaking the bitterness in Clive's voice when he said, "The payment being his bringing me up according to your strict specifications!"

"Just so! However, you have no cause to be bitter. Your life has not been exactly one of hardship, has it? Would you say that you have been exposed to poverty, dirt, disease, or the life of a bastard child in Malaya?" His tone became sharp, "You *are* a bastard child! If it were not for the organization I represent, you would be begging on the streets of Kuala Lumpur or pimping for the whorehouses of Singapore! Give thought to it, young man! Consider it when the time comes for me to explain what the future holds for you."

Clive Hunter was visibly shaken. Bastard was a word seldom used at Eton. That *he* was a bastard in the true sense of the word stunned him. (It was the point at which he had ceased to doubt anything he had been told by the man opposite. It was the moment of his becoming a man.) He found a reserve of strength that allowed him to ask calmly, "What happens now?"

Sung studied him for a long moment before replying, "For now, nothing. You will return to Eton in a few days and resume your education. You will go to Cambridge as planned, and you will attend to your studies diligently. Yours will be the good life because that was always the intention of the organization. When the time comes that you have completed your studies at Cambridge, you will continue them in the Orient. You will communicate what has passed between us to no one or you will die. Do you understand that?" His voice took on a cutting edge, "You will die a death befitting one who betrays friends who rescued him from being a bastard beggar!"

The young man digested this, then asked, "What happens to my so-called grandfather?"

"Sir Gerald is, as everyone knows, elderly. He is in poor health, and you have been summoned home because of his health. He will return to this house later today, and subsequently suffer a fatal heart attack. The doctor will pronounce him dead from natural causes, and there will be a funeral. After a suitable period of mourning, you will return to Eton. Chin will remain here for a few months until your grandfather's estate is settled. You will sell the house and Chin will return to Hong Kong."

The Chinese had pronounced Sir Gerald's death warrant in conversational tones, and Clive could feel cold shivers at the small of his back. Everything was so precise, so orderly. The strange part of it all was that *he* could appreciate the logic of it. Instinct also told him that Chin was not destined to grow old.

7

Before he slept that night, Clive Hunter went carefully over the events of the day. His whole world had been turned upside-down in the space of a few hours. From being the grandson of a man who was socially accepted and respected for the service he had rendered to his country, he was, henceforth, the tool of some organization or other. From being the *legitimate* son of a British diplomat and his wife to being the son of a British army officer and a Chinese woman of dubious morals—in other words a *bastard*—was mind-boggling. To be told calmly that his "grandfather" was about to die was incredible. And now he was to go back to school and then on to Cambridge as though nothing had happened.

What was the alternative? If he *was* a bastard and had been selected for the role the organization had chosen for him, would they *allow* him to do other than what *they* wanted? Obviously not. He would follow his grandfather to an early grave. On the other hand, he had been excited by the story Mr. Sung had told him. He was still excited. Why not accept the situation as it was? If he was to believe Mr. Sung, life, apart from the demise of his "grandfather," would go on. Nothing would change for *him*. Go back to Eton and on to Cambridge. It would be fatal to do anything else.

What Mr. Sung had told him had to be the truth. What possible useful purpose could have been served in his learning Chinese as a child? Prior to today, he had accepted that it had been because his career was to be in the Diplomatic Corps but, on examination, that appeared pretty flimsy. If parents wanted their son to be a doctor, did they have him tutored when he started walking? Of course not! It was a lot more logical that his being taught to read and speak Chinese in the important formative years was for a purpose he had yet to learn of. Not many people could write Chinese characters. He could! Countless millions of literate Chinese could, but how many British schoolboys? He fell asleep pondering the question and trying to hazard guesses at the reason for his being chosen for the role the "organization" planned for him.

In the morning he awakened refreshed. A few moments after coming out of a deep sleep, he recalled every detail of the previous day. As he washed and dressed, he felt satisfied with the calm manner in which he had accepted the turn of events. He felt almost reborn. As though everything in his previous life had been the dream. Now was the time of reality. If he found Mr. Sung downstairs it *would* be reality. He decided to go forward in whichever direction the fates decreed.

Mr. Sung was indeed downstairs. He was seated at the breakfast table and when the young man entered the room, he said, "Good morning, Clive! You slept well?"

"Yes, thank you."

Sung smiled blandly as he said, "Excellent! A good night's sleep refreshes one for the day." He waved an indolent hand in the direction of the sideboard, "I can certainly recommend the kippers—best I've had in a long time."

Clive sat at the table and ate. The morning greeting from Chin was the same as it had always been. Coffee was poured for him in just the same way as it had been a thousand times before. The only difference was that Mr. Sung was at the head of the table where Sir Gerald Hunter normally sat. Sir Gerald would be buried behind the *Times* and breakfast eaten in silence. Today it was eaten in silence, but Clive felt he was being carefully scrutinized by the silent Mr. Sung.

After he had some of the kippers and was munching on toast and marmalade, Clive ventured to look at the man at the head of the table. Mr. Sung returned the stare but said nothing. Clive wanted to avert his eyes, but a streak of perversity wouldn't allow him to do so. For long minutes the two gazes were locked. At length Mr. Sung smiled and said, "Congratulations. I would never trust a man who was afraid to look me in the eye. Would I be correct in assuming you wanted to look away but were determined to stare me out if it took all day?"

The young man continued to look into the other's

eyes as he asked, "Isn't that the way it always is when two people find themselves staring at each other?"

"Yes. The eyes are the mirror of the soul. If someone immediately withdraws, it is because he—or she—is weak and unsure. Eyes tell more about the person than a thousand words." Mr. Sung wiped the corners of his mouth with his napkin, then placed it carefully on the table. "If one person is contemptuous of another, it is conveyed in the meeting of eyes for a fleeting second. A person can be made to feel his inferiority in that merest glance. Likewise, hatred can be clearly discerned in the eyes, no matter how one strives to hide it. There is nothing quite so easy to read as the trust in the eyes of an animal, or a child." He sat back in his chair, "I can tell you—and it is important to a young man to know this—never to avert your eyes from those of a woman you desire. She will read everything that is necessary from your eyes. Boldness will break down resistance. She will know you desire her, and if she can win the battle within herself, she will be yours."

Matter-of-factly, Clive said, "I hadn't thought about it that way before."

"You should have." An edge came into the voice of the Chinese, "I want you to think of it from now on. Develop the skill of using all of your animal instincts; that is what separates great men from the herd. Use your eyes to see into the souls of others. Use your mind to reason out situations. Trust nobody and never leave yourself open to blackmail because of weakness." He stood up, "If you have a weakness and indulge it, never leave evidence that can be used against you. Do you understand?"

"The weakness should be fought." Clive also stood up.

Sung smiled. "Don't fight weaknesses too hard, my young friend. The greatest men of history had them. My point—which I hope you did not miss—was that indulgence of them should never make you unnecessarily vulnerable. As it did your 'grandfather.'" He walked to the French doors, "Will you join me for a walk in the garden?"

It wasn't an invitation, and Clive knew it.

They walked in silence for some time. When they came to a bench, Sung sat down and the young man joined him. After a few moments, the Chinese said, "You have had time to think about yesterday. What have you decided?"

Clive had been expecting a question of this nature and he waited a few moments before he said, "I don't have a choice, do I?"

"No, we established that yesterday."

"I thought so, too. It will take some time for me to adjust to the new situation, but I have thought about it carefully. I am quite willing to do whatever it is you—or your organization—want me to do."

Sung turned and appraised him. "You will not be sorry. However, I want to warn you"—his eyes bored into Clive—"don't try to be clever at any time. The slightest sign that you are playing a devious game, you die!"

Clive did not trust himself to speak. He was afraid. It was a new feeling for him. He could not recall ever having experienced fear like this before in his life. However, the feeling passed quickly, and he felt quite calm. He waited quietly for Sung to speak again.

The Chinese looked deeply into the young man's eyes and seemed to read something of prime importance there. Whatever it was, he did not comment on it. Instead, he asked, "Are there any questions you want to ask me about the things you were told yesterday?"

"No," shaking his head, "I have gone over it all several times in my mind, and it all seems clear and logical. There are certain questions I would like to ask about the 'organization' you spoke of, but I feel you will not answer them."

Sung smiled. "Just so, you will be told more in good time." He folded his hands in his lap, "There is a question I want to ask *you*. What do you think it was that inspired us to select you to be the one who will serve us?"

Clive was puzzled. "I don't think I quite follow you. Do you mean when I was a baby?"

"I mean now. Let us suppose that we have others who could serve our purpose. Why do you think you were selected?" The Chinese was still smiling, but it was now a cold smile without a trace of humor. "Do you think it was chance—luck—"

After a long pause, Clive said, "I doubt that you do anything that hasn't been carefully considered. That rules out the elements of chance and luck. I have to conclude that you had a test of some kind."

"Excellent," Sung smiled. "There was a test. What do you think it was?"

"I have no idea," Clive said.

"You do, if you think about it." Sung closed his eyes, then spoke again, "Think back to last winter. You were home from Eton for Christmas. Do you recall going to a cinema in Brighton? Do you recall an incident at a certain bus stop?

Clive recalled the incident vividly. He had been bored and decided to see a movie. It had been cold when he left the cinema, and the next bus wasn't due for thirty minutes. He decided to walk to the next stop to keep himself warm. He set off at a leisurely pace, paying little attention to his surroundings. Christmas was over but the New Year was to come. Another week or so of holidays and then back to school. He had a lot to think about. The three young men came from behind. He found himself being pushed into the mouth of an alley. He stumbled slightly but quickly regained his balance. The tallest of the three who had jostled him laughed and said, "Got a cigarette, mate?"

"I don't smoke." Clive knew he was in trouble.

"How about giving us the price of some?"

"I haven't any money."

"Hear that, lads? Pretty-boy here hasn't got any money!" The tall one, who appeared to be the leader, laughed again, "Maybe he'd like to earn some!" The other two laughed with him and one of them, a heavyset youth of about Clive's age, pushed him. "You're one of these fancy public-school boys, ain't you? That's where they don't have any girls, eh? Have to toss yourself off, or do you go in for the young boys?"

Clive made no answer. He knew that no matter what he said, it would just provoke them further. He would have to act. Take the initiative before they did.

The third youth poked a finger into Clive's chest, "Lose your tongue?" Still Clive said nothing. The leader, who seemed fond of laughing, laughed again and asked, "Fancy sucking me off for a few bob?"

Clive swung at the one nearest him and had the satisfaction of hearing him groan as his fist bit into the youth's midriff. The satisfaction was short-lived. The other two youths attacked and their manner of fighting was new to Clive. No Marquess of Queensberry rules governed at the schools *they* had attended. It was no holds barred, and within minutes Clive was on the ground being kicked, punched, and butted by all three of his attackers. The one he had punched in the stomach was especially vicious. Instinctively, Clive covered his head with his arms, but his body as unprotected. He was kicked mercilessly before they stopped. From a haze of pain, Clive heard one of them say, "Let's get his pants off and have a look at his dick." He struggled as hands fumbled at his clothing but it was useless. He could feel the cold air on his buttocks. Clive heard the leader laugh as he said, "Fancy a shot at that lovely white ass?" There was answering laughter, then one of the others said, "Take what money he has and let's get the hell out of here." A long pause, a final brutal kick, and he was left alone.

It was cold and silent. There was almost no traffic —just an occasional car moving past the mouth of the alley. Slowly, painfully, Clive got to his feet. Thank God they hadn't taken his trousers with them! He got dressed. They must have been in a hurry to leave because a few coins jingled in one of the pockets. His billfold lay on the ground. He picked it up and found that all the currency was missing. He counted the coins they had left and found there was enough to cover his bus fare.

At home, Clive found his face unmarked. His body had angry red bumps and scrapes on it, and he knew he would be badly bruised and stiff in the morning. He pretended not to feel well and spent a couple of days in bed. His grandfather came up to see him twice a day. Chin brought his meals. He rubbed himself with liniment and massaged himself frequently to fight the stiffness. He found sleep difficult, but it didn't matter. He spent the hours remembering the faces and planning his revenge.

On the third day after his encounter, he felt able to go downstairs. After lunch he went to the workshop behind the garage. He lit the gas ring beneath the melting pot of lead. When the pot was hot and the metal began to bubble he cut off a length of rubber garden-hose about a foot and a half long. He plugged one end with a piece of steel and placed it in a vise. When the lead in the pot was molten, he took it from the gas ring, gently poured the contents into the open hole of the tubing, and plugged the open end. When the metal had cooled, he was ready.

Finding the youths presented little difficulty. He kept watch around the coffee shops, and on the second night the fates were kind. One youth left before the others. Clive followed him until he entered a deserted street. He gave no warning, but ran up behind him and hit him squarely on the back of the head. Without a sound, the youth crumpled and fell. Clive dragged him by the collar into an alley and bent over him to make sure he was still breathing. Satisfied, he proceeded to kick the unconscious boy. His efforts were deliberate and methodical. He concentrated on the joints and finally the groin. He found that he was detached and cool. He had expected to be exhilarated but there was nothing. Just the body on the ground and him taking revenge. An occasional groan came from the lips of the unconscious youth as a particularly painful blow struck home but it was over in a few minutes. Clive removed the trousers and underpants from the body and rolled them into a bundle. He threw them over a garden wall on his way back to the coffeeship.

Again he was lucky. The other two were still there and he had to wait for a while, but finally one of them left alone. His treatment of the second was similar to that of the first, and when it was over, he went back to complete the job. However, the third youth—the leader—almost got away. He was laughing and joking with a group of friends his own age when Clive looked in at the window. It looked as if he would leave with the group, but Clive waited anyway.

Suddenly he heard a motorcycle engine fire and race as it was revved up. Something told him to look into the coffeeshop. Sure enough, his victim wasn't there. He must have left by a back door. Clive turned away and ran to the end of the street. A glimpse of the face under the crash-helmet told Clive that the rider was his final target.

The driver of the motorcycle was revving the engine unnecessarily. He seemed to be filling the street with noise for the fun of it. Finally, he kicked the machine into gear and was ready to take off. It wasn't the way Clive had planned it, but it was his only chance. He lunged forward and swiped the front of the helmet with the loaded hose-pipe. The protective sides of the helmet took the main force of the blow, but the pipe smashed the rider's nose. With a loud scream, he slewed over to one side. The bike tilted with him and as the youth's fingers released the clutch the bike careened across the street, dragging the rider with it. Clive took to his heels and ran.

All of this flashed through Clive's mind as Mr. Sung watched him. Now Clive looked at the man cagily as he asked, "What do you know about that?"

"Shall we say I arranged it?"

"What do you mean 'arranged it'?"

Sung smiled and there was humor in it as he said, "I mean that a certain someone paid those three young men to set upon you—we were interested in seeing how you would react."

"Baloney!" Clive was on his feet. "I can't believe you had anything to do with it—it's too pat!"

"How do you think I know of it?" Mr. Sung was quite unperturbed. "I have to confess that the incident cost us much more than we had planned for, but, money aside, it paid off handsomely. You didn't—as one might expect an Eton schoolboy to—report the matter to your grandfather or to the police." His voice took on a note of approval, "No, you were motivated by deeper instincts than those of your class. You took personal revenge and, may I say, in a way that surprised us."

Clive took this in. It *was* possible—he was coming to believe *anything* was possible that concerned Mr. Sung! He shook his head in admiration, then said, "You are a very surprising man, Mr. Sung."

"So are you, Mr. Hunter." The Chinese rose to his feet, "That is why you have been chosen by the organization I represent. It is to be hoped that you fulfill your early promise." He turned and walked toward the house, leaving Clive to follow.

8

The years at Cambridge were largely uneventful for Clive Hunter. He took his studies seriously, played cricket and rugby, and enjoyed a full social life. He applied himself assiduously to mastering Chinese. This had been at the suggestion of Mr. Sung, who had arranged for a teacher for him. Playing rugby kept him in peak physical condition, and he played for his college on several occasions. He discovered that he had a large sexual appetite but had the good sense to satisfy it mainly in London. He had a number of short affairs with the girls of his social set, but did not allow any of them to develop to the point where he could not extricate himself without difficulty.

He saw Mr. Sung for the last time the day he returned to Eton. During his first few weeks he suspected everyone with Oriental features of being at Cambridge for the specific purpose of spying on him. Mr. Lee met with Clive at intervals during his university years, and it was he who dispelled his early fears of being under constant surveillance. Clive was shrewd enough to realize that there had to be some degree of surveillance, but he closed his mind to it and applied himself to the collegiate life.

Financially he had no problems. Though his "grandfather" had left very little in terms of hard cash, "dividends" from his Far East "investments" arrived with almost monotonous regularity. The sale of the house raised enough money to ensure that at the end of his studies he would be able to enter the world of business. Just what form that business would take was not clear to Clive, but Mr. Lee assured him that it would be taken care of when the time came. It was a comfortable situation to be in.

In his final year, he was instructed to let it be known that he intended to continue with his studies in the Far East for the next two years. This news surprised no one. He had no family ties, was independent financially, and had never traveled. Though he had many acquaintances, nobody was close to him. He joined in social activities and had occasional parties at his flat, but avoided situations which seemed likely to ripen into close friendships. Alone when it suited him, but never a loner.

He succeeded in getting a good degree, relinquished the lease on his apartment, and spent two weeks in London buying suitable clothes for his travels in the Orient. Before leaving for Hong Kong, he had one last meeting with Mr. Lee. It took place in his hotel room and lasted a few minutes—just time enough for him to receive the congratulations of the "organization" and instructions regarding making contact with his mentors in Hong Kong.

After he boarded the aircraft at Heathrow Airport, Clive felt tremendously elated. Things would soon fall into place. All his speculations would be resolved. As the giant jetliner rose above London, he located Windsor Castle and Eton College through the blue-tinged glass of the window at his elbow. Cambridge would be on the right-hand side of the plane but too far off to be visible. His life, until now, had been spent almost entirely in these two places, preparing him for what was to come. The future lay ahead and he was ready to face it.

Hong Kong!—Place of the Sweet Lagoons. From the first moment of approach by air, he loved it. Clive was captivated by the panorama of the mountain-ringed harbor of Hong Kong itself—peaked hills rising from the capital, Victoria. Kowloon peninsula jutting out from Mainland China. The New Territories. From books he had devoured, he was able to locate Macao, some forty miles to the west of Hong Kong, and surrounded completely by China. This was truly the Orient, and its magic floated up to him in waves.

Hong Kong itself was everything he had read about. Nothing he saw in the first few days of sightseeing disappointed him. Returning to his hotel one evening, he had just inserted his key in the door when the telephone rang. Later, he realized that someone must have been posted in the lobby. The caller gave no name, but instructed him to take a taxi to a certain address and to arrive precisely at 9:00. He would be met and given further instruction at that point. He was asked to repeat the time and place and, when he had complied, a click terminated the conversation.

Outwardly calm but inwardly tingling with excitement, he paid off the taxi driver outside the designated rendezvous at precisely 9:00. It was the Connaught Center skyscraper which seemed like a strange place to meet. However, as the taxi drew away from the curb, a Chinese in Western clothes approached and pointed to a car parked a few yards away. The rear door swung open, and when Hunter was seated, it was closed behind him.

The journey was short, made in silence. Hunter paid no attention to the man seated next to him nor the driver. He wanted to turn his head but knew it would be a breach of etiquette to do so. The man was obviously only an escort—if he were other than that, he would have started a conversation. At the destination the driver opened the door for Hunter. The other man joined him and indicated with a gesture that Hunter should follow.

It was a perfectly ordinary house of a middle-class Chinese family. Once inside, Hunter's companion indicated a chair in the hallway and disappeared through a door opposite. Taking the chair, Hunter settled in what he felt was the correct attitude. Not too stiffly, but not too comfortably. As he waited, he had the distinct impression that he was being observed. Fully five minutes elapsed before the door opened and Hunter was beckoned to enter.

It really was no surprise to him that the man seated behind the desk on the far side of the room was Mr. Sung.

54

Sung dismissed the third man with a gesture and, when they were alone, he bowed to Hunter. "Welcome to Hong Kong. May I offer you refreshment in what may seem to you less incongruous circumstances than the first time we met?" Hunter could not suppress a smile. The intervening years had left no marks of age on the Oriental features of Sung. As though divining his thoughts, the other man said, "You have grown to a man and it pleases me that you should be exactly the image of an upper-class Englishman." He smiled with a hint of malice, "Your activities in athletics and in ladies' beds appear to keep you in good physical condition!"

"Thank you." The younger man returned the smile, "A little tea, perhaps?"

Sung chuckled delightedly, "Excellent, excellent! Exactly the way to treat my observations on your leisure pastimes!" He resumed his seat behind the desk and indicated a comfortable chair next to it. "Sit down. I'll have the tea served before we talk of serious matters concerning your future."

When they were once again alone, Sung finished his tea and waited until the other man had done the same. Then he began. "First, I must extend the congratulations of the organization to you for obtaining your degree with honors. I must also congratulate you on the manner in which you have conducted yourself since we last met. Reports have been most satisfactory and, should you prove equally satisfactory in the course of the next two years, yours will be a place within the organization to be envied." He toyed idly with a paperweight for a moment, then said, "Your curiosity with regard to the nature of our activities has been contained with difficulty, I assume."

Hunter smiled and said, "It has consumed me for a long time but the curiosity of youth has been replaced by patience of manhood."

"Aptly put, your Chinese studies have not been wasted. Have you no theory or calculated guess?"

Again Hunter smiled, "Speculation is the wasted time of fools."

"Just so." Sung placed the paperweight on the desk with exaggerated care, then said, "You have, of course, encountered the history of the Triad during your studies?"

"Yes."

"You followed the role of Triad in Chinese history?"

"Yes, I made a special study of it at one point."

"There is no need, therefore, for me to waste time in outlining that history to you?"

"No, I am familiar with it."

"Would it come as a surprise to you to learn that the organization which I represent is the Triad?"

Hunter digested this for a moment, "No, I would accept that Triad could be a likely possibility."

"More than a possibility—" Sung broke off and stood up. "There is something I want you to do for me," he came around and stood before the younger man. "Remain seated but extend your right hand."

When Hunter had done so, Sung took a small, delicately carved knife from the inside pocket of his jacket. Deliberately, he pricked the cushion of his own right thumb until blood welled from the puncture. He reached for Hunter's extended hand and, intoning the words, "With this blade, fresh with the blood of Triad, I prepare you." Then, with solemn deliberation, Sung cut Hunter's thumb. When the blood flowed, he placed the two thumbs so that one wound covered the other. After a moment, he said, "For as long as you shall live your blood will be that of Triad and, in gratitude for this, your life will be dedicated to Triad, though it may mean death." He wiped the blade of the knife carefully on a silk handkerchief from his breast pocket, restored it to the inside of his jacket, and resumed his seat.

Hunter sucked at the wound on his thumb while he watched the cleaning of the knife. It was all so unexpected and theatrical that he couldn't quite believe it had actually happened. Something from a comic book or some farfetched tale in a novel. Any impulse he may have had to laugh was quickly stifled when Sung said, "Despite the reports in what are normally responsible newspapers, you have been initiated into Triad by my simple act. No elaborate ceremonies are conducted. The mingling of my blood with yours has tied you to our Society with bonds that only death can sever. From this point on, your role in life is to do our bidding. There are others who will do your bidding and, in due course, you will be instructed in the ways of dealing with those subordinate to you. Also, you will learn how to respond when challenged by those superior to you. Be assured that the Society will have no hesitation in taking a life that is rightfully theirs—as your is."

Hunter contented himself with nodding understanding of what had been said. From what he had read of Triad, he did not doubt for a moment the truth of Sung's statements. Having experienced the efficiency of the "organization," he did not doubt that they were Triad. And now that he was one of them he belonged somewhere. In a way, the Society would be surrogate for the mother and father he had never known.

Sung allowed the silence to last for a few minutes. Time for the initiate to recover. Time for Sung to decide just how much he was prepared to divulge to Hunter. At last he said, "Progress within the Society is determined by the suitability of an initiate to fill a position. In your case, there is a very important position to be filled, but I must tell you there are other candidates for this role. This is the way of the Triad —nobody is indispensable. Our system has proved to be foolproof over the centuries, and no other organization in the world wields the power that we do. You have studied our history, and you are aware that obedience without question is the rule. However, because you are a very special case, I will permit you to ask the question I know is uppermost in your mind right now."

Hunter did not hesitate. "Why was I—to all the world a Caucasian—chosen to be initiated into what has been strictly a Chinese secret society?"

Sung nodded approval, "Excellent. You show promise. The reason you were chosen was that to us your soul is Chinese. I am sure that you appreciate that the obvious drawback of integrating a Chinese into the Western world is Oriental features. I have stated that the Society has unparalleled power. Power of a magnitude and extent you could not possibly comprehend. I do not know the full extent of it—only that which is necessary for me to be aware of. Because of the ways in which the world has changed and shifted in the balance of power held by nations of the world, we have found it necessary to change also. It is of prime importance to our future as Triad that we have access to decision-forming process at the very highest level in the West. To achieve this, we must have people placed in strategic positions within the power structure of the West. Need I go on?"

"No, I quite see what you mean."

"Good. You will also see that traitors of the West are of no interest to us. We require our own people. People who have been tried and tested and met with the highest possible demands imposed on them. Men who are totally dedicated to the Triad Society." He used a pointing finger to emphasize his next sentence. "You—my friend—could be one of these men!"

After allowing Hunter a moment to digest this, he went on, "During the next two years, you will be introduced to the operation of our organization. You will learn all you need to know. The ramifications of Triad are extremely complex and entrusted only to those who prove worthy. I must stress that the interests of Triad must be served above all other considerations." He sat back and considered Hunter for a moment, "When did you last see Mr. Lee?"

"Last Monday in London."

"That is the last time you will see him."

"He is dead?"

"Precisely. He knew of your existence and the details of your education. He could have proved a potential danger. One man cannot be allowed to jeopardize a project which has cost time, effort, and money. Not one man—or a hundred men!" Sung spread his hands in a fatalistic gesture. "The Society before the individual."

Hunter nodded, "The logic of Lee's fate is perfectly clear to me."

"I'm pleased that is your attitude. There will be times when you will have to take similar action. You must never hesitate. Show no weakness to your subordinates because I can assure you that you will receive no mercy from your superiors." He eased himself into a more comfortable position in his chair, then went on, "Under normal circumstances, you would not have been told of the demise of Lee, but it is so very important to your future that you appreciate fully what being a member of Triad means. Now, to other matters. I mentioned to you that you are a candidate for a very important position in the organization. I now tell you that there were ten in all. Each one was conceived by a British father and a Chinese mother. Each was placed in an environment such as yours and each educated according to our requirements. Four of the children showed signs of having Oriental features, and they were disposed of. One died of natural causes, and two proved to be below the standard of intelligence necessary for our purposes. That leaves three—yourself and two others. It follows that your chances of success are two-to-one. Understand?"

"Yes."

Sung examined his fingernails for a moment as though they were of importance, then said, "The decision of how much you need to know during these next years will rest with me because I will be your *Ahkung*—" He broke off as a slight smile appeared on Hunter's face, "What amuses you?"

"That you of all people should become my grandfather."

Sung smiled in return, "Ah, yes, it is ironic. However, in the structure of Triad, the controller of an area or an important project is called Grandfather. A venerable title in the Chinese tradition of family. We are structured in a way that one knows the identity of all subordinates but only of one superior. Another thing, you no doubt have read from time to time in the newspapers of tong and gang warfare, of squabbles over territories and secret rituals. There has always been a fascination about tongs and mysterious Chinese with pigtails for Westerners. We encourage them to believe in all of it. An elaborate smokescreen to obscure reality. To put it simply you will become a very dangerous man to the West and also a very dangerous man to us."

III
London
1976

9

A woman asked to describe Clive Hunter in one word might call him "eligible." A man, on the other hand, might call him a "lucky bastard." Hunter was aware that he was a "lucky bastard" and had no regrets about his parentage. With regard to luck, he did not believe in it. All experience confirmed that a man weighs each situation and determines his destiny by decision. The element of luck played no part in his existence.

Questioned further, a woman might describe Hunter's eligibility in terms of degree of attractiveness, marital status, charm, manners, and wealth. If she knew him intimately, she would speak complimentarily of his body and sexual ability, but never of the fact that he tired of women quickly. A man, in similar circumstances, would probably define a lucky bastard as a man with a flat in Regent's Park, a weekend cottage in Suffolk, several cars, a successful import business that allowed for trips abroad, and the benefit of a "good" education. If the man had had dealings with Hunter and had survived the experience, he would know that he was utterly ruthless and extremely dangerous. Such a man would never divulge this knowledge.

A policeman might describe Hunter as being thirty-four years old, medium height (5' 10"), weight 170 lbs., hair black, eyes blue, clean-shaven, no distinguishing marks or scars.

If asked for a word to describe himself. Clive Hunter would have said "enigma." The world at large regarded him as such, and people who had known him and shared his educational background found him to be good company, extremely well-connected socially, and possessed of good taste. That he had the wealth to indulge his tastes was attributed to inheritance and business acumen.

Ascot, Goodwood, Henley, Cowes were annual musts for Hunter, and he genuinely looked forward to them. He enjoyed sentimental journeys to Eton and Cambridge. The Boat Race, Lords, the Oval and Twickenham were attended with enthusiasm. His choice of clubs was in keeping with his needs and position and, being a bachelor, his having a Chinese manservant was regarded as perfectly normal. That the Chinese doubled as chauffeur on occasion was accepted, and everyone assumed that the man had served Hunter while he pursued postgraduate study of Oriental languages and customs in the East. To bring such a servant back to England on completion of these studies was in the best tradition of British behavior.

Hop Tang prepared a pot of tea and placed it on the silver tray beside the matching water jug, sugar bowl, and milk jug. As always, he put two cups and saucers on the tray. He glanced at the clock and, noting it was five minutes to the hour, covered the teapot with a cosy, and lit a cigarette. His master kept late hours but insisted on being roused at precisely 7:00 each morning. As he smoked he looked across Regent's Park and deduced from the light mist that it would be a fine day. After years of living in England, he still hated the climate. In all other things he was happy. His master had proved worthy of his position in the Society, and Hop Tang's role was now purely to serve and protect. In early years, he had disliked his assignment and longed for his own kind. Now he knew that Hunter *was* his own kind, and Tang was content.

He crushed out his cigarette, washed his hands, removed the cosy from the teapot, and lifted the tray. He knocked at the bedroom door and allowed a moment to pass before entering. An embarrassing situation would cause his master to lose face. This morning Tang's discreet delay had been unnecessary; Hunter was sitting upright in bed while his companion was still asleep. Hop Tang wished his master a good morning and furnished a weather report as he set the tray down on a bedside table. He then opened the curtains, ran a warm bath, and withdrew.

Hunter sipped from his cup and smoked a cigarette as he quickly reviewed matters to be attended to in the course of the day. Each matter had previously been examined in detail, and he had taken a decision on it. Satisfied that the important aspects of his day were in control, he put the cup and saucer on the bedside table and gently drew the sheet down. The smooth roundness of the woman's buttocks excited his desire. He maneuvered himself so that he was between her legs, inserted his hands beneath her pelvis and raised her until he could mount from the rear. The act was one of basic gratification and soon over. The woman responded, but Hunter had finished before she was satisfied.

When Hunter had shaved and bathed, the girl was sitting up in bed drinking tea. He commented briefly on the promise of good weather and passed through to the dressing room. As always, Hop Tang had laid out his clothes for the day and, as always, the choice was impeccable. He dressed quickly. The girl watched him and as he crossed the bedroom, she asked, "When shall I see you?"

"Who knows?" he shrugged. "I'll be around. It was a great night and we must do it again sometime."

She nodded but did not trust herself to speak. She had wanted him for a long time and had planned her strategy. She had hoped that a night in bed would be followed by an association that would lead to some sort of permanent relationship. Others had tried and failed, but she had believed she was different. She had realized in the course of their lovemaking that he only wanted to use her body. He had done so with great skill, and she had exhausted herself in reaching heights beyond previous experience. She had no regrets, but her pride made it difficult to accept the totality of his dismissal.

Hunter paused with his hand on the door handle, "Tang will attend to your breakfast and arrange a taxi for you." He indicated the bathroom, "You'll find everything you require in there. As I said, it was an excellent night." The door closed and he was gone.

The administrative affairs of Far East Importation Ltd. were conducted in a suite of well-decorated offices in New Bond Street, where a staff of competent people skillfully dealt with the complicated procedures of meeting the requirements of Board of Trade, Customs & Excise, and shipping regulations. The business was highly successful and the legitimate activities effectively disguised the true function of the company. The staff were all ordinary British citizens and completely unaware of the existence of Triad.

There was no familiarity between Hunter and his employees. That Hunter spoke Chinese and Japanese with visitors was not unusual, and the fact that Hunter spent little time in his office was attributed to the efficiency of Mr. Fotheringham, his general manager.

On this particular morning Hunter, had been at his desk for half an hour before Fotheringham arrived at precisely 9:00. Hunter was studying a complicated contract involving the import of machine parts from Japan. The general manager showed no surprise at finding Hunter at work and, after a polite exchange of greetings, the two men discussed straightforward business matters for an hour.

At 10:00 two Japanese gentlemen were shown in and a satisfactory negotiation was concluded for the future of their machine parts.

At precisely 11:30 two Chinese gentlemen were shown in to discuss matters concerning the distribution of foodstuffs for use in restaurants. As these men were fairly frequent visitors and discussion was to be in Chinese, there was no need for Fotheringham to be present.

The two Chinese paid respects to their Leader and acquainted him with the results of their last instructions. Each was an *Ahkung* or "grandfather." Eng Soon Cheong controlled London and the South, and Hup Wah Kee, Birmingham and the North. (They, together with Ming Sut Poo, controller of Scottish activities, and Tsang Lo, who controlled Wales and West, shared the secret of the identity of the Leader in the United Kingdom.) As *Ahkungs* they were subject to Hunter's authority. As far as they were concerned, there was no one beyond Hunter. Anonymity had to be preserved at all levels. Such is the structure of the Triad.

Hunter listened attentively to the reports. The method employed by Hunter in making decisions applied at all levels of the Society operation. He did not solicit opinion nor enter into discussion. He asked questions and ascertained the facts, but he had the sole responsibility for decision. The function of the other men was to execute his decisions.

Eng Soon Cheong was concerned about a "protection" racket run by non-Chinese hoods in the Greater London area. Shopkeepers, traders, and restaurateurs were being forced into buying "insurance policies." In exchange for a weekly "premium" they were permitted to carry on business undisturbed. If the premiums were not paid, nasty accidents would befall the unfortunate owner of the business. There would be embarrassing disturbances on the premises, mysterious fires, broken windows, or perhaps a car accident.

Hunter weighed the factors, then decided. "It is obvious that this is purely a local organization. The two brothers who control it are, by normal standards, clever and fairly ruthless in their methods. Their activities do not directly conflict with those of the Society, but if we allow them to harass Chinese businessmen we will lose 'face.' Since your warnings have been ignored, we must take strong measures that cannot be ignored."

He lit a cigarette and blowing a plume of smoke toward the ceiling, Hunter watched the wreaths of feathery blue dance in a shaft of sunlight. Direct confrontation with the gang would attract police attention, investigation, and possible newspaper coverage. The situation required that pressure be placed on the leaders of the gang in such a way that no publicity would result. He shifted his gaze from the shaft of sunlight to Eng Soon Cheong. "From what you have told me, it would appear that the elder of the two brothers is too well protected for us to succeed in inflicting harm without a good deal of unfortunate publicity. Our efforts must therefore be directed against the younger brother."

Mr. Cheong nodded agreement, "What will be the procedure?"

"Simple but effective," Hunter laughed softly. "We

will permit the younger Mr. Galston to indulge his taste for exciting women and, in consequence, be in the position to convince the elder Mr. Galston that we are serious about his discontinuing protection for Chinese businessmen." For the next few minutes, Hunter outlined in detail the procedure to be adopted.

Hup Wah Kee faced a situation in Birmingham that required immediate action. Since it was Triad's policy to cloak all activity with situations calculated to confuse investigation, a chain of Chinese restaurants with branches in major towns and cities provided a perfect cover for Triad. Clever bookkeeping ensured that no connections could be established. Furthermore, by permitting—and in some cases financing—perfectly innocent Chinese to operate restaurants, it was impossible for an outsider to distinguish one from another.

Wholesale companies supplying items necessary for the restaurants made up a perfect distribution network. Some wholesalers conducted a perfectly legitimate business, and others combined Triad activity with normal grading. All Chinese are aware of the Triad but, as with the *omerta* that shrouds Mafia activity, a wall of silence surrounds Triad. Like the Mafia and *Union Corse*, Triad depends on fear and anonymity for their very existence. Anything that might threaten Triad's hold over the Chinese populace had to be dealt with swiftly and effectively.

A young Chinese immigrant had recently opened a restaurant in Birmingham with his own money. The man spoke fluent English and was well educated. In Hong Kong, as a son of wealthy parents, he had enjoyed a high standard of living, but the future promised little for him. An elder brother would inherit his father's business, and he would have to be content with second place. Education had broadened his outlook, and he resented the restrictions placed on him by custom and tradition. When he married, his bride was approved by his father, and when he had voiced his intention to go to England, no major objections were raised. He and his wife liked their new life, and the coming of a son completed their happiness. He knew of the existence of the Triad but had never experienced personal dealings with them. Unfortunately, he had voiced opinions in the Chinese community that there was no place for Triad activity in a democracy. Being respected in the community, there was some danger that his opinions might carry weight.

The situation demanded swift and decisive action. Hunter gave instructions to Hup Wah Kee. "You will arrange for this man to be warned against making further remarks that could be detrimental to the Society. You might suggest to him that a few favorable remarks to his friends would go a long way toward his enjoying good health. If, for any reason, it appears necessary for the warning to be repeated"—he spread his hands expressively—"you will remove the threat."

"I understand," Hup Wah Kee inclined his head, "I will attend to the matter."

When the two *Ahkungs* had gone, Hunter spent some time in reflection. All was well with the Society's activities in the U.K. The two problems were in the nature of being a nuisance—nothing more. The setting up of the organization in Britain had taken a long time, but now the machinery was running smoothly. It was time for Hunter to concentrate on his most ambitious project.

Hunter's idea had received warm approval from the Inner Council. He did not, of course, have direct access to top level, but he had submitted the plan through channels. The answer had taken a long time, but he finally received the message: "Brilliant plan, progress at your discretion." He had lived with it for more than a year now, but the year's delay had strengthened his position. He had been able to cultivate people necessary for its successful launching.

It had begun with a chance suggestion in his club that he should stand for Parliament. Hunter had laughed at the suggestion at first but, on reflection, the possibilities the House offered intrigued him. As a Member of Parliament, he would be in a position that could be invaluable to the Society. He had explored the idea and put together a plan. The cottage in Suffolk qualified him as a resident of the area, and he had spent a good deal of time there during the year. He had become involved in local affairs but had been careful not to seem too eager. He had cultivated a friendship with the Member of Parliament for the constituency and was accepted by the local Conservatives. The seat would be perfect for Hunter to enter the House on the back benches.

The only drawback to the plan was that the incumbent Member—the Rt. Hon. Peter Hays-Aldington—was forty years of age and enjoyed perfect health. A general election would certainly return a Tory candidate for Suffolk East, but it would be Hays-Aldington. Hunter would be elected only in the event of Hays-Aldington's resignation or death. In the *natural* course of events, both were unlikely.

In the meantime, Hunter continued to meet with the right people in London and discuss, in general terms, the likelihood of his standing as a Conservative candidate at the next general election. The party assured him they would find a constituency where he would be elected, and already there had been suggestions that Hunter's proficiency in Chinese and Japanese could be of considerable value to the government. With regard to any investigation by the party, Hunter had no fears of adverse results. The Society had long since established an impeccable lineage for the Leader in Britain.

10

Charlie Hong's kitchen was a hive of activity in preparation for the lunchtime trade. In just under an hour, all the tables in the dining room would be occupied. Charlie Hong took pride in the standard of meals and service in his establishment. He divided his time between supervision of the dining area and tasting the contents of pots and pans. He had just come through from the kitchen when his attention was attracted by a rapping on the front door. That two Chinese should want to enter this early in the day was not unusual; representatives of suppliers frequently called during slack business periods. He admitted them, but his welcome smile froze when the two suddenly became six.

The manner in which they executed their task demonstrated professionalism. The dining-room staff was forced to join those in the kitchen; Mrs. Hong and their infant son were brought down from the living quarters, Mr. Hong found himself wedged into a corner of the kitchen with the business end of a wicked-looking automatic pressed into his stomach.

Once the intruders had everything under control, the leader adopted a deceptively casual manner. He nodded encouragingly to Mrs. Hong, frowned at her husband whose lips were framing words of protest, tasted the contents of the pots and pans with lip-smacking approval, lowered and raised oven doors, and made clucking sounds to the infant Hong.

Silence hung heavy, and even the beloved ginger cat paused in her elaborate cleaning ritual to watch the stranger move about the kitchen. Finally the man walked slowly up to Charlie Hong. "You are a most imprudent man. You have a fine wife and child and a flourishing business. You are respected in the Chinese community and yet you speak against a Society that has been honored in China for many centuries. You have no reason to do this. The Society has never interfered with your life. You have behaved very badly." The words were in polite Cantonese, but the tone carried menace that caused prickles of ice-cold fear along Hong's spine. Panic seized him as he remembered whispered stories of the ruthless methods employed by Triad.

The leader sighed. "It is essential that you cease to speak of our activities. Unfortunately, we are aware that a verbal warning would carry no weight with you. It is necessary, therefore, to demonstrate that we are not to be trifled with." He moved to where Mrs. Hong held her child tightly. "As I have said, you have a fine son." His fingers rested lightly on the boy's cheek. "I should hate to think of him being the victim of an unfortunate accident."

Hong's cry of protest became a groan as the muzzle of the gun bit deeply into his belly. His wife turned away instinctively to protect her child. A smile flickered briefly across the man's face. Then, with a smooth movement, he lifted the cat. Cradling it in one arm, he murmured reassuringly as he stroked its head. It appeared that his attention was temporarily distracted.

In the silence that followed, only a faint bubbling from the stoves and the purring of the cat were audible. A kitchen helper, motivated by reasons which he hardly understood, made a sudden movement toward the man with the cat and was felled by a guard. The leader slowly raised his head and glanced around to ensure that the situation was completely under control. Then, apparently satisfied, he grasped the cat by the loose fur and skin at its neck and held it at arm's length.

The animal hung in this suspended position without struggle. Everyone in the kitchen focused on the leader and the cat. They sensed something was about to happen, but were totally unprepared for what followed. The leader smiled grimly and lowered one of the oven doors with his free hand. He addressed Hong, "Watch carefully, my friend—it could just as easily be your son!" As he finished the sentence, he hurled the cat into the baking heat and slammed the door.

The six left as the kitchen resounded with the cries of the demented animal seeking escape from the agonies of hell.

The girl eased her body away from that of the sleeping man, then lay quietly at the edge of the bed. Knowing she had exhausted him, she allowed a few moments to elapse before her feet slid to the floor. Noiselessly she crossed the room to the door. With long, slender fingers she gently released the catch. Then she returned to the bed with equal stealth and awaited developments.

When the men arrived, she was aware only of their presence as three shapes silhouetted against the light from the window. Her feet again found the floor, and she moved away from the bed. At a signal the three moved as one to the bed. A gag was placed over the mouth of the sleeping man, and his legs and arms secured before he was fully awake.

When the light was switched on, it took a few moments for the bound man's eyes to adjust to the glare. When he saw that his three captors were Chinese, his immediate frantic conclusion was that they were related to the girl and were about to exact revenge for his having had her. He turned his head to her in mute appeal but found only beautiful inscrutability.

If the Chinese found the perfect nakedness of the girl attractive, discipline was stronger. Not once did their gaze shift from the bed. The leader motioned with a hand, and she began to dress. When she finished a second gesture dismissed her. Only then did the leader address the man on the bed. His face was expressionless as he said, "Despite warnings, you and your brother have continued to harass Chinese business interests in London. We must ensure that no further harassment takes place." He took a flat leather case from a side pocket of his jacket and measured his words by tapping it lightly in the palm of his left hand. "Because of your activities, we have lost a good deal of 'face.' 'Face' is important to us." He paused, opened the leather case, and removed a surgeon's scalpel.

Frank Galston was terrified. Like many of his kind, he took sadistic pleasure in inflicting pain but he was terrified of it. Basking in the reflected glory of big brother Billy was the story of his life. Frank was shown respect only because of the protection of his older brother. Frank's bravado had grown from this. The girl tonight was a good example. He believed she wanted him because he was such a stud. He had never fucked a Chinese girl, so it was back to the flat he kept for his sexual adventures without a thought that she might represent trouble. Now he was facing the most dangerous situation of his young life. He struggled with his bonds and made sounds in his throat that promised money in exchange for mercy. He knew little of the code of Triad.

The leader of the group spoke again without emotion, "Your brother should take heed of what we are about to do to you. If he were less prudent, we would have done it to him, but he takes many precautions to protect himself." His tone hardened, "However, you may tell him that we will pay with his life if we have occasion to cross paths in the future." Then, taking a hypodermic syringe and a bottle from his inside pocket, he inserted the needle through the foil lid and drew the contents into it.

Galston redoubled his efforts to free himself and the strength of stark terror caused the bed to shake. The cord bit deeply into his wrists and ankles. At a nod from the leader, the other two men moved to either side of the bed and took hold of the captive. The needle was plunged into the fleshy part of Galston's left thigh.

It took ten minutes for the local anesthetic to take effect. The three Chinese watched their terrified victim in complete silence. At length the leader of the group signaled that it was time to proceed. He took all four pillows and placed them behind Galston's head and shoulders so that he was propped in a near-sitting position. A cruel smile spread from the leader's mouth to his almond eyes. His words were hissed as he said, "You are a man who prides himself on his sexual prowess. In your own foolish mind you prize what hangs between your legs and the pleasure it affords you." The smile widened, "You are a big man when you are thrusting into a female. You like them small because of the pleasure it gives you in hurting them!" He lifted the man's genitals with the blunt edge of the scalpel blade and relished the terror in his victim's eyes. A tone of mocking reassurance crept into his voice, "Don't be afraid for your prick—I'm leaving you that to pass your water!" The surgical instrument was withdrawn and a flood of relief engulfed Galston. It was short-lived. In the next breath, the Chinese said, "No, you can keep that—it is your balls I'm going to take."

Galston watched in fascinated horror as an incision was made on his scrotum and the keen edge of the scalpel deftly removed his testicles.

Clive Hunter took pleasure in savoring the good things of life. Dedicated to his life's work, he applied himself to it and never allowed personal needs to take precedence. Even now, after an excellent meal prepared and served by Tang, he was preoccupied with

Diana Grosvenor's place in his plans rather than her seductive presence. He had decided that as Member for Suffolk East he should assume the respectability of marriage. Her background was right and she was certainly attractive. It would be no hardship to limit his sexual appetite to the marriage bed—for a time, at least. She would fit in with country life and provide the proper social status for a Member of Parliament. He would, of course, keep the London flat as a base from which to attend the House. Yes, all in all, he was pleased with his selection of a mate.

The girl snapped her fingers to rouse him from his reflective mood, "Penny for them!"

"Worth more than that," he smiled, "I was thinking of you."

"Dishonorable thoughts, or were you thinking of taking me home?" she said seductively.

"Both—I think it would be a pity to expose you to the night air."

She smiled lazily, "When you decide, let me know."

"The decision is yours." He hadn't yet attempted to make love to her, careful not to overplay his hand, but the prospect excited him. He slowly took in the sweep of her long legs and the swell of her breasts. The sensation of his roused maleness was pleasurable.

He interpreted her silence as invitation and moved to her. He stood before her for a moment or two, sure that she must be aware of his desire. She did not resist when he drew her to her feet, and her hunger for him was apparent as she drew his tongue greedily into her mouth. She pressed her thighs against his hardness as he deftly freed her straining breasts. When he took their weight in the palms of his hands, his thumbs teased the hardening nipples and soft moans of pleasure encouraged him to slip his hand down between her legs. The softness of her pubic hair led to the moist folds of her vulva, which he parted with tantalizing skill.

She showed her inexperience as she struggled to bring his swollen organ from his trousers. When she finally succeeded, he winced as she seized it in both hands. Her inexperience was further evident during the night when she adopted only the conventional position each time he had her. He vaguely regretted that someone else had taken her virginity, but consoled himself with the thought that completing her education would be something to look forward to.

IV

11

Inspector James Maxwell drowsily contemplated the stewardess, trying to decide whether or not her breasts were larger than those of his girl in Kowloon. She certainly had better legs, but Chinese women are not noted for legs. Her buttocks excited him and, as the girl leaned over, he could make out the lines of very brief bikini panties. No doubt she had a man somewhere, and Maxwell doubted he could get any on the strength of one flight and a bit of talk, but it was certainly worth a try. A bit of British would be a welcome change even though his experience had shown him the Chinese had a much more extensive repertoire. No doubt his girl would be with somebody else by the end of the week, but that was part of the way of life. He would have to find someone himself for the duration of his stay in England. Someone who didn't have to be paid for and certainly nobody who wanted him to write every day when it was over.

His temporary posting to the United Kingdom would be a welcome change. He was totally pissed off with the frustrations of Hong Kong, the graft and corruption, and the sluggishness of his superiors.

Little had changed in this last year for Maxwell. Still an inspector and, he thought bitterly, bloody likely to be when he packed in. His superiors had the force running around in ever-decreasing circles that threatened to wind up with everyone disappearing up their own arse. Any bunch of young hoodlums who got together still became, in the eyes of the authorities, a "tong." Exotic names like Red Dragon, August Tigers, Golden Dawn of the Sleeping Cat were bandied around as "lodges" or "secret societies." It was crap! He knew it and they knew it. But none of them were willing to take serious action against the Triad. He had shot his mouth off on several occasions, but it was a waste of time. His conclusion was that most of the bastards were on the take like Watson had been. Time had only slightly mellowed Maxwell since the Watson incident and the murder of his friend Towers.

Maxwell sipped from his glass. The Triad must be laughing up the narrow sleeves of their Western jackets at the failure of the West to recognize that they were being manipulated by powers beyond the government of Red China, by string-pullers who made the dragon dance to their tune. Maxwell sighed, if a dummy like him could see it, why the hell couldn't the bright boys at the top of the totem pole see it?

For a kid from the East End of London, he hadn't done too badly. Out of school at fifteen and working in a butcher's shop was a far cry from his present situation. National Service in the army had taken him out of the environment that would otherwise have stifled him and exposed him to Hong Kong. Then three years with the police in London, but life with a house full of hungry kids and a wife who would dole out sex as if it were some kind of a Sunday-school treat was not for him. He watched the others get bogged down and applied for Hong Kong.

He had never allowed himself to get involved in the graft and corruption of Hong Kong, but as his hopes for making serious progress against the Triad faded, he had devised his own method of providing for his old age. When opportunity presented itself, he held onto money that should have been handed in as evidence. The money would be forfeit to the Crown at the conclusion of the case and it would be squandered anyway. He had better use for it. Over the years he had amassed a bit more than 20,000 pounds. Not a fortune, but a bloody sight more than he would ever have saved working in some supermarket as a meat cutter!

He ordered a fresh drink to find out if the stewardess would repeat her teasing routine. Sure enough, she took longer than was necessary to serve him and exerted pressure on his arm with her thighs as she did so. When he fixed his eyes on hers, she blinked long lashes and the pressure remained. In a soft voice that only she could hear, he said, "If you have a telephone number in London, I'd love to call you sometime. Like tonight." She picked up his empty glass and walked off as though she had not heard him. He consoled himself with the thought that she was probably wearing a padded bra.

His thoughts wandered to his assignment. The briefing had taken all of ten minutes and consisted of his being told that the Home Office had requested the loan of someone who had firsthand experience of Triad. It appeared that they were encountering Chinese problems in England since the influx of Chinese immigrants. Some bright boy had been doing his homework and probably read newspaper reports that Triad and tongs were behind the gang warfare in the Far East. In Maxwell's opinion, the bright boy was likely to be some chinless wonder who wouldn't know Triad from a *mah-jongg* tile.

The upshot of the briefing was that he was packed on a plane within four hours. He was sure that nothing would come of the assignment. Probably somebody just wanted him and his views removed for a few months. He noticed that the stewardess was making her way up the aisle but decided to ignore her. No point in pressing the nose against the baker's window if you know you can't get a taste of the goodies.

He was surprised when she replaced his drink with a fresh one he hadn't ordered—and more surprised when he saw a telephone number neatly printed on the paper napkin.

12

Tony Macdonald badly wanted a cigarette, but knowing the Old Man's views on tobacco, he refrained from lighting up. Nothing would be said, but exaggerated coughs and raised eyebrows would rob him of pleasure before he had taken more than a few drags. A flicked ash would assume the proportion of a Sahara sandstorm, and a crushed butt in the ashtray an obscenity to be removed by the disapproving secretary. Nothing worse than smoking in the presence of a reformed addict. It was easier to fold one's arms and concentrate, rather than be inconsiderate. Macdonald did just that.

Sir Archibald Sanderson took his time finishing the job he had been working on when Macdonald was shown in. Beyond a curt nod toward the chair he wanted Macdonald to occupy, nothing had passed between them. The minutes ticked away and Macdonald pretended to take an interest in the clock. He couldn't count the number of times he had sat in this same chair and examined the same clock. He was sure he could have drawn it from memory and faithfully placed every scratch on the polished surface of the wooden frame. Why the chief bothered to act out the same old charade was one of the mysteries of the department.

At last Sir Archibald closed the manila file. He carefully screwed the cap onto his fountain pen, "Given up smoking, Macdonald?"

"No, sir."

"Just sacrificing your comfort in consideration of mine, eh?"

"Not exactly."

"Never mind, I don't intend keeping you here for long. You have a lot of reading to do." He pushed several files from the corner of his desk toward the other man, "Make a change, won't it? Haven't had much to do for a week or two, have you?"

Old bastard, thought Macdonald as he reached for the files. *First quiet spell I've had in years, and he has to make a big deal out of it.* Aloud, he said, "I manage to fill in my days, sir."

"I daresay." Sir Archibald dismissed Tony's remark and pointed to the files in Macdonald's lap. "I want you to read every word in those. I want you to read every word several times. Read and inwardly digest, as my old English teacher used to say. When you have finished, I want you to be the world's greatest living expert on the subject matter. Got it?"

Macdonald nodded, "Got it."

Sir Archibald fixed his eyes on Macdonald. "This is one of the more important assignments we have undertaken since the end of World War II. I'm giving it

77

to you because I think you are the man for the job." He pointed once again to the files, "In these you will find every scrap of information the department could beg, borrow or steal on the Chinese Triad." His eyes were penetrating, "You have heard of the Triad Society, I trust?"

"Yes, sir, I have heard of it. More rumor than fact most of the time. I sometimes wonder if Triad really exists or whether it's just a myth."

"Hardly one of your most intelligent remarks, Macdonald. Do you imagine I am filling in my day talking to you about myths?"

Old bastard! This time Macdonald almost said it aloud. Sir Archibald's sarcasm always had the effect of making him feel like a schoolboy. One day he was going to be pushed too far, and that day would probably be his last one with the department. He placed the manila files on the floor and lit a cigarette. Sir Archibald's glare was a source of satisfaction.

The older man picked up a paper knife and suspended it between his index fingers at either end. He held it in this manner for a few moments, then, with a deft movement, balanced it by its point on one finger. Then he grasped the handle in his right fist.

His eyes fixed on Macdonald and he said, "The Triad Society are without doubt the vilest criminal organization in the history of man. By comparison, the Mafia is a fragmented bunch of thugs and the *Union Corse,* rank amateurs. When you have read the case histories contained in the files, you will see what I mean. They have been around for a long time, and their existence has plagued law enforcement agencies around the world for the last two hundred years or so. Until the end of the World War II—when we still had a bloody empire—Britain only had to contend with Triad activities in the Far East. Always the will-o'-the-wisp kind of awareness that was an annoyance—frustration, if you like—but never direct confrontation. Since the end of World War II—when the socialists gave chunks of our empire to any group of bastards that shouted for independence—we have found evidence of Triad activity in new places."

He looked with distaste at the crushed cigarette

78

butt in his ashtray, then at Macdonald, and went on. "It has been suggested that Triad has established itself in this country, and Washington is also uneasy. I subscribe to this. The police files, both here and in the United States, record isolated incidents which, if taken over a period, are very, very disturbing. For one thing, drugs have been on the upsurge since the mid-forties. We have encountered Mafia and *Union Corse* involvement to a high degree, but it is very difficult to come across specific evidence of Triad involvement. We hear about the Far Eastern traffic in drugs, but this is hardly surprising when the bulk of drugs originates in the East. For anyone who knows the power and influence of Triad, it is impossible that they are acting as errand boys for the Mafia and *Union Corse.*"

He sat back in his chair, "Here in Britain we have had an influx of Chinese immigrants these past few years. Every village seems to have one Chinese restaurant in addition to the proverbial pub and post office. In the towns and cities they outnumber fish-and-chip shops. Supermarkets have a section where one can buy all the ingredients to cook by numbers as well as eat by them! Beansprouts . . . water chestnuts and all that kind of garbage! Even my club had the audacity to have sweet-and-sour pork on the menu the other night!"

Macdonald grinned, the picture conjured in his mind of the members of Sir Archibald's club struggling with chopsticks was too much for him. He couldn't resist asking, "Did you have some, sir?"

"Of course not! Don't mind the odd curry dish now and again—but there is a limit." He gave the younger man a look that discouraged further comment on the subject, then went on. "The police in this country encounter very little evidence of Chinese businesses being 'protected' by local thugs. We know that the Chinese have a reputation of being well able to take care of themselves and handle any trouble that arises with customers in their restaurants, but I refuse to believe that this is achieved by individual efforts. My every instinct tells me that organization lies behind it. Not the tong system beloved of mystery writers, but Triad. Your assignment is to check out all Chinese activities that might confirm Triad presence in Britain. I give you three months to have a full report on my desk. Two for your investigation and one to compile the results into acceptable English. I don't want any heroes and I don't want people charging all over the place on a crusade. I want a report with facts in it, and I will decide how to handle it from there." He moved forward and suddenly flashed the knife at Macdonald. "Do I make myself clear?"

"Abundantly clear, sir." Macdonald eyed the paper knife with some apprehension. It was sometimes rumored that Sir Archibald was slightly unbalanced as a result of his wartime activities. "I'll read these files thoroughly and proceed with caution."

Sir Archibald sat back in his former position and tossed the knife on his blotter. "Don't ever underestimate these Triad people. Dangerous in the extreme, as you will discover from your reading material." He stood up to indicate Macdonald's dismissal, saying, "As usual we are short of manpower. Pick your team carefully and use it to maximum advantage. I have arranged for a man from Hong Kong to assist you in your inquiries—name of Maxwell. We had him checked out thoroughly, and you have a copy of the report on his background in your hand. Bit of a rough diamond, but apparently the best Hong Kong could come up with."

Macdonald rose and headed for the door. To his retreating back, Sir Archibald said, "We have booked your man into the Skyline Hotel for a week, and you will meet him there this evening. One week of splashing around in the tropical pool, and you can move him to somewhere more in keeping with the department's budget!"

Macdonald paused with his hand on the doorknob and looked back. He allowed a trace of sarcasm to creep into his voice, "Perhaps I could find him a bed-and-breakfast place somewhere on a direct subway line to the City."

Not to be outdone, Sir Archibald replied, "How about a Salvation Army hostel—I understand they are very comfortable!" Then, as Macdonald opened the door, he said, "By the way—would you believe that

Maxwell started out as a butcher's apprentice?" A malicious smile creased his face, "However, you and he have one thing in common."

"What would that be, sir?" Macdonald asked.

"I understand he has been something of a thorn in the flesh of his superiors over the years." Sir Archibald drew a file toward him and bent his head over it.

13

Back in his own office, Macdonald arranged for his secretary to provide a large pot of coffee and two extra packs of cigarettes. He intended to spend the rest of the day without interruption, reading the files Sir Archibald had given him. Rumors aside, he held Sir Archibald in the highest respect, but there were times it took a good deal of self-control when coping with him. The reference to Maxwell having been a butcher's boy was a good example. Macdonald recalled some of the "right" people he had met in counterintelligence—total disasters when it came to thinking for themselves or squeezing a trigger before they had their brains blown out by someone with fewer scruples than they. One thing Macdonald had learned above everything else in his years in the field: to judge a man by his capabilities.

When he was comfortably settled with coffee and sandwiches, he gave instructions that he was not to be disturbed except for emergencies. He had had several run-ins with the Mafia over the years and was no stranger to the *Union Corse*. Though he had heard many stories of Triad, he had been inclined to skepticism. Now he would examine the available facts and reach his own conclusions.

He bit into a sandwich and read. . . .

The Triad Society came into being toward the end of the seventeenth century and was originally formed to resist the Manchus who had invaded China. The last Ming emperor was executed by the invaders, and his followers were ruthlessly pursued throughout the country and forced underground. For their own safety, they formed secret cells and adopted signs and passwords. Recruits were required to undergo strict investigation before being accepted and had to swear blood brotherhood oaths on initiation. Anyone who violated the strict code that governed the activities of Triad was tortured and put to death by extreme measures of cruelty which were designed to serve as an example to others. The Manchu dynasty in China lasted from 1644 until 1912, and during this period Triad waged guerilla warfare against it and swore to drive it out of China.

By the early 1900s the Chinese had penetrated Manchuria to the extent that they formed 80 percent of the population, and the few remaining Manchus were restricted to the Aigun area of the Amur valley. As the former invaders lost power, Triad gained it. Throughout China they had lodges which exerted ruthless influence, and the original concept of a patriotic brotherhood changed to that of furthering the illegal activities of the Triad Society.

When, in 1841, Hong Kong was ceded to Great Britain under the terms of the Treaty of Nanking (signed in 1842) Triad was well established in the southeast sector of Kwantung province; including Hong Kong Island, Stonecutters' Island, Kowloon, and the New Territories. The British very soon became aware of the Triad threat, and severe penalties were inflicted on anyone proven to be a member of the Society. They were branded on the left cheek, imprisoned, and finally deported to mainland China. However, very few were caught, and total Triad membership in the colony is estimated today to be one Chinese in six.

Not all of the membership are active but they are sworn to aid and protect those who are. The Society has penetrated at all administrative levels, and their intelligence techniques are such that they conduct their illegal activities with impunity. If a Triad member is arrested and bribery fails to secure his release, he will accept imprisonment, no matter what the term, secure in the knowledge that his family will be taken care of by the Society. The oath of silence is rarely broken and, if it is, the one who breaks it is quickly silenced forever. Because of this, the authorities are virtually powerless to combat Triad activity.

Similar situations exist in all countries where there has been an influx of Chinese immigrants. Criminal activity, such as prostitution, drug trafficking, illegal gambling, and protection rackets, are controlled throughout the Far East by Triad. At lower levels rivalry exists between lodges, and this at times flares up into open "gang warfare," but these incidents are quickly brought under control by pressure from higher levels.

In China Triad was assured continued influence when Dr. Sun Yat-sen (a member of the Society) formed his Republican party. When China became a republic and the infant ruler, Henry Pu Yi was deposed, Dr. Sun became president of the republic. Triad members were established firmly in the government. Dr. Sun Yat-sen died in 1925 and civil war broke out in China. The two sides were the Nationalist Kuomintang under Chiang Kai-shek and the Communist party, the leadership of which was assumed by Mao Tse-tung. Individual members of Triad supported both sides, and the situation was exploited to the full by Triad headquarters until the Japanese invaded the country in 1937. At the conclusion of World War II, when China, under Chiang Kai-shek accepted the surrender of Japan, civil war resumed. The Triad supported the Communists and with the withdrawal of the Nationalists to Formosa, they were once again in a position of power in China. In Formosa they also have people in positions that assure the Society of immunity.

The emergence of China as a major world power and her involvement in Korea and other areas of the Far East increased the need for an intelligence network. The rift with the U.S.S.R. made it imperative that this network become international. The obvious difficulty in establishing an espionage system in the U.S.A., Great Britain, and West European countries was that of facial features. Russia and the Eastern bloc presented less difficulty in that mongoloid features are fairly commonplace in these countries. At first China was forced to place overreliance on double agents. But from recent evidence of successful espionage and counterespionage activity by the Chinese, it must be concluded that they found an alternative to employing double agents. It is the opinion of this department that the alternative network is furnished by Triad.

Macdonald closed the file and refilled his cup with coffee. It took little imagination to deduce that the establishment of an espionage network in Britain or the United States could easily have taken place under the cover of Chinese restaurants. The difficulty was separating the sheep from the goats. Short of outlawing Chinese restaurants and deporting all Chinese people in the U.K., the task was an impossible one.

He turned to the three thick files in which case histories of Triad activity were recorded. These covered some fifty years and gave a comprehensive picture of bribery, corruption, and every crime imaginable. The brutality, callousness, and disregard for human life staggered him. He had to force himself to read the sordid details of some of them. It was late afternoon by the time he finished the case histories and he ordered a fresh pot of coffee before starting on the file headed "GENERAL NOTES":

In at least twelve countries, a perfectly legal opium-poppy industry operates. The revenue from opium derivatives forms a large proportion of the economy of these countries, and the rest of the world depends on these producing nations for supplies for medicinal purposes. Until a means of producing drugs by synthetic process is found, the growing of opium poppies will continue.

Turkey, the second largest producer of opium-poppy derivatives, has placed a ban on growing the flowers. The reason was that the fields were, in the main, located in wild terrain inaccessible to government inspectors. It was estimated that 20 percent of the total yield from the harvest found its way onto the illicit drug market. The growers are paid five times the government price by drug traffickers. It should be appreciated that drugs bought illegally in Turkey can be sold in the United States at a profit of at least 500 percent if pure, and twice that if adulterated. World demand for opium-poppy derivatives for medicinal use, coupled with Turkish dependence on the export revenue, will force resumption of the industry and, consequently, the resumption of illegal traffic from this area.

Southeast Asia is the world's main poppy-growing area. It is known as "The Golden Triangle," and it is generally accepted that the governments of the countries within the triangle have little control over the marketing of the opium and its derivatives. A similar situation exists in Central America, especially in Mexico, where declaration of crops and harvest yield are a farce.

It is estimated that total world production (legal and illegal) of raw opium is 4,000 tons per annum. Requirements for medical uses and scientific research purposes are estimated at 1,000 tons per annum. This leaves 3,000 tons finding its way onto the illegal market. In the United States it is estimated that the Mafia grosses $6 billion a year from drug trafficking. Production of raw opium in mainland China exceeds 2,000 tons per annum—at least half of which is marketed through the Triad Society. Triad income from drug trafficking must therefore be in the region of $20 billion per annum.

Having read all of the material thoroughly, Macdonald could only agree with the conclusions of his chief. It took little imagination to see that Triad offered the perfect espionage network. The Chinese government would have to be fools not to avail themselves of it, and there was every reason to suspect that Triad and the government of Red China had very close ties.

He buzzed for his secretary and had her bring some fresh coffee. He also instructed her to contact Maxwell at his hotel and confirm their meeting for 8:00 that evening. As he relished the fresh coffee, he read the report on Maxwell's background and service with the Hong Kong police.

14

From the moment they met, Macdonald and Maxwell felt a strong rapport. Though their backgrounds were poles apart, each recognized a dedicated professionalism in the other. Neither man was given to the exchange of niceties. Macdonald divorced his social life from his professional activities. He was able to function quite comfortably in the social world, but in his professional world, it was rarely appropriate to observe the social graces with con men, thieves, and killers. One could respect an adversary as well as a colleague, but respect was usually won or lost when men were stripped of everything but sheer guts and determination to survive.

Maxwell avoided banalities because his early years had been totally devoid of them. His dislike of hypocrisy bordered on being a passion. He liked people or disliked them. Not afraid to demonstrate affection, he made no effort to disguise contempt. He did not resent his own background, nor was he proud of it. He was what he was, and people had to accept or reject him.

Maxwell had resigned himself to the possibility that the man from the Home Office might be a desk-bound civil servant who had stumbled on Triad by accident and was using his investigation of it as a shortcut to promotion. He would pick Maxwell's brain for evidence, and in three months or so he would have a thick, bound report as a passport to the next stage of his career.

If this were the case Maxwell had decided that the civil servant would still be passing his water in the same old stall when he—Maxwell—was making his return flight to Hong Kong. No way was the guy getting the key to the executive restroom by his efforts. A second possibility was that it would be the old-school-tie and old-boy-network routine. Maxwell wasn't about to buy that deal either.

Meanwhile, Macdonald had made no prejudgments. The man from Hong Kong had been drafted to the department at the request of Sir Archibald. Macdonald was in charge of the investigation. If Maxwell's experience could help, fine. If he proved to be a liability, he would go. Simple as that.

It was pleasant to sit at the poolside and sip at a drink. The sarong-clad waitress could easily have qualified as a bunny at any Playboy Club. Maxwell, on his guard since hearing Macdonald's public-school accent, was surprised when the other man said, "She reminds me of a girl I fucked when I was on holiday in Greece last year. I had to leave three days early while I still had the strength to walk to the elevator."

"Greek girl?"

"Through and through! I arrived on a Friday night —met her in the bar—was fucking her inside the first hour. Spent the next four days and nights eating, drinking, fucking, and sleeping! I knew her name and one or two other things, but conversation was limited. After the first night it became an endurance test, but I was determined to last as long as she could."

Maxwell grinned, "But you didn't make it."

"No," Macdonald said with mock bitterness. "She produced a vibrator on the morning of the fifth day. I decided it would take a better man than I to keep up with her. Later in the day I made an excuse about having to move on somewhere else."

"Was your ego hurt?" Maxwell asked.

"Not a bit." Macdonald signaled to the waitress, then went on. "Not being able to make it after chatting some dolly up and having too many drinks in the process would hurt my ego. But in this case I can assure you that my ego was the least of my worries."

When the girl had supplied fresh drinks, Maxwell raised his glass in salute. "I have been the route of not being able to make it, and it's no joke. As a matter of fact, I'm hoping to spend my first night back in England in the bed of a delicious stewardess, and I plan on measuring my drinks from now on. I'd hate to be a flop on my first night in England."

Macdonald's story had served well as an ice-breaker. The two men had sized each other up and liked what they saw. Macdonald lit a cigarette, then said, "I think you will find the project we will be working on very interesting. I have to tell you that I have no firsthand experience with Triad." He drew deeply on his cigarette. "I have been looking at the files today and I was staggered by the magnitude of the whole setup."

"Pity a few more people didn't get around to reading them!" Maxwell scowled. "I feel as if I have been flogging a dead horse in Hong Kong for years."

Macdonald smiled, "I wouldn't be too sure about that. A lot of the stuff I read came from Hong Kong, and much of it was gathered recently."

Maxwell took a long swallow from his drink. "That's typical! I have been told that I had rocks in my head every time I brought up the subject of Triad." He emptied his glass, "Same old story—people like me bust their asses filing reports, and some guy at the top takes the glory!"

Macdonald raises his glass, "I'll drink to that!" When he had finished, he looked at Maxwell, "Will one more impair your performance?"

In reply, Maxwell called the waitress and ordered another round.

When they had been served, Macdonald led the conversation back to the files and briefly outlined their contents. Maxwell was impressed and asked to see them. Macdonald considered, then said, "Why not? We might as well start out by sharing what information is available." He grinned. "That way it might become a habit with us, and we will share whatever we manage to dig up over the next couple of months."

"Suits me." Maxwell was pleased. "I like to work that way." He gave Macdonald a shrewd glance, "I'm the simple type. But I should tell you that nobody ever screws me twice. I play along, but if I find that the other guy has a set of rules I don't know about—then that's it!"

"Understood. And I'm glad you raised the point. I would take a very dim view of it if I discovered you holding anything back from me."

Maxwell lit a cigarette, "I am beginning to suspect that you are a civil servant in name only." He held up a hand to ward off any explanations. "I'm not being nosy. You tell me what you want me to know—I figure that is your intention anyway—but I want you to know that as far as I'm concerned, the deal we just made stands. I'll give the job all I've got, but don't screw me."

Macdonald looked at him searchingly for a moment, "I am—at least on paper—with the Home Office. However, my line of work has nothing to do with the sign on the door that says Urban Development Department. You will see the setup for yourself in the morning. All very Whitehallish on the outside, but it ends there." He grinned suddenly, "By the way, my chief has a phobia about expenses. I swear to God he would have me buying paper clips out of my own pocket if he thought he could get away with it. Trying to get him to pay for anything is like trying to get shit from a wooden horse." His tone became serious. "Kidding aside, I will try to be as open as possible with you about the department but only regarding the project we are both involved in. Beyond that you will have to accept that I can tell you nothing."

"Fair enough."

"Good." Macdonald got to his feet. "I'll leave you to sort out your sleeping arrangements; though I'm sure my chief would lie awake all night if he thought he was paying for a bed here that was empty."

The two men shook hands and their bargain was struck.

15

Maxwell and Macdonald worked very closely during the next couple of weeks. Their early rapport developed into the kind of kinship that seldom happens more than a handful of times in a man's lifetime: a relationship that will last for the rest of the lives of the men involved. They did not discuss it, and neither could have put his finger on the point at which he recognized it, but they were both aware of a special feeling for the other man. They also found themselves developing an obsession about Triad. They shared information and Maxwell told Macdonald about the peaches incident. The intensity of Maxwell's feeling infected Macdonald. Their work together became a two-man crusade. From the information they quickly concluded that Triad was operating in the British Isles and that the network of Chinese restaurants and supply houses provided the perfect cover for their activities. Whether these activities were politically or criminally inspired was anybody's guess. But Macdonald and Maxwell believed the network served a dual purpose. They decided the best course of action was to compile a list of every Chinese establishment in the country. This, together with a list of every person of Chinese origins in the country, would give them a starting point.

In addition to Maxwell, Macdonald had selected a

three-man team from the agents available in the department. They were told of the basic purpose of the investigation but ordered to instruct clerical staff that the compiling of the lists was purely for purposes of a census. The three agents were each given a third of the country to cover and told only to observe and report on activities in his particular area. It was stressed that a low profile must be maintained. Macdonald and Maxwell would work at the office and plot all Chinese establishments on wall maps. Macdonald knew it would be a real slog for all concerned, but it was the only logical method to be employed. It would be relatively simple to keep the lists and the maps up to date once they were established. Until then, however, it was just one foot in front of the other. The important thing was to keep it all nice and quiet. No suspicions aroused and no incidents.

Macdonald and Maxwell soon found themselves bogged down by a deluge of paper. The sheets of listings, customs forms, and ships' manifests arrived as fast as they could dispose of the ones on hand. The different-colored pins on the maps soon became a forest: blue ones for restaurants, red for supply houses and black for ports-of-entry. They devised a separate color code to indicate the saturation of Chinese close to areas important to national security. At the end of each weary day, they got into the habit of washing the dust from their throats at a local pub.

They always found a corner where they couldn't be overheard to discuss the day's work. There was no doubt they were progressing, but the question was where the hell were they progressing to? They examined possibilities until they were exhausted. What they were doing was frustrating to men of action, and Maxwell asked a hundred times what the point was coming from Hong Kong to stick pins in a map when any fool who wasn't color-blind could do it equally well. It became a joke between them.

Maxwell had changed hotels for the sake of convenience. The trip to and from Heathrow each day took up too much time. As a gesture against Sir Archibald's parsimony, Macdonald found a hotel where the rate was higher than the Skyline. To compound it further, both men ate dinner at Maxwell's hotel several times a week and made sure the wines they had were expensive. Often they would go out on the town together. It gave Macdonald pleasure to take the other man to places he had never been—clubs where the "in" people congregated. It was all a bit of a bore to Macdonald who had always had access to these places and had outgrown them, but it was brand-new to Maxwell.

In return, Maxwell took Macdonald to cockney pubs in the East End. Places on the waterfront where a public-school accent would be greeted with derision at best. Pubs where mongers got together for a "knees-up" or an old-fashioned singsong with patrons taking turns at the microphone. He took him to drag bars where it was men only—though some of the queens looked so much like beautiful women that Macdonald could hardly believe it.

If Maxwell had a weakness, it was that he couldn't resist attractive women. The propect of an unescorted lady was a challenge he had to meet. On two occasions this weakness led to embarrassing situations. The first was at an East End pub where Maxwell spotted what he considered to be a likely lady. He had bought her a drink and was talking with her when her husband, who had been playing darts, came over to the bar. He didn't pay a lot of attention to what was going on between Maxwell and his wife—probably figuring she could get high at someone else's expense. But when he heard Macdonald's educated accent, that was a different matter. The man moved to where his wife was seated and, in a loud voice, said, "Bleedin' toffs! Come to the East End looking for a bit of spare arse! You, mate"—he poked a finger into Maxwell's chest —"piss off or I'll kick your bleedin' head in!"

Maxwell was getting off his stool to deal with the man when Macdonald intervened and attempted to smooth things over. The belligerent husband turned on Macdonald and shouted, "You fuckin' poofter, keep out of this or I'll have me sister slap your face!" That was too much for Macdonald, so he hauled off and hit the husband full in the face.

Unfortunately, the man had a number of relatives

and friends in the place, and in the battle that followed, both Maxwell and Macdonald had ample opportunity to work off the frustrations of sticking pins in wall maps. They managed to escape relatively unharmed before the police arrived.

The second occasion was at a gambling club in the West End. Both men had observed a particularly attractive woman sitting by herself just outside the gaming area. While Macdonald was at the men's room, Maxwell tried his luck with the lady. She politely snubbed him, but it passed over his head and he persisted. Her husband chose that moment to join his wife, and a nasty situation could have developed had not Macdonald returned in time to prevent it. It was a matter of little consequence to anyone involved but, by a quirk of fate, Macdonald would have occasion in the future to remember it.

16

At the end of the two-month period allowed by Sir Archibald to gather the necessary material for his report, Macdonald had everything his team could find. He had everything—and nothing. He had a month to collate the material into a readable form. That would be his report—a list of Chinese restaurants, companies, residents and their deployment, etcetera, etcetera. Two months of diligent search by countless clerks, three highly trained agents tramping the streets of villages, towns, and cities throughout the country, and a man brought in from Hong Kong. . . . They had compiled thorough records, but beyond that, their efforts had been a waste of time.

Macdonald was seething with frustration. A month to write a couple of introductory paragraphs and then pile one list on top of the other. He closed his eyes and could visualize the scene—Sir Archibald, purple-faced, with the report in one hand and the expense account in the other. That would be something to see —Sir Archibald demanding sarcastically to know whether the whole department was now in the business of census taking—and if they were, why was the Department of Counterespionage paying their wages and expenses. . . . Speaking of expenses, etc., etc. . . .

The pile of lists seemed to mock him. Deliberately, he drew them toward him and carefully arranged them into one neat stack. He then rose to his feet, picked up the stack with both hands, and exclaimed loudly, "A pox on all Chinese! May their balls turn square and fester on the corners!" With that he heaved the mass of paper against the far wall.

Maxwell glanced up, looked from the fluttering paper to Macdonald, and said mildly, "Not the kind of remarks that further détente, Tony." Macdonald kicked savagely at his metal wastebasket and sent it crashing against the wall. "That pile of shit is what we have to show for two months' work." He sat on the edge of his desk and lit a cigarette. "A pile of bloody lists with a couple of introductory paragraphs and the good news that you and I firmly believe that Triad is operating in Britain." He sucked heavily on his cigarette. "Not a scrap of evidence to support our belief—just a feeling in our water!"

Maxwell shrugged his shoulders, "What can I tell you? A report is a report . . . is a report. . . ."

"I know," Macdonald shook his head wearily. "I just wasn't cut out for sitting behind a desk. With other assignments, at least I was getting secondhand excitement from what came in from the men in the field. I compiled my reports with images of their actions in my head. Like some old warhorse, I could hear the sound of the bugle or whatever it is old warhorses are supposed to hear." He pointed at the pile of lists. "With that load of rubbish, I get mental images of my agents getting foot-rot from tramping the bloody streets! As for the chief . . ." he broke off. "I leave his reactions to your imagination, James."

Maxwell grinned and swept a hand to indicate the wall maps, "You have this beautiful decor. Quite the 'in' thing, I understand." He rose to his feet and surveyed the room critically. "I would say you have been a bit heavy handed with the blue pins but if that's what turns you on, sweetie, who am I to knock it?"

"Balls!" Macdonald crushed out his cigarette. "Seriously, James, what the hell have we got?"

"Nothing, we both know the only way to get evidence is in the field. Somebody has to make contact somewhere and play it by ear."

Disgustedly, Macdonald replied, "We went all through that the first day you were here. We have explored the possibility of using a Chinese to infiltrate, but you keep pointing out that in Hong Kong they were sent back to the office in a box. Even if I could find a Chinese with the proper qualifications, having his dismembered body delivered in a cardboard carton at the back door would be counterproductive—but for Christ's sake, what else is there?"

Maxwell examined his shoes. He had been waiting for the opportunity to make a proposal for several weeks but knew it had to be handled carefully and at just the right moment. Now seemed like a good time. In measured tones he said, "There is always me."

"Disguised as a Chinaman and opening up a restaurant?" The other man laughed, "You speak Chinese about as well as my granny could make doughnuts!"

"How were her doughnuts?"

"Lousy!"

"A pity," Maxwell pretended to be hurt, "I thought my mastery of the language had impressed you."

Snorting derision, Macdonald resumed his seat behind the desk. When he looked again at Maxwell, he was surprised to hear him say, "I am serious, Tony. I can at least make contacts and get some evidence that the Chinese are into dope in a big way here in London."

"How?"

"You furnish me with a fair quantity of morphine to use as bait and I'll do my colonial-on-leave act and try to sell it." He warmed to the plan. "After all, I *am* a colonial on leave! There is nothing to connect me with your department, and a simple drug deal will give your report some weight. I'll be in and out of it inside a couple of weeks."

It was a tempting proposition, but Macdonald shook his head. "No way. What happens if they cut you up in cubes? Do I have them reduced to ashes for scattering or dried for posterity?" He shook his head again. "Do you know what my boss would do to me if your scheme didn't work? If I had to go to him and say that I had carelessly lost the man from Hong Kong he had kindly provided—would it be terribly inconvenient if I asked for another?"

Maxwell grinned at Macdonald's humor, "You have a better idea?"

"No, but I sure don't like yours." He reached for his cigarettes, "I am grateful to you for offering, but it is just too risky."

"The desk has got you, eh? Secondhand bugles for the rest of your life and memories of how it used to be." Maxwell was deliberately needling the other man.

Macdonald took the unlit cigarette from between his lips and asked harshly, "You think I'm turning you down because I'm chicken?"

"I don't know—maybe you are just losing your touch."

"Losing my touch, hell! I would do the job myself if I thought that there was an even chance of it coming off."

"What cover would you use?"

Macdonald squinted thoughtfully, "I could come up with something."

"Not as good as a genuine colonial policeman on leave."

"Perhaps not, but it would be my risk, not yours."

"Maxwell smiled, "I was just needling you to see how you would take it. You know my plan has more than even chance of success. How about it? Take the risk." He held up his right hand as though swearing an oath, "I promise I'll take no risks that I can avoid. I have a very healthy respect for the Triad—I'm not going to do anything stupid."

"What quantity of morphine would you want?"

"A fairly large one." He considered for a moment, "Could you get fourteen blocks?"

"That would be seven pounds in weight—worth around a hundred thousand pounds."

"Right. If I'm to get a significant response, it would have to be that quantity."

Macdonald thought for a moment, "No problem getting that much. My only reservation is that I wish I could be sure you'd come back alive." He lit the

95

cigarette he had put aside earlier, "Having your ashes in an urn on my desk would be of little consolation to me."

Maxwell grinned, "Are you prepared to let me have a go?"

"I guess so."

"Good. One very important point about the morphine is that it must bear the '999' mark. All the Chinese stuff has that trademark."

"I know. You would be a goner if you turned up for the meeting with something from Turkey."

"We will have to plant it somewhere. Nobody in their right mind would meet with these people carrying the stuff. And I'll have to move to another hotel. The one you put me in is not the kind of place I would have chosen as a cop looking for a good time."

"I'll leave it up to you. What do you plan to do from there?"

"Spend my time hanging around likely places." Maxwell began pacing the room slowly, "Put out some feelers and hope they rise to the bait. It might take some time, but I would imagine ten days at the outside. Once I make the contact, I'll try to get a message to you. Failing that, I'll meet them and play it straight. They agree to the price, and I'll meet with them again."

The enthusiasm of the other man was infectious, and Macdonald found himself getting excited at the prospect of some action—even if it would be secondhand for him. He interrupted Maxwell to say, "They will certainly search your room before any preliminary meeting takes place. Why pay for what you can get for free?"

Maxwell's pacing increased, "That's why we have to plant it somewhere. Could you arrange a place that the Chinese would accept as logical?"

"I'll have to give it some thought, but I'm sure we can figure out a place."

Maxwell laughed, "So we're on our way!"

Macdonald nodded but the wave of enthusiasm had left him. Echoes of Sir Archibald's "no heroes" warning rang in his head. Deliberately, he lit a cigarette, "James, we're behaving like idiots. If we go ahead with this scheme, at least we have to be professional. Turning you lose without backup is worse than stupidity."

The other man's head jerked up. "Backup? You've been watching too much TV! Are you suggesting putting a tail on me?"

"Something like that."

"Well, it just won't work. These people are going to be watching me every moment until they make their move. They will pick up my tail and that will be the end of it. The only chance we have is for me to work solo. I'll get a message to you somehow when I make contact, and you get me the hell out of it before they take me apart."

Macdonald stared at him for a moment or two, "You have made up your mind to do this with—or without—whatever help I can give, haven't you?"

"That's right." Maxwell's face hardened.

"Commit suicide is what you're going to do!"

"Not if I can help it. I've been around this deal for a lot longer than you, and I don't like myself anymore. I've watched these yellow bastards push the button on too many people. I lost a girl who did nothing but the mistake of being *my* girl. I lost a friend who did nothing but be *my* friend. I've watched boys and girls of twelve and fourteen years bought and sold!" His voice had risen and the words were pouring out of him. "Sold for the sole purpose of having a prick rammed into them. At twenty these kids are old and diseased. Other kids—all over the world—have a drug habit before they get out of their teens! Triad does whatever the hell it likes in the East, and they are getting stronger every day in the U.K." His face was savage now. "I've seen it all happen and I've done nothing about it. I owe them for Towers and I owe them for the girl. Aside from anything else, there are personal debts, and I'm bloody well going to do something about them!"

Macdonald drew hard on his cigarette. Now he knew where the other man's head was. Years of frustration had brought him to the point of taking maybe superhuman—but more likely insane—action. He loathed the Triad and, perhaps, he loathed himself. He blamed himself for the deaths of his friend and the girl, and he had to do something about it. Macdonald crushed out his cigarette. "I *could* stop you. I hear what you are saying and I know that you genuinely mean it when you say you'll play it cool, but I have to tell you that I doubt your chances of getting any kind of message to me after you make contact."

"But you *won't* stop me," Maxwell said. "I'm offering you a chance to penetrate this organization. It might be only half a chance, but it's more than you're ever likely to get from any other quarter. I'm a professional and I'll be using everything I've learned to stay alive. I'm not about to commit suicide. I have my airline stewardess to consider." He grinned again, but wickedly, "There's still a lot of mileage in that young lady. I've been working hard on her, but there's still a couple of dozen positions we haven't tried."

17

Maxwell did proceed with caution. He spent ten days hanging around the strip-clubs and clip-joints of Soho and got precisely nowhere. Each night he would telephone Macdonald and report zero. They had decided that they would not risk meeting until the man from Hong Kong had finished with his job. As each boring day followed another and the nights dragged by in a procession of females, colored lights, and bad liquor, Maxwell began to feel he would never make contact with Triad at any level. But experience told him it would take time, and he was convinced that they were aware of his existence. A sixth sense told him he was subject to continuous scrutiny after his first day in the area.

He quickly discovered that a small group of girls served the dozens of strip theaters in the area. He saw them hurrying from spot to spot carrying small cases—on an endless round of exhibiting themselves in what were supposed to be erotic artistic poses. The fact was that the most popular girls were the ones who indulged in obscene pantomimes. The names of the performers changed from establishment to establishment, but the high admission prices, sleaziness of decor, and exorbitant prices for inferior liquor were the same in all of them.

He played around with a number of girls, but it took a week to find one who was Chinese. Fluent enough when playing her wares, she pretended language difficulty when he introduced drugs to the conversation. It was the same when he tried with owners of Chinese restaurants. They refused to enter into any conversation that touched on drugs. Maxwell refused to believe that *all* of them could refuse the lure of a huge profit.

So he continued in the role of colonial-on-leave, spent money as though it were going out of fashion, and waited for the other side to make their move. Maxwell wondered whether his liver would pack up before his penis.

The eleventh day he finally made contact. He was approached in a bar by a Chinese who was clearly just a messenger boy. It was obvious to Maxwell that he was being tested. He quoted the figure of £100,000 sterling for the goods he had for sale. Two days later he received instructions at his hotel to wait in the bar for a man to take him to his prospective buyer. He telephoned this information to Macdonald.

His guide was punctual, well dressed, and polite. He appeared quietly on Maxwell's side and said, "Please finish your drink. I have a car waiting, but a minute or so will make little difference. Maxwell was annoyed with himself. He had been watching for his guide's approach, but the man had succeeded in reaching him unobserved. He took a last swallow from his glass and slid from the barstool. "Let's go. I don't like keeping people waiting."

"An admirable quality." The remark was followed by a slight inclination of the head, and the Chinese led the way to the door. The car at the pavement was not distinctive—a medium-priced family sedan. The interior was drab and the Chinese driver wore nondescript clothes and didn't turn around when Maxwell got in the car. Maxwell settled in the back seat and his companion joined him. The vehicle moved smoothly from the curb and threaded its way through traffic. They drove in silence until the car emerged from Piccadilly. Then Maxwell was handed a pair of dark glasses with side pieces. "You will wear these please." The request was polite but did not encourage argument.

The lenses cut out all vision, and the side pieces effectively shut out all daylight. These were a professional tool of the trade. The wearer was, to all intents and purposes, blind. As though divining his thoughts, the Chinese said, "I would advise you to refrain from removing your spectacles until I tell you to do so. I have a gun pointing at your heart, and the slightest movement of your hands will result in instant death."

Maxwell turned toward the speaker, "Would my having a smoke be too much for your nervous system?"

The sarcasm was wasted. He became aware of the pressure of a pistol barrel in his left side and the polite voice said, "You may smoke, but I shall light it for you."

It was impossible to follow the route taken by the car. Maxwell had spent too many years away from London, and as the vehicle swung through a series of turns he resigned himself to ignorance of their whereabouts. At length the car came to a halt. He allowed himself to be drawn from the car and shuffled blindly forward. They mounted a short flight of steps, entered a house and then ascended two long flights of stairs connected by a half-landing. A short pause preceded the sound of a door opening. After some steps forward, the dark glasses were removed.

It was a few moments before his eyes adjusted to the light and, when they did, he found himself in a medium-sized room. The curtains were drawn and illumination was from a standard lamp in the corner. The furnishings were simple and the only occupant, apart from the guide, was an indistinct figure seated behind a large old-fashioned desk. It was obvious that the people he was dealing with were truly professional. He knew he would have to exercise caution in presenting his story.

A chair was brought forward, and a gesture indicated he was to sit. He complied and used the lighting of a cigarette to attempt to make out the features of the man behind the desk. It was a useless exercise, and he had the uneasy feeling his play was obvious. After studying him for a moment, the man spoke, "I trust for your sake, Mr. Maxwell, that you are what you say you are. It would be unfortunate if it turns out that you are extending your professional duties to the United Kingdom."

"I'm on leave," he tried to be both casual and convincing, "the merchandise I have to sell is something I have been waiting to get rid of for a long time. This leave affords me the opportunity of combining business with pleasure."

"Business and pleasure are entirely separate and should be conducted as such." There was censure in the man's tone. "However, I did not have you brought here to discuss such matters." His voice took on an edge, "You have been trying to sell a quantity of morphine valued at £100,000 sterling. You must take us for fools!"

"Why?" Maxwell drew calmly on his cigarette.

"Because, my friend, the weight of such a quantity would be seven pounds, some fourteen blocks. Did you bring it hidden in your luggage?"

Maxwell ignored the sarcasm and said calmly, "You must think *I'm* a fool! It's obvious that a police officer would get ten years if he were caught at that game."

"Just what game did you play?"

"That is my business. I have fourteen blocks to sell. The price is £100,000. Do you want them or not?"

A moment of silence followed, then the voice said, "Yes, I am interested in such a quantity—and the price is right if the quality is high."

"Nine-nine-nine—is that good enough?"

"Excellent!" the man sounded impressed, "But tell me—what was the source of this consignment?"

"Confiscation." He lit another cigarette from the butt of the previous one. "Policemen aren't paid all that much, and the pension could hardly be called attractive. I decided to make provision for my old age."

The Chinese digested this, "A very wise move on your part, Mr. Maxwell, but the sum involved is by present-day standards hardly a fortune."

"Granted—but a bird in the hand, etcetera."

"Quite." The voice took on cunning, "Have you a further quantity still in Hong Kong?"

Maxwell was tempted to answer in the affirmative. It could be arranged and might lead to his getting closer to the organization. However, he decided he was in a bad position to improvise. "No, it would be too risky; £100,000 is quite enough for me."

"I see," the head moved as though considering his answer. Then the man went on, "I find you a man of mystery, Mr. Maxwell. You arrange a considerable quantity of refined drugs to be smuggled into this country. Then, like a fool, you try to sell it by approaching people in clubs and public houses. When I speak to you, I find you a cautious man, yet you have exercised little caution in the past few weeks. I have had your hotel room and luggage searched, and there is no trace of the morphine you speak of. Perhaps you would care to explain these circumstances."

Maxwell shrugged his shoulders. The Chinese was after something more than just the drugs, and it was up to him to find out what that something was. He sat back in the chair and spread his hands as though in surrender. "I must congratulate you on your efficiency. But you certainly can't believe I would leave the evidence where it could be found. I had the merchandise but no market for it. I figured that the way to do it was to let the market find me. It was a certainty that the small-time crooks of Soho wouldn't have the kind of money I was after, but I knew word would get back to the people who had. I figured my only danger was from police agents, and if they couldn't find the goods, they had no case. I figure I am in no danger from you as long as I have the goods, and I'll take bloody good care that, when I exchange the morphine for the money, I have a way of hiding the money as well as I have hidden the drugs." He spread his hands again, "If you can't get the money back, you'll leave me in peace!"

The Chinese had been listening attentively, and he now seemed more relaxed. "It would appear that you have your wits about you. I can see that finding a market was your major difficulty, but you are wrong in your assessment of danger. As a policeman, you should know that your colleagues are not stupid. As a whole, they are hidebound by petty regulations but as individuals they can be very clever. This is so because the people with whom they have to deal destroy faith in human nature." His voice had taken on the manner of a lecturer. "When people are stripped of the security that civilized society offers, they revert to animal instinct. Your experienced policeman, by association with criminal elements, also reverts to animal instinct. Is this not so in your own case?"

"I suppose so," Maxwell shrugged, "but what has it got to do with your buying my drugs?"

"I mention it to illustrate my point about danger. The elaborate security precautions employed in bringing you here were for two reasons. First, I had to ensure that you could not return of your own accord nor direct anyone else here. But secondly, and probably most important, there was the possibility that you were being followed. Let us not be naïve—the blundering inquiries you made in Soho must have reached the ears of Scotland Yard, don't you think?"

Maxwell nodded, "There is that possibility, but I was a bit more discreet than you give me credit for."

A short silence followed, then the man behind the desk said musingly, "Possibility—that is a good word —I now come to a further one. Suppose for a moment that you yourself are the police spy. It is then possible that a car was detailed to follow you here. My precautions would be justified. If you were not followed, I am faced with the difficulty of determining just how you intend to proceed from this point."

"Don't be ridiculous!" Maxwell got to his feet, "I want to sell just one lot of drugs, and that's the end of it!"

"That is where you are wrong! Sit down!" There was no mistaking the command in his voice, and when Maxwell had obeyed, he went on, "You have two things to sell, and I am more interested in the second than the first."

The moment of truth had arrived. Maxwell stared at the man, "What are you talking about?"

"Think, Mr. Maxwell, think. You have fourteen

103

blocks of morphine that you smuggled into this country. It is a useful quantity, and the sum you ask for it is reasonable. You deliver the goods and I will pay you the money. You will not be molested. However," he hung on the word, then repeated it, "however, we both know that obtaining drugs in Hong Kong is not difficult. What is difficult is shipping them over here. You apparently have overcome this, and I will pay a further £100,000 for details of how it was done."

Maxwell's stomach tightened into knots. So that was it! He had made a serious mistake in not covering this possibility. He tried bluffing, "You don't really expect me to reveal that kind of thing!"

"But I do," the voice was silk, "I not only expect it —I demand it!"

"I'll have to think about it." Maxwell's mind was working at a furious rate, "There are other people involved, and I don't think they would risk it again."

"I will devise a way of convincing them that they should. I am a reasonable man and, to prove it, I will give you a day to think it over. You will be my guest here. I'll have someone bring your clothes from your hotel. When you have explained the method you used, I will see that you are paid for the drugs you have and, if your method proves of value to me, I will pay you the second sum when you have returned to Hong Kong."

No way out—he was caught! Maxwell knew he didn't have a prayer of devising a story that would satisfy these people. They would check and counter check—and he would end up very dead.

18

Macdonald knew something had happened by six o'clock that evening. No report from Maxwell—and the girl at the hotel switchboard stated that Mr. Maxwell had checked out. He hurried to the hotel, but the receptionist said that someone had paid the bill and left. No, she couldn't remember what the man looked like and, anyway, she didn't know Maxwell by sight.

It was a busy hotel catering to tourists with people checking in and out all the time.

It was too dangerous to pursue things further. To speak with the manager and grill the staff would only draw attention to the fact that Maxwell's disappearance was of interest to the authorities. All he could do was curse himself for his stupidity. He regretted now that he had agreed not to keep the hotel staked out and that he hadn't had a tail on Maxwell. The whole deal had been flimsy—downright unprofessional —and they should have realized that Maxwell would be caught one way or another. Chances were that the man from Hong Kong was already dead. If he wasn't, where the hell could he begin to look?

A tail would at least have known where Maxwell had met the contact and, if they had left by car, the license number and a good description of the vehicle. Instead, they had a city of nine million people and no leads at all. An impossible situation. He telephoned his office and left instructions that all messages were to be relayed to him at the hotel. He then returned to the reception desk and enlisted the aid of the girl on duty. Having flashed an identification card, he arranged with her to signal him if anyone inquired whether a friend of Maxwell's had asked about his leaving. It wasn't much, but it was the best he could do.

He bought a newspaper and sat at the bar where he could keep the reception desk in view. After he had ordered a drink he glanced at the paper. Britain's trade deficit for the previous month had been £185 million. . . . Peter Hays-Aldington, Member of Parliament for Suffolk East, had been killed in a car accident . . . four people shot in Northern Ireland. . . . He crumpled the newspaper and thrust it disgustedly under the bar.

Clive Hunter read of the death of Hays-Aldington in Hong Kong. It brought a smile of grim satisfaction to his lips. Tang was an excellent lieutenant, and Hunter was confident the accident had been arranged with his usual cold efficiency. In many ways Tang reminded him of Chin, his grandfather's manservant. Poor Chin, he had been rewarded by death for his efforts in educating Hunter. Knowledge in the head of a live man was a threat. When the threat was greater than the usefulness of the individual, he had to die. He hoped that Tang would live a rich, full life, but for Hunter, the Triad was the only way.

His summons to Hong Kong had come as a surprise, but his absence from London did present an ideal opportunity for disposing of Hays-Aldington and he had taken advantage of it. The next step—his adoption as Conservative candidate—would take a little time, but after that would come his eventual election to the House. Time was something he could afford, and patience was a quality he had long since developed.

He had been in Hong Kong for three days and spent the time calling on business associates. He was to spend the weekend at the home of a wealthy Kowloon family, and a fishing trip, ideal for his transfer to another craft and his first visit to mainland China, had been arranged for Sunday.

On the appointed day, the cabin cruiser proceeded out to sea at a leisurely rate. To the casual observer, it was the well-to-do enjoying the facilities their social position afforded them. After they had threaded a course through groups of small fishing vessels, the cruiser's engines throbbed and they took a course that, had they followed it, would have taken them between Formosa and Canton. They continued on it for just one hour, lowered the sea anchor, and started fishing. The sea was calm but a slight offshore breeze ruffled it occasionally, causing the crests of the wavelets to sparkle in the sunshine.

Only motorized fishing-junks would venture this far from Aberdeen and the menace of Red patrol boats reduced their number to a privileged few. British boats also patrolled the area, but these were carefully kept out of Chinese territorial waters. In their present anchorage, they would know of the approach of a British naval vessel long before it presented a threat. The three crewmen took spells at scanning the waters with the aid of powerful binoculars.

Around noon, a motorized junk approached and came to within twenty yards of the cabin cruiser. After exchanging the password, Hunter was transferred to the other craft. Outwardly the junk was old and weather-beaten, but this was camouflage. Beneath the half-rotten timbers was steel, and two powerful diesel engines thrust it forward at a rate that patrol boats would have been unable to keep up with.

Hunter arrived in China in a large wicker basket. The container was slung on two poles with a coolie on each corner and dumped with similar baskets on the back of a truck. The load was driven to a warehouse. Inside Hunter was removed from the basket and, wearing a blindfold, was taken to a room that smelled of spices. He was placed in a chair and cautioned not to uncover his eyes until he was told to do so.

Hunter did not feel fear as he waited. He knew that something of tremendous importance was about to take place. If he had offended, his disposal would have taken place in England. He knew he would not have been given the chance to justify the offense. The code was absolute. So Hunter waited with confident expectation, inhaling the spicy aroma and listening for footsteps.

The footsteps finally came and a hand was placed beneath his left elbow. He was guided to another room where incense sweetened the air and a cool draft brushed his face. Though still in complete darkness, he sensed that there were a number of people in the room. Pressure on his arm indicated he should halt and, when he complied, a voice, speaking in Cantonese, said, "Welcome, brother. Many years ago our Leader, a man blessed with wisdom beyond that of ordinary mortals, proposed that a Caucasian be raised to the highest level of our ancient Society. So it is that you, outwardly British but in your heart Chinese, have been chosen for a place in the sacred Inner Council of the Triad. You will be led from this place to exchange your Western clothing for attire more fitting to the occasion. When you return, you will undergo initiation into this Society."

As he changed clothes, Hunter was elated. As he had progressed in the Society, he had learned of the existence of the ruling body, but that he would ever be a member of it had seemed impossible. Despite the simplicity of his initiation years before, he knew that elaborate intiation ceremonies were held when an *Ahkung* was appointed. That he—the Leader in Britain —had been ignored, he attributed to the fact that he was, to all appearances, Caucasian. Over the years, he had resented this discriminatory treatment but was wise enough never to have given voice to his feelings. And now he had been chosen to join the Inner Council of Triad. The door opened and a Chinese cast approving eyes over the silk pantaloons and loose-fitting robe in which he was attired. He was again blindfolded and led barefoot to the chamber where the Inner Council awaited.

When they entered, Hunter was told to stand absolutely still. A moment later, he felt the prick of a sharp instrument on his left breast, and the voice that had addressed him earlier said, "In front of you is a sword. Should you be foolish enough to attempt to remove your blindfold before being told to do so, you will die. This sword is symbolic of the power of the Triad—we always find the traitor. He may travel to the farthest corners of the earth but we will find him. The sword also symbolizes restraint. In the Triad you advance only as far as the Inner Temple Council allows. Should you ever conspire to upset the established hierarchy of the Inner Council, you will die."

The sword was withdrawn and the voice continued, "You will now advance ten paces to the altar and kneel before it."

Hunter followed the instruction and found a cushion placed beneath his bare knees. A hand rested on his right shoulder and the now familiar voice said, "There are thirty-six oaths to be sworn. I will recite these and you will repeat them. Think on the words as you speak them, for they are ancient and binding."

It took some time for the oaths to be administered. At length the intoning voice ceased and a different one replaced it. The tone of the new one was authoritative, but the words were spoken with almost parental affection. "I am the Leader of the Society. I am Number One and you are Number Ten. The Inner Council is comprised of ten members. You have justified my faith in your abilities and that is why you have the exalted position you now occupy. We use no names in council and each member is addressed by number. You will be advanced according to your achievements for the Triad. However, I have a duty to repeat the warning given you earlier by the Conferring Member." A deadly edge replaced that fatherly overtone, "Never be tempted to conspire with your fellows to advance your position in the council. The higher a member's position, the greater his responsibility and the greater the price he pays should he ever betray his oath. You have sworn all the oaths of the Society and have reached the highest level. Should you betray us you will die at our hands by the Death of a Thousand Cuts—the most terrible manner of dying ever devised by man."

A silence of several minutes followed. Then, without warning, the blindfold was whipped from Hunter's eyes. Startled, he rose to his feet and stood in blinking bewilderment as his eyes accustomed themselves to the light. A large carpet occupied the center of the room. On it, in intricate needlework, were depicted scenes of life and death. Around the carpet were ten cushions. He was facing an altar and the only objects present were a large bowl, ten smaller ones, a silver knife, and a metal pot suspended over a small spirit lamp. Incense smouldered in sockets and three silken banners hung above the altar. To the right of it were three grotesque effigies in papier-mâché suspended by the neck from gibbets.

There were nine men besides himself present. All were Chinese, and all had their arms folded so that their hands were hidden in the loose folds of the tunic sleeves. Six men formed an aisle—three on each side, at the head of this stood the other three. The white-robed figure was on the right and the figure on the left wore a silver sword and scabbard that hung from his waist and almost reached the floor.

The man in the center bowed deeply, "I am Number One." His head inclined to the right, "This is the Incense Master. He is the Conferring Member for our rituals and is Number Three in the Inner Council."

His head indicated the man on his left, "Our Vanguard is Number Seven." A hand emerged and gestured to the line of men on his right, then to that on his left, "The Deputy Leader is Number Two . . . and we have Numbers Four . . . Five . . . Six . . . Eight . . . and Nine respectively." He smiled and bowed again, "You are, of course, Number Ten." He beckoned with his free hand, "Come forward."

Hunter obeyed. He was incapable of speech and his limbs shook uncontrollably. It took an effort to advance until he stood opposite the Leader. He stopped there and waited. The Leader made a sign and the two lines of men opened out into a single line facing the altar. Hunter, in the center of the line, turned also until he, too, faced in that direction. The Leader took up position to the left of the focal point, and the Vanguard took his on the right. Intoning a chant that was incomprehensible to Hunter, the Incense Master moved to the center. He took a sheaf of parchments from his left sleeve and, continuing his chant, dropped them slowly into the metal pot on the altar. Black smoke curled upward from the charring paper, and acrid fumes mingled with the sweet ones of the burning incense.

The chant ceased when the last of the parchment had been reduced to ashes, and the Incense Master emptied the contents of the metal pot into the large bowl. He stirred the ashes and then turned around and addressed Hunter, "The parchments I have just destroyed had the oaths you have sworn to uphold written on them. The ashes have been mixed in the ceremonial bowl with wine, blood, and spices. We will now seal your initiation by adding the last ingredient." He took the silver knife from the altar and led the initiate to the large bowl. A quick movement of the blade pricked Hunter's right thumb and a drop of blood was squeezed from it into the mixture in the bowl.

The contents were carefully decanted into each of the smaller bowls. These were distributed to all the members. The Incense Master raised his bowl toward Hunter and intoned, "After drinking the Red Flower-wine, you will live for ninety-nine years. When nine is added to this number, you will live for one hundred and eight years." He then drank the contents of his bowl at a single swallow and indicated that Hunter should do likewise. When he had done so, the other members raised theirs to salute him and also drank.

At this point the Vanguard placed his drinking bowl on the floor, drew his ceremonial sword from its scabbard and advanced toward Hunter with deliberate tread. Hunter stood his ground even though the fury on his face suggested the man had gone beserk. Hunter glanced quickly at the others to gauge their reactions, but his eyes were met by total inscrutability. The swordsman's advance seemed inexorable and Hunter knew if he were to make a move it had to be now. He decided against it, stood erect and faced the man with fatalistic calm.

The Vanguard bared his teeth, uttered a blood-curdling shriek, and swirled the sword around his head. He rushed forward, past Hunter, and decapitated the three papier-mâché effigies. The three sets of heads and trunks hit the floor in rapid succession.

After a moment the Leader bowed in Hunter's direction, "You did well, my friend. You have shown proof of your courage." He waved a careless hand at the remains of the dummy figures. "This little charade is of symbolic significance. The figures represent Emperor Hong Hei and two notorious traitors who betrayed our Society." He smiled sardonically, "They did not meet death any better than they lived."

When he finished speaking, the Leader walked to the head of the carpet and sat on the cushion there. The others also took their places, and the Leader silently indicated the only vacant cushion. After bowing in acknowledgment of the invitation, Hunter joined them. The Vanguard looked at the Leader and on receiving a curt nod of permission, rose and left the room.

Silence reigned while the man was absent and continued when he returned. He was carrying a large bottle of wine in one arm and had a live white cockerel tucked under the other. When he reached the carpet, the Incense Master rose and, taking the bottle from the other man, ceremoniously walked around the perimeter of the carpet partially filling each of the small drinking bowls. While this was taking place, the bird struggled wildly to free itself, but the Vanguard had it firmly secured. A feeling of excitement possessed the men in the room.

The Incense Master finished pouring the wine. He put the bottle to one side and walked to where the Vanguard waited. Seizing the head of the cockerel in one hand, he grasped the body expertly with his other and dragged it from the Vanguard's arms. He extended the frantic bird at arm's length toward the altar, and then swiveled back to face the Vanguard. Out came the sword, and with a single stroke the Vanguard severed head from body.

With an expression of joy on his face, the Incense Master filled each of the drinking-bowls with the blood spurting from the still-twitching carcass. When all had been served the Leader rose to his feet and said, "We drink to your good health. *Yam Sing!*" "*Yam Sing!*" the others jumped to their feet and returned the salute. The ceremony was over.

19

The room Maxwell was locked in had probably been part of the servants' quarters once. There was just enough space for a single bed, a chest of drawers, and a kitchen chair. A narrow fanlight, soiled by decades of London filth, was the only source of light by day. At night, a naked electric blub of low wattage provided a foggy yellow illumination. The floor was covered by a grimy carpet and the walls stained with watermarks that gave off a dank odor. The door was solidly constructed.

By placing the chair on the chest of drawers and mounting the rickety structure, Maxwell could look out beyond the guttering to the street below. It was a long way down. In his desperation, he had considered writing notes and throwing them from the fanlight. But first he had to get the fanlight open; besides, he had no paper and he didn't know where the hell he was.

When necessary, he could use the toilet by kicking

the door to attract attention. Two Chinese with guns accompanied him on these trips. The same two men brought food and drink on a tray. Examination of the room failed to uncover any object that could be used as a weapon or tool. The only utensil provided with his meals was a spoon, and he certainly did not like the odds of that against two automatic pistols.

During the early hours of his captivity, he debated whether to try to bluff by saying that he had brought the drugs into the country himself. But they would never believe that he had carried the morphine in his luggage. No, there had to be another way, and it had to be simple enough to sound convincing. His only hope was to try to buy time and hope for a chance to escape. He racked his brains and finally constructed a story that—even though improbable—was possible.

A full day passed before he was escorted back to the room where the first interview had taken place. Maxwell sat on the chair he had occupied previously and attempted to take the initiative by complaining loudly about his accommodation and protesting against being held prisoner. The man behind the desk heard him out, then said, "You know why you are here. You have had ample time to review your situation, and I am now prepared to listen to you." A note of unmistakable warning crept in, "I shall listen to *one* story. I want no changes of heart. Your life depends on your convincing me that you speak the truth. Now, get on with it."

Maxwell began his story slowly and deliberately. "Just over a year ago, I picked up two Chinese fishermen with a cargo of contraband opium. It wasn't much, but it was obvious they weren't operating on their own. I decided to follow the thing up and made a point of questioning them myself before taking them to headquarters." He grinned, "You know how it is." If his listener did, he made no comment. "We have to observe the rules—and these state 'no violence.' But how do you get anything out of these people without putting the fear of God into them?"

A paperweight was raised and brought down on the desk with a crash. Maxwell hurriedly resumed, "It took a fair bit of persuasion but eventually I got the truth out of them. They had been hired by another man to ferry the stuff in, and this was the last of eight trips —I think it was eight. Anyway, I put the two in a local jail and decided to see the other man. I took half a dozen constables with me. Of course the man denied that the opium was on the premises, but when I said it was my intention to search the place, he owned up. Now I was in a peculiar situation." Maxwell lit a cigarette. "The man had admitted guilt, and I didn't have a search warrant! I had left the constables out in the warehouse, and here was the man offering me a bribe to postpone the search. The sum he named was £5,000 and he assured me that it would be in my hands within an hour." He leaned forward to lend credence to his words, "Believe me, I had never taken a penny in bribe money in my life." He waved a disparaging hand, "Sure, I had taken the odd gift of drinks, meals—and girls, but never big money. Yet here I was with the opportunity to make more than a year's salary in ten minutes." He sighed heavily, "It was too much of a temptation."

The Chinese had been listening attentively, "Go on. What happened then?"

Maxwell shrugged. "Like he said, I had the money in my hand within an hour. To keep the books straight, I obtained a search warrant next day and carried out a proper raid. Needless to say, we found nothing. I was happy having a few extra pounds to fall back on, and the Chinese had saved his shipment. I kept well clear of the place afterward and was determined to accept no more bribes."

"This man, what was his name and address?"

"Sorry, can't tell you that."

"No matter, we will let it pass for now. Proceed with your story."

"Well"—Maxwell lit a fresh cigarette—"it was about six months later that I came into possession of the morphine I want to sell you. It was pure luck, an accident, call it what you like. A simple raid, like so many others, but among the stuff we found was a briefcase with the fourteen '999' blocks in it. I knew the trademark guaranteed it to be quality. I removed the morphine and stuffed the briefcase with odd papers from the filing cabinets. Then I handed in the brief-case. It was as neat as pumpkin pie."

"Then what?"

"I held onto it for awhile. Let the heat die down, if there was any. After that I made a few inquiries. It turned out that what I had was worth very little in Hong Kong—probably about £10,000. It was, how-ever, worth ten times that in England." He crushed out his cigarette, "I knew I had this leave coming up, and I felt sure I could get rid of the stuff once I got here. The difficulty was how. I could, of course, take a chance on bringing it in myself—but the ten-year sentence if I was caught stopped me cold. I had to find another way."

The Chinese leaned forward, and for the first time Maxwell got a glimpse of his features. It was just an-other Oriental face, and he wondered irrelevantly why the man had troubled to hide it. His voice was eager, "Just what was that way?"

"Simple, really. I paid another visit to the man with the warehouse. I pointed out to him that I could have his place put on the surveillance list and it would only be a matter of time before he would be serving a nice long sentence. I also implied that I had been investigating his activities and associates since our last encounter and that I had a pretty incriminating dos-sier at headquarters. He got nervous and when I touched on the subject of having a little package shipped to England, he jumped at it. In exchange for his getting it over here, I would see that nothing hap-pened to him.

"And this man arranged it for you?"

"Yes. I passed him the package and he attended to it."

"Delivered it to you here?"

"No, I had to collect it." Maxwell could have bitten off his tongue, as soon as he uttered the words. They would be able to check a London address in less than an hour.

"Just where—exactly—did you collect from?"

"Sorry," he shook his head, "I can't tell you that."

"I did not think you would," the man was almost laughing now. "You tell a very interesting tale, Mr.

Maxwell. It is, however, more entertaining than enlightening. You have neglected to furnish the two most important details—the names and addresses of your contacts here and in Hong Kong." He extended a hand, "You must realize that I require these."

"Sorry," Maxwell shook his head again, "I can't betray this chap who has helped me."

At a signal from his interrogator, a pistol barrel slashed savagely across Maxwell's face, laying his cheek open to the bone. He came to on the floor. Blood poured around his jaw and filled his mouth. The kidding was over and he would gain nothing by being stubborn. He made a gesture of surrender, "It looks as though I'm being pretty stupid."

"You are indeed." The Chinese pointed to the overturned chair, "Please, be comfortable—I wouldn't want you to make any mistake about the answers." He waited until the bleeding man was seated, "As soon as you are ready."

Maxwell dabbed at his face. He looked the other man straight in the eye, "The one in Hong Kong is Hop Koo Su and the address is Victoria Road in Aberdeen. In London I collected the package at a restaurant in Fulham Palace Road—Golden Dragon is the name of the place."

"Good," the Chinese nodded his head approvingly; then, making a signal to one of the guards, said, "You understand that we will now check on these."

"Yes," Maxwell had to fight to keep helplessness out of his voice. Without protest be obeyed the prodding of the pistol barrel and left the room.

One hour later he returned to the room. His guards had stayed with him all of the time which prevented any attempt to escape via the fanlight.

There were two men in the room and the overhead light was burning. Maxwell recognized his interrogator as the one standing at the side of the desk and assumed that the new man seated behind the desk was his superior. This man spoke to the guards in rapid Cantonese and Maxwell was thrust into the chair. Strong ropes secured his body and legs to the chair. For some reason his arms were free. The man spoke again in Chinese. Despite the rate of delivery, Maxwell

116

got the gist of it—enough time had been wasted already—either get the truth or kill him.

One of the guards was instructed to place Maxwell's right hand on the desk and hold it there. When this had been done, the man behind it picked up the heavy paperweight and with cold deliberation broke each of his fingers. He did it in just five seconds, paying no attention to Maxwell's screams. Cold water was thrown in Maxwell's face and when he was conscious the man said in English, "You are a police spy. Since I cannot believe that you are a one-man crusade, it follows, therefore, that you tell me the full details of your assignment."

"Get knotted!" The agony of his hand was excruciating, but he would have attempted to strangle the man, given the opportunity.

His left hand received similar treatment. When he climbed out of the darkness the pain caused him to retch and vomit. When the sickness passed he shook his head to clear it. He knew he was going to die. No matter what he told them, they would not let him live. They would inflict pain by every method they knew to extract the information they wanted but, in the end, death would release him. It was at this point that he decided he would talk. He would talk and talk and tell them nothing. He segregated a part of his brain and filled it with a story. That would be it! He had heard somewhere that the only way to survive torture was by concentrating on one thing. He would fixate on his story.

The guard placed a thumb on either side of Maxwell's face at the points where his upper and lower jaws met and exerted intense pressure. The effect was a searing pain coursing upward in waves until he thought his skull would burst. Maxwell did not know whether he was screaming or not. He lived only inside the pain and concentrated a section of his brain on the story.

It was a surreal experience, and he became a witness to the scene. The torture continued and his screams rose and fell as intense pressure was applied to various parts of his nervous system. The man inflicting the pain was an expert and the divorced section of Maxwell's brain followed the proceedings with interest. The victim withstood the efforts of his tormentor admirably but it gradually became clear that the amount of pressure applied to any particular point was purposely limited. It was an object lesson to show how frail the human body is when subjected to torture by a master of the art.

At length, the guard exhausted his repertoire and looked to the man behind the desk. Maxwell heard him address his superior as Hop Tang. He saw the man shake his head. "We have just demonstrated the methods that will be employed if you continue to be uncooperative. You will now tell me the details of your assignment."

"Yes," the slumped head nodded weakly as it was slowly raised to the questioner. The divorced section of Maxwell's brain fed the words and carefully monitored them as they gibbered from the mouth. "I was considered to be an expert on drug trafficking in Hong Kong and the New Territories. . . . Police here worried by increased traffic in England . . . wanted someone to try to penetrate the ring. . . . I was given the job. . . ." The face screwed up in an effort of concentration, "Nothing much to go on. . . . A few picked up over past year or two . . . some drugs at docks and Heathrow. No pattern . . . but I knew there had to be one. Too big an operation for small-timers. . . ."

"Who are you working with?" Tang interrupted. He was not happy about the turn of events. Hunter's absence had forced him to assume command. His actions would reflect on his Master. He had to get the truth from this man.

The victim's mouth moved several times before words came. "I am working with Scotland Yard. . . . Drug Squad . . . but only top brass know of my existence. Know from experience in Hong Kong that people are open to bribes . . . insisted that I have a free hand."

"The name of the man you were briefed by?"

"Sir Andrew Balfour." The well-known name could do no harm, and the police commissioner had adopted unorthodox methods in the past.

"He alone?"

"Yes."

At a nod, pressure was applied by thumbs placed beneath the earlobes. It was increased until the screams from the man reached an inhuman pitch. When the thumbs were removed the question came again, "He alone?"

"Yes, yes, I swear to God. . . . Please don't let him touch me again. . . . I'll tell you anything but don't hurt me anymore." Sobs racked the body and the divorced section of the brain was well pleased with the performance. Pleased, but illogically contemptuous.

"And you have been working alone?"

"Yes. I figured I could infiltrate the ring by selling drugs. . . . I swear to you I thought this was the way. . . ." He sobbed convulsively. "I wish to God I has stayed in Hong Kong. . . . Please let me live—I'll do anything you want." He strained forward, "I could work for you . . . get information for you . . . I could be of value to you . . . feed back what you want them to know. . . ."

At a signal, the thumbs found the pressure points at the base of the skull and pressed until the victim hovered at the limit of human endurance. The tongue babbled and the details of the story were repeated monotonously without deviation. Eventually Tang was satisfied. The human wreck opposite had to have exhausted the truth. All questions had yielded the same pattern of answers. It was an isolated one-man crusade that was ill conceived, badly planned, and executed with blundering incompetence. He issued a string of instructions to the effect that the body was to be robbed of what little life remained and disposed of. With that, he exchanged bows with the *Ahkung,* Eng Soon Cheong, and left.

The part of what had once been James Maxwell waited patiently. Far in the recess of his brain it bullied, coaxed, and cajoled. It took a long time to coordinate the actions necessary to raise the body from the bed and move to the chest of drawers under the fanlight. One of the small drawers was removed from the dresser and placed on top of it. The broken hands relayed protest to the brain, but the brain ignored them and urged further effort. The body clambered up and, raising the drawer, it smashed away glass and wood. Noise was of no importance now—you can't kill a dead man.

The body emerged from the aperture, oblivious to tearing cloth and skin. It maneuvered until, feet first, it slowly slid down the pitch of the roof and was arrested by the guttering. The head turned left, then right, and eyes searched the street below. A line of parked cars was broken by the shape of a truck. The truck's contents were protected by a tarpaulin. The feet edged along the guttering until the body was directly above the truck. Slowly, the body assumed an upright stance then toppled over and downward. The tarpaulin sagged with the impact cushioning the fall. The body gathered its strength then clumsily worked its way to the edge and half-climbed, half-fell to the pavement. It rose and shambled off into the night.

The guards, confident that their charge was incapable of action, had retreated to a comfortable room on the floor below. In response to the sound of smashing glass they ran upstairs. From the shattered fanlight one of them saw the body topple from the roof. He leaped down from his ramshackle platform, and the two rushed to the street.

The body had gone. They exchanged glances of horror and extended their area of search. When they realized that the prisoner had escaped, they each were tempted to follow his example. Discipline prevailed, and with dragging steps they returned to face the wrath of Eng Soon Cheong.

20

Macdonald was asleep when the telephone rang. It took him a moment to comprehend what the voice was saying but, when he did, he said, "I'll be there in ten minutes." Two days with no word from Maxwell, and now this. He made it in twelve minutes.

The uniformed inspector was apologetic. He said the man was badly injured but had insisted on being brought to the police station rather than a hospital. He had kept repeating Macdonald's name and telephone number over and over again. A doctor was with the man now, but in the inspector's opinion, they should go straight in. When they did, the doctor came across to meet them. "How is he?" Macdonald asked.

"Hopeless." The doctor shook his head, "It's a miracle that he is alive at all!"

Macdonald stepped to the bed and looked at his colleague. He found it difficult to believe that this was the same man he had seen just a few weeks ago. Suffering had aged him. A terrible gash on his right cheek was crusted with dried blood, and a series of ugly bruises stood out against the chalk-white pallor. The eyes were sunken in deep shadows.

Macdonald called Maxwell's name. The eyelids flickered then, and with effort, Maxwell's eyes opened. The semblance of a smile showed and was gone. The lips moved but no sound came. A spasm convulsed the whole body; when it was still, the lips moved again and a whisper emerged, "You've made it, Macdonald. . . . I almost gave up. . . . The bastard we want is Tang—heard him called that . . . Don't let him die quickly. . . ." The whisper was intense with hatred, "Please don't let the bastard die quickly. . . ."

Macdonald leaned closer. "Where did they take you?"

"Don't know—couldn't—," the voice faded and his eyes closed.

It looked as though he had gone, but the lips moved again and said, "I didn't tell him about you . . . I didn't tell. . . ."

"Tang—what does he look like?" Macdonald was unaware that he was shouting. He could see Maxwell slipping away. The body struggled to a sitting position and the eyes opened wide. A grotesque grin twisted the face and he said, in near-normal voice, "When you've seen one of them, you've seen 'em all!" He died upright and slowly toppled.

Macdonald caught him and gently eased him to a reclining position. The doctor moved forward. Macdonald did not wait for the official verdict; he strode to the door and wrenched it open with unnecessary violence. The inspector followed him, "I'm sorry. We'll mount a full investigation."

"You'll do fuck-all the kind!" He turned on the other man. "Who brought him in?"

"A patrol car found him." The inspector remembered his position, "But wait a minute, sir, I'll ask the questions!"

Macdonald dragged his wallet out and flashed the inside cover at the policeman, "See that? I'll tell you what you'll do and won't do!" He stuffed it back in his pocket, "Now, where was he found?"

The inspector had been shown a card that carried top-level authority. He was not about to challenge it. He swallowed, "It was just off Kings Road—Steven Street."

"When?"

"Around one o'clock. The patrolman said he insisted on coming to a police station. Took them ten minutes or so to get him here. . . . I phoned the doctor and then you. Doctor got here just before you did."

Macdonald glanced at his watch, "Less than an hour." He paced up and down, came to a decision, and stopped in front of the inspector. "You have a plainclothesman on duty?"

"Yes."

"Good. I want to take the body back to where it was found and leave it there. He's to put it in a doorway or somesuch place . . . where it will be found by a passerby in the morning."

The policeman was aghast, "You're not serious!"

"Never been more serious in my life. I want it done now. Time is of absolute importance. Get on with it!"

The doctor had entered unobserved by the other two and had overheard the latter part of the conversation. Now he came forward and addressed Macdonald, "Are you some kind of a maniac?" He was having difficulty controlling his temper, "Have you any conception as to the extent of the injuries suffered by that man in there?" He held both his hands in front of the other man's face, "Every finger—including the thumbs—had been deliberately broken! He had been tortured beyond the limits of human endurance! The doctor's hands waved with fury and his voice shook, "Did you see the bruises on his face and neck?" Not waiting for a reply, he went on, "These are the so-called pressure points of the nervous system. Some sadistic bastard had worked on him—a sick mind that knew exactly where to exert the worst possible pressure to obtain the maximum possible pain. I've never. . . ."

Macdonald interrupted impatiently, "Don't bother with the details—we have more important . . ."

"More important?" the doctor shouted. "Do you realize that that man had an injured spine from a fall? Have you any conception of the agony he suffered?" He shook his head in wonderment, "That man should have died many hours ago. I just don't know why he didn't!"

"He stayed alive because he wanted to tell me something." Macdonald's temper boiled over, "That's why he did it. Your skills are of use to the living but they can't help him now!" His voice rose slightly, "Now I can help him—and I intend to—and you can help by forgetting you ever saw him." He turned to the inspector, "You can help by getting on with what I instructed you to do!"

The inspector nodded curtly and turned to go. Macdonald placed a hand on his sleeve. "I want no tongues wagging about any of this. You put the fear of Christ up your lads because I will have their guts if any of them open their mouths!"

The inspector shook Macdonald's hand from his arm and there was resentment in his eyes, but he nodded his head. He wanted to tell this cold-blooded sod a thing or two, but caution kept his lips sealed.

When they were alone, Macdonald gave his attention to the doctor. He could depend on discipline keeping all of the policemen quiet, but the doctor had to be won over. It took two cigarettes and ten minutes of explanation. He told him nothing that mattered but convinced him that it was a security operation of the highest priority. While they were talking, the macabre cortege passed through on Maxwell's last official journey.

Later that morning, having washed and changed, Macdonald checked with the police. Maxwell had been found by a passerby; the body was pronounced dead on arrival at the hospital and now lay in a mortuary. The police were treating it as a case of death in suspicious circumstances. The newspapers were to be given certain facts regarding the victim's activities in Soho. Obvious conclusions would be drawn, and the coroner's verdict would be in accordance with the evidence. The police files would contain another unsolved crime, and hopefully the Triad inquiries would yield nothing more.

At 9:00 precisely, Macdonald presented himself to Sir Archibald's secretary. She was surprised at his unbidden appearance but made no comment. Sir Archibald expressed surprise and had to be told twice that it was Macdonald before he advised her to send him in. Sanderson indicated the usual chair, then sat back and listened.

It took fifteen minutes for Macdonald to tell the whole story. He left out no detail and his chief heard him through without interruption. A silence fell when the younger man's voice stopped and the muted sound of traffic could be heard through the double-glazed windows.

Sir Archibald was livid and he made no effort to disguise the fact. His lips curled, then he asked quietly, "What were your instructions?"

"To compile a full report on suspected Triad activities in this country—together with lists of possible chains of distribution for drugs. Two months to gather the information and one month to collate it. No crusade—just a report."

"How long have you been with the department?"

"Ten years, sir."

"Your fitness report came to me two months ago. It was excellent. Would you say the M.O. and chief of staff are incompetent?"

"No, sir."

"I can only conclude, therefore, that you have been afflicted by some brain disorder during the past two months?" His voice rose, "Have you?"

"No, sir."

"No?" The eyebrows rose, "Perhaps then you might care to enlighten me as to why you are here two weeks before your report is due. Why you permitted Maxwell to do what he did—and last, but by no means least, where you get the gall to sit there and calmly tell me

124

that you have screwed up your assignment from start to finish!"

Macdonald wanted to point out that the assignment could be successful only if a means could be found to penetrate Triad. He wanted to express regret for Maxwell's death. He wanted to apologize for his incompetence but didn't. He did not move and his voice was steady when he said, "I have given you the facts, sir. I have nothing to add beyond that we had a theory. It was clumsy, and Maxwell paid with his life for my stupidity."

A further silence ensued, then Sanderson said, "When I was an adolescent I had a theory that babies came from womens' back-passages. Time proved that I was two inches off in my calculations . . . and I have been disenchanted with all theories since." He rose and walked to the window, "Theories always remind me of cunts!" He stared for fully five minutes at the street below, then returned to his seat, "I am not going to take you off this assignment. However, from now on, you will stay within the confines of your brief."

"Yes, sir."

Sir Archibald studied the younger man and considered the decision he had just made. Macdonald had made a major blunder, but he had been a first-class operative in the field and had proved an excellent coordinator. Ten years in the department hadn't aged him all that much; a few gray hairs at the temples, but the black hair was thick and the strong-featured face unlined. The dark brown eyes were hard and the set of mouth and jaw firm. No sign of the body going to seed, and the records showed that Macdonald was still more than capable of handling himself in the gym. An extract from a report sprang into the chief's mind: "A nasty piece of work this man. Broke the arm of the instructor in a mock-disarming exercise." That was just three months ago and he knew, as he knew everything that went on with his people, that Macdonald was held in awe by many of the younger men in the field. To take the Triad assignment away from him would be a blow to Macdonald's self-respect and his effectiveness. No, he had earned the right to regain his dignity. Sir Archibald knew that his decision was the right one.

Macdonald kept his eyes on the older man's throughout the scrutiny. He was well aware that he was the object of inward debate, but he was certain the decision would not be altered. It was up to him to vindicate himself.

Sir Archibald leaned forward, "You may or may not locate this Tang. It is bloody unlikely that you will trace him by consulting the Greater London telephone directory . . . but, if you do, you will take no field action without the go-ahead from chief of staff or myself. . . . Is that clear?"

"Yes, sir."

"Good! he scowled. "You are well aware of the set up in the department—myself, chief of staff and four coordinators. Field operatives are either eliminated by the opposition or gradually added to the "inactive" list. They open country pubs or grow roses. Nobody gets fired—and nobody resigns!" He smiled, but his eyes were hard. "I can't see you playing host to the natives of a rural community, and you're a bit too active for roses. As an efficient coordinator you are worth five thousand a year, tax exempt, and we waive the tedious details of deductions. As a failure, you become a worthless embarrassment to your colleagues and a well-informed liability to me. A luxury I couldn't afford!" He sat back. "You have, in line of duty, killed, to my knowledge, six people. Do you regret their passing?"

"No, sir." He shrugged his shoulders. "I have killed only in instances when it was them or me."

"Exactly. I have also had to choose killing or being killed. It is an occupational hazard. I have even had to sacrifice a colleague for the success of an assignment." His tone became sharp, "I will sacrifice you if I have to. Nothing as dramatic as having you meet with a nasty accident; rather, I would have you incarcerated in Broadmoor!" His lips twisted in a bleak smile. "I believe the term is 'Detained during Her Majesty's pleasure.' You would be padded from a hard, cruel world." He made a gesture of dismissal. "Now, get out of my sight. The thought of you in a straightjacket is a tempting one at this moment."

21

After the interview with Sir Archibald, Macdonald was in no mood to sit behind a desk. He needed fresh air and space to breathe in. The loss of Maxwell—a friend as well as a colleague—had hit him hard. It was pointless to dwell on his guilt for the death of his friend, but he could not easily forget the punishment Maxwell had taken. The best he could do was promise Maxwell—and himself—that he would exact retribution when the day came. Maxwell would be in his thoughts for a long time to come.

Macdonald walked aimlessly for a while but found himself hating the crowded streets. What he needed was the feel of grass beneath his feet and solitude. He headed for St. James's Park. As he entered the gates of the park, he felt he was in a different world. Nannies strolling with their charges or gossiping on benches. A few down-and-outs were scattered on the grass—intermingled with dropouts drinking in sunshine as they dreamed of Utopia. The river sparkled and excited cries of children filled the air. The traffic noise receded as he went deeper into the park and only the vapor trails from aircraft marred the blue of the sky. Civilization would be tolerable as long as oases such as this existed.

Macdonald sat on a empty bench. He removed his jacket and stared lazily around him. A perfect day, with the trees, grass, and shrubbery green as only England is green in summer. Gradually warmed by the sun and lulled by the sound of military music from the direction of Buckingham Palace, he dozed. When he awoke his mouth was dry and he considered going for a cold beer. That would mean returning to civilization and he wasn't ready for that, not quite yet. Instead he found himself watching the approach of two boys, accompanied by an attractive woman in her mid-thirties.

The boys—one about nine and the other a year or so younger—each carried a model sailboat. They were chattering excitedly in eager anticipation of reaching the pond. The woman was aware of Macdonald's interest in them. She carefully kept her eyes averted as they approached and drew level, but her retreating figure swayed in a tantalizing rhythm, just a shade more pronounced than before. She would have been disappointed to learn that it was her sons who were the focus of his attention. Time had gone back thirty years for Macdonald.

It was in this same park that he and his brother Andrew had sailed their boats. As a breeze filled the tiny sails, they became sailors on the high seas. On land they could be soldiers, explorers, cowboys—any one of a hundred things. How many people become what they want to be? Macdonald laughed inwardly. His brother did! What about him? Given the opportunity, would he change places with big brother Andrew? No way. The only thing he envied Andrew was that he lived in the Scottish Highlands. He wasn't ready for it yet but someday, when he had fulfilled himself, he would live in the Highlands. There the air was clean and a man could be as free as the deer and the eagles. A harsh climate, but the seasons brought their separate rewards. He loved the great, brooding mountains from which crystal-clear torrents rushed to waiting lochs, shores where tempests blew in winter and miles of unspoiled sands stretched in summer, forests, bogs, heather, and bracken merging colors in unparalleled beauty. Someday, but not now.

Now. What was he now? Irritably, Macdonald forced the question to the back of his mind and concentrated on the past. He was the second son of a second son. His father had run the London office of the distillery owned by his grandfather. Uncle Andrew, the elder brother after whom his brother was named, managed the distillery in Perthshire. When World War II came along, his father had gone into the army. Major Macdonald of the Black Watch gave his life as the victorious Allies pushed through to the heart of Germany. His grandfather, Sir Andrew Macdonald, was proud of the sacrifice his second son made, but was even more proud of the job Uncle Andrew did at the distillery.

However, Uncle Andrew and his very socially acceptable wife failed to have children. It was a sad disappointment to them and to grandfather. As the begetting years dwindled, grandfather and Uncle Andrew took more and more interest in the older brother, Andrew. Tony was given the same public school education as his brother and everyone in the family treated the two boys alike, but it was obvious that Andrew was being groomed for the star role. Tony became aware that *his* role was to be secondary. He did not actively resent it but he was determined he would not be treated like his father. Major Macdonald's widow remarried. This alienated her from the "family," and it meant the boys spent most of their holidays in the Scottish Highlands. The arrangement suited all concerned. Mother and stepfather were happy together. Uncle Andrew and his wife had a family denied them by nature, and grandfather knew there was another generation to continue the line and keep the distillery in the family.

University followed school for both boys. Andrew got his degree and Tony was sent home after his first year. Both brothers were drafted for military service. Andrew easily obtained a commission in the Royal Air Force, but Tony struggled through Mons Officer Cadet School, to become a second lieutenant in the Black Watch. Unlike his father, Tony was not a hero, but he *did* survive. Korea matured him and convinced him his destiny did not lie being in charge of the London office of the Macdonald Distillery.

When the young men returned to civilian life, Andrew settled in happily as understudy to Uncle Andrew. The consensus of the family was that Tony should go back to university to get his degree—a prelude to his taking over in London, like his father. Tony, bored and restless, went to Canada instead. He bummed around for a couple of years, then went to the United States and did the same for two more years. He had so many jobs that he lost count. His years abroad brought awareness of what life was all about. The grinding existence that was life for countless millions made him appreciate the finer things he had previously taken for granted.

After four years, he returned home. Although he felt closer to his family, he had no desire to fill the role

129

they expected of him. He stayed at home two weeks and left for London. There he met an army colleague who was now a mercenary in Africa. Tony threw in with him and spent the next three years moving around the Dark Continent. When he next returned to the United Kingdom, he was twenty-eight years old and had just £200 in the bank to show for ten years of adult life. Grandfather was dead and Uncle Andrew semiretired. Brother Andrew had married suitably and was occupying his niche in life to the satisfaction of everyone concerned.

Andrew made no bones about the fact that he resented Tony's presence in Perthshire. As far as he was concerned, his brother should go to London to take his place in the scheme of things. Tony preferred drinking the family product—Grand Clanranald—to selling it. It was, as far as his palate was concerned, the finest whiskey in the world, but it was for enjoying, not something which inspired his commercial instincts. Enjoy it he did, but in local bars, not at home or at the golf club as a Macdonald—in his brother's opinion—should. He soon ran through the £200 in the bank, but his grandfather had left him shares in the distillery so money wasn't a problem. But the local bank manager kept the family advised of the rate at which the black sheep was spending it. Furthermore, Tony's choice of female companions did not meet with family approval either. The end came when he got into a real drag-them-out-in-the-alley fight with one of the distillery workers in a local bar.

At a family conference, an ultimatum was delivered. Tony was to take the job in London as manager, or else! He told them to shove the distillery. When the row subsided, it was agreed that his holding in the company would be increased to give him an income of £10,000 a year on condition he withdrew from the family scene. Tony agreed with alacrity to the proposal and was on the London train next day. He found a flat in St. John's Wood that suited his needs and, having the money to indulge his good taste, he spent a few happy weeks setting himself up for the good life. But when the flat was finished he was bored.

Introduction to the department came from the

most unexpected person. Out of a sense of duty he visited his mother and stepfather once a week. It wasn't a hardship, as he had found his stepfather an understanding ally during his years of wandering. One evening, after his mother had gone to bed, his stepfather tentatively suggested there was a government job that might suit the black sheep. He hinted it was in the field of intelligence and, for the first time, told Tony that he had been in intelligence during the war. He suggested an appointment be set up. Having nothing more promising in view, Tony agreed. The appointment led to several interviews. The whole process intrigued Macdonald, and eventually he was given a few test assignments.

Reflecting on it all now, Macdonald did not regret his ten years with the department. It had been exciting, dangerous and, most important, fulfilling. He had had enough adventures to satisfy ten men and come out of it all relatively unscathed. It was only since he had been promoted to controller and had been given a desk that he was depressed. It was logical that he pass on his experience to the younger men, but he wanted to do it in the field, not as a shadowy figure lurking in the background. The nine-to-five world of desks and filing cabinets was not for him. He was a restless soul, and his destiny was to wander. Maybe it *was* time he called it a day. Sir Archibald had said nobody retired, but to Tony, being desk-bound was worse than retirement. He was "inactive" though he continued to work for the department. He sure as hell wasn't doing it for the money! What was he doing it for?

Before, it had been for the excitement. He had loved traveling around from place to place. He had done it because he was an escapist. The only responsibility he had ever carried had been the success of an assignment. The extent of his responsibilities had never exceeded the immediate situation: to keep the people in his care alive and bring an assignment to a successful conclusion. From the day he was commissioned in the army until now, that had been his life. No wife or family to provide for. Never any major financial crisis. No community involvement. That had been his life and he had loved it. Perhaps the mode of life indicated some character deficiency but that was the way it was. Maxwell's death was his first failure. Was he now trying to escape because of that?

Being a controller carried with it a kind of responsibility that was new to him. He hadn't really considered it before. Resentment against being brought "inside" had blinded him to it. In the field he had been responsible for people, but he had shared their risks. He hadn't shared the risks with Maxwell. *That* was it. Could he continue to send men to their deaths and wash it all away over a glass of port in the clubs? Tough luck, and all that kind of thing. The job is bigger than any one individual. Several bastards had happily sent *him* to possible death over the years. That he had survived was due to his skills, ruthlessness, and sense of survival. He had never seriously harbored a grudge against any of his superiors for sending him on an assignment. It was all part of the game. Thing was, did the people he had in the field resent his sending them there? More important, did he really give a damn whether they resented or not? Truth was that he *didn't* give a damn if the field operatives resented him or not. He had taken his chances in his time. If they found it too hot, they could get the hell out of the kitchen.

V

22

In all, Hunter was away for ten days. Tang met him at the airport and reported fully on developments during Hunter's stay in Hong Kong. As expected, the day-to-day operations of the Society had run smoothly. As this had been a test period, Hunter was pleased with the performances of his *Ahkungs*. He was less pleased to hear about the Maxwell incident and questioned Tang closely on all details. The handling of the situation to the point where the prisoner had escaped was above reproach, but the untidy conclusion angered Hunter.

Assurance that those responsible had paid the price for their negligence did nothing to appease him. He did not like the time lapse between the escape of Maxwell and the subsequent discovery of the body. It was an imponderable factor. Further questioning on this aspect of the incident did not yield any unsettling information, but Hunter's unease persisted.

As a new member of the Inner Council, Hunter did not want to be bothered by problems due to carelessness. He was now familiar with the full extent of Triad's international influence. He was in a position of great power, and the lengthy briefing sessions he had received from the Leader in China had left him in no doubt as to the responsibility his position carried. He had been staggered by the sheer weight of the statistics, the colossal sums of money involved, and the power wielded by the Society. The political influence that Triad funds and generations of infiltration could bring to bear at the highest levels of government was such that the economics of many Far Eastern states could be manipulated almost at will.

The Leader had illustrated the ways in which Hunter could contribute to the international activities of the Society when he reached a sufficiently high level in the

British government. The Common Market presented opportunities that could be exploited in favor of China's position in world affairs; also, the emerging nations of Africa, together with South America. The Triad had to extend its influence to these two continents and build organizations there. Aid from China had placed many of the new nations in debt. As the Chinese sphere of influence grew, so did Triad power.

In the United States there were two Caucasians occupying high positions in Triad affairs. On the subject of Vietnam, the Leader had explained that the conflict there had served the Triad cause in two ways. While the Americans were exhausting their economy and national will to prop up what was a war in name only the Chinese were consolidating their position in Africa. Korea, as an object lesson, had served to prove that open confrontation with the West was too expensive. The war in Malaya, fought by guerrillas trained by China, was far less expensive, and the Far East was a theater which could provide enough small wars to keep the Americans occupied for years to come. Also drug traffic to Vietnam had been a lucrative business for the Triad and the increased drug addiction, together with racial problems and political upheaval such as Watergate, served to create internal strife in the United States. It was important to Chinese development that a fairly high level of unrest was maintained in America.

The Leader's frankness in explaining the details of Triad influence through the world had flattered Hunter. He had no illusions about how this knowledge bound him to the Society. His interests and those of the Triad were inseparable now.

All in all, Hunter's trip had been enlightening, and he was now eager to pursue his election as member for Suffolk East. It was unfortunate that this Maxwell incident had occurred, but he would just have to rely on Tang's explanation that there had been no opportunity for the man from Hong Kong to contact anyone, if indeed he was not working alone.

The election was a triumph, and Clive Hunter was duly returned to serve as member of Parliament for Suffolk East. The turning point of the campaign had been a charming wedding in the village church where the bride's family had worshiped for several generations. A beautiful bride, a handsome groom, autumn color stealing over the countryside, and a guest list that was a miniature *Who's Who*. The voters loved every moment of it, and follow-up pictures of the happy couple on honeymoon clinched it.

Hunter played it cautiously on entering the House. He made a point of assuming a modest air when the subject of his knowledge of the Far East was raised. It was only a question of time before he was invited to sit on a select committee. Those who mattered began to take an interest in the member for East Suffolk. It was whispered confidentially, "Hunter is a young man going places in the party."

On the domestic front, Hunter was as happy as he would ever allow himself to be. His wife satisfied him sexually and didn't complain when her husband spent most week nights in London. The weekends began early Friday evening and lasted through late Monday morning. Her home was close to her parents and she did go up to London occasionally for a day's shopping, followed by dinner and a show. Mrs. Hunter was the envy of her female friends and happy as only a new bride in love can be.

The Far East Importation Co. Ltd. conducted business as it had done before Hunter became an M.P. Mr. Fotheringham was given added responsibility and never asked questions about certain negotiations that were best handled by his managing director. The affairs of the Society flourished under the four *Ahkungs* and Tang, in turn, supervised their efforts. Hunter was kept advised of all activities but did not allow himself to be involved beyond making major decisions. As a member of the Inner Council it was important that a two-way channel of communications with China be constantly open. This had been arranged before he left Hong Kong. The code employed amused Hunter. Only a Chinese scholar could have read the words and without the key, no codebreaker would ever crack the code. It had been used by the Inner Council for centuries.

The leisurely pace at Westminster and the apathetic

approach with which a number of M.P.s carried out their duties tried Hunter's patience. Procedure ruled in government. The individual's identity could be swallowed, reducing him to a mindless body. There were, of course, the "brilliant" men whom the media latched on to. The real trick was to gain acceptance. This was the task Hunter set himself and being in the right place at the right time became second nature. Careful cultivation of the right people became a habit. A beautiful wife, a place in the country, the correct social scene, and having the kind of money necessary to indulge all of these were the tools he employed.

He had to exercise self-discipline regarding women. It was his nature to be attracted by the challenge of a beautiful face or a sensual body. But he resisted temptation. He used his wife for all his sexual needs and was fortunate in that she developed healthy appetites of her own. She became capable of meeting his every demand. In time he knew it would be necessary to have fresh adventures, and he hungered for them. Chinese girls were what he wanted most, and it would be a simple matter to arrange. He could import them and export them when he grew tired. The prospect amused him, and he discreetly set up the necessary arrangements.

With time the Maxwell incident faded in importance. Hunter arranged a complete overhaul of security within the Society and requested a similar tightening up in Hong Kong and the New Territories. He did not doubt that the British police were aware of drug traffic from the Far East but, apart from Maxwell, there had been no indication of any major investigation. As always, small quantities of drugs were allowed to fall into the hands of customs, and minor arrests made. It was important to keep the authorities happy.

23

Macdonald lay in bed and litsened to the water boiling in the automatic teapot. He had been awake for the best part of an hour but had been reluctant to get up before his scheduled hour of 7:00. He was looking forward to a cup of tea. Propping himself on his left elbow, he poured a quantity of the amber Nilgiris, no milk or sugar to destroy the delicate flavor, and sipping from the cup he reflected that it was going to be another nothing day.

He lit his first cigarette of the day and rehashed the thoughts that had been going through his head since he awakened. Two months ago he had submitted the completed Triad report to Sir Archibald and since then his duties had consisted of one mundane assignment after the other. He was still officially responsible for the investigation, but it was only a matter of sticking a few pins in the map when new Chinese restaurants opened and removing them when they closed down. Apart from that, progress was nil. It looked like a long, long winter.

He refilled his cup and lit a fresh cigarette. He felt jaded despite his four hard sessions at the gym every week. The cigarettes didn't help, but he wasn't about to give them up. Nor was he about to give up Grand Clanranald. His depression had nothing to do with tobacco or whiskey. It was the cumulative effect of nine-to-five days at the office where the most dangerous encounter was likely to be the bloody-awful coffee. Nine-to-five and every weekend off. Christ almighty! What the hell was one supposed to do with the free time? The present routine was driving him crazy. Maybe he should enroll for classes at some night school or other. Take up a hobby. He *had* a hobby! Right now she was called Avril. Before that it had been Jean, Mary Frances, Elizabeth, etc. etc. No, he thought to himself, there had never been one like Avril. He crushed out his cigarette and thrust the bedclothes aside. His feet hit the floor and he strode barefoot to the bathroom.

Standing in front of the mirror, he subjected his face to critical examination. It wasn't a *bad* face, considering how long he had had it and some of the beatings it had been subjected to. It *did* reflect maturity—that he couldn't deny—and women prefer mature men. Certainly Avril preferred him.

He bathed, then sluiced off the soapsuds under the shower. As a matter of routine, he made the water as cold as he could and forced himself to stand under the freezing needles of water until he had difficulty catching his breath. After a brisk toweling, he felt totally invigorated and went through to the bedroom to dress. Clothes were important to Macdonald. His wardrobe was extensive and the tailored suits and shirts bore the labels of famous makers in London, Rome, Paris, and New York. Shirts, ties, and socks were coordinated with the grays, blues, and browns of the suits—his favorite colors.

By the time he had dressed, it was 8:00. He made coffee and lightly toasted two slices of bread. As he ate he glanced through the mail but there was nothing of interest. He turned to the morning paper. His habit was to scan every column but read only items of interest. He seldom missed an article and could usually recall the broad details of any story. A headline on page three caught his eye. It ran: "Soho London's New Chinatown?" and the subheading was "Heroin Haul Traced to Gerrard Street." The text stated that a quarter of a million pounds worth of heroin had been found at the Liverpool docks and that the destination of the haul was an address in London's Gerrard Street. Probably the biggest haul the police and customs had made this year. Macdonald was amazed. There had been too many stories in the newspapers recently that touched on Triad. The last thing he needed was a crusading journalist coming up with an exposé. There was no way he could muzzle the press and no way he could get his hands on any useful information journalists might come up with unless he could get Sir Archibald to arrange it with responsible editors. Even if he did there would remain the irresponsible editors. Unhappily, he left for the office.

The department insisted that all staff have good cars, and special funds were available for damage incurred in the line of duty. Each man had to supply his own car and replace it when the mileage demanded. Macdonald had a '76 Mercedes 600. He could well afford it as it was a write-off against his dividends from the distillery stock since he was, on paper, a director of that company. He had owned the car only a few weeks, and it was barely broken in. To and from the office every day, and a few pleasure miles was hardly enough. What it needed was a good run on the Continent to build up a few thousand miles and give the powerful engine a chance to settle down. As he pulled into the parking area he resolved to take a holiday soon. He had the time coming and he could afford it.

His secretary was already at her desk when he entered the outer office. She raised her head and said, "Sir Archibald has been asking for you."

To satisfy his ego, he sat and did nothing for five minutes. Then he left for Sir Archibald's office.

The old man wished him good morning but spoiled it by glancing at his watch as he spoke. Macdonald sat in the usual chair and waited for the chief to start the session. Sir Archibald picked up a sheet of paper and held it up in front of him. The newspaper article was neatly Scotch-taped to it, "Seen this, of course?"

"Yes, sir, I've seen it."

"Followed up on it?"

"I'm just about to. I didn't want to rock any boats."

"Don't bother, I've done it—nothing in it for us. Either the customs and police got lucky or the Chinese *allowed* them to find the stuff. Customs and police are taking credit, but my considered opinion is that they were allowed to find it.

The stress on "considered" did not escape Macdonald. He nodded and contented himself with saying, "If *you* say so, sir."

Sir Archibald scowled as he said, "I *do* say so!" He toyed with his paper knife, "Would you believe, Macdonald, that the owner of the establishment where the heroin was going is on vacation in Hong Kong?"

"I would believe it."

"Would you also believe that the establishment was a hole-in-the-wall with merchandise in stock that wasn't worth more than a couple of hundred pounds?"

Macdonald nodded and said, "I'd believe it."

"That's good!" Sir Archibald swung in his chair and stared at the wall. After a moment he said, "It is my

considered opinion that the whole thing is a dead end."
He swung back to face Macdonald, "Do you know
why?"

"You tell me, sir. You checked it out and you know
the facts."

"You are doing very well today, Macdonald." The
older man smiled as he went on, "No guesses—you
might get used to your desk in time!" He pointed the
blade of the paper knife at the younger man, "Would
you believe that the heroin was of such low quality it is
almost useless."

Macdonald digested the information. The whole
thing was obviously a setup. It was nice and pat and
fell in with the pattern he and Maxwell had discussed
so many times. Keep the police and customs happy,
but only when convenient to Triad. He shrugged, "I
can't argue with your view."

"Glad to hear you say that." Sir Archibald nodded
sagely. "Would you believe, Macdonald, that there are
people in high places who think the department is
staffed with well-intentioned idiots?" He came as close
to a grin as Macdonald had ever seen him. "Well-
intentioned—but nonetheless idiots. Do you believe
that?"

Trying not to shift uncomfortably in his chair, Macdonald nodded and said, "It can't be easy, sir."

"It *isn't* easy, but then nobody said it would be!"
Sir Archibald tossed the paper knife on the desk and
picked up a ruler. "As you get old and, I hope, wiser
in the ways of sitting behind a desk, you will learn
how to handle situations such as the one you have been
involved in these past months. We are going to back
off from this heroin haul and let the police investigate
to their hearts' content. We are going to let the newspapers report on the police activities to *their* hearts'
content." He allowed his voice to drop, "You see, Macdonald, we are going to play our Chinese friends at
their own game. When the police come to a dead end,
the papers will be fed up with the story. Do you agree
with that?"

"Yes, they're onto Triad already—several reports
have appeared in the past months."

Sir Archibald shook his head sadly, "And too bad

about that. They make Triad out to be like Fu Manchu or characters by Edgar Wallace."

"It isn't funny, sir!" Macdonald snapped back. "Maxwell didn't die laughing. I don't laugh at it, and I sure as hell won't let anyone else do it either!"

"You're quite right. It *isn't* a laughing matter." The older man shot him a glance that was a mixture of approval and rebuke. "Don't forget it and don't let any of your men forget it. We are dealing with the best-organized and most ruthless criminal element in history. The full extent of their activities isn't known to us but, given time, we will destroy them. Time is the key factor. It is going to take a *lot* of time. Triad influence was built up over centuries, and there is no simple way to put them out of business. The secret of defeating an enemy is in knowing the deployment of their troops and being in a position to cut off their supplies. The same principle applies here. In all armies there is a hierarchy of command leading up to the commanding officer. The troops in the field are aware only of the battle they are involved in. It is the commanding officer at headquarters that sees the whole picture. The officers in the field carry out *his* instructions. Conditions in the field when an actual battle takes place are imponderables. The commander in the field reports back, but the commanding officer is a fool if he depends entirely on his field commanders. He must always have a contingency plan in case the battle is lost."

Sir Archibald was running short of breath. He paused for a moment, then went on, "What I'm saying is that the commanding officer is concerned with winning a war! Do you follow me, Macdonald?"

"Yes, I'm with you, sir."

"That's good, because *if* you have been listening closely you will appreciate the importance of desk jobs in the field of intelligence." The older man threw his ruler onto the desk. "I hope you have got it clearly fixed in your mind because I'll be *damned* if I'm ever going to go through it all again with you—ever!"

Macdonald nodded his head but made no reply. He was flattered the Old Man had taken the trouble to talk to him at this length. It was unusual, to say the least.

He began to feel that he was accepted. Sir Archibald had obviously wanted him to fully appreciate the importance of being behind a desk. Nostalgia about adventures in the field was one thing, but the past was over and done with. The man behind the desk had to be committed—committed to the present. It was a coming of age for him and what Sir Archibald was really saying was he would be accepted only if he accepted *his* role in the scheme of things.

Sir Archibald must have pressed a buzzer on his desk, for his secretary put her head around the door. The head of department said, "Let's have coffee for two."

"For two?" The woman's voice held a note of surprise.

"Two!" Sir Archibald was emphatic.

Macdonald *was* surprised. Acceptance had really arrived. It would be the first time he had ever taken coffee in this office.

24

After the coffee had been served—an improvement on the quality brought around the lower offices—Sir Archibald pushed the ashtray toward Macdonald and said, "You might as well smoke, I suppose."

Another surprise. Macdonald accepted the invitation. When he had a cigarette lit, he said, "This is very good coffee."

"Help yourself to another cup." Sir Archibald leaned back in his chair, "We were talking about a war against Triad. I have asked the Prime Minister if there have been any discussions with the United States, and he assures me there haven't been. I did tell you before that I know Washington has files on Triad, but there hasn't been any official joining of forces between us and the Americans. We are each involved in campaigns of containment. My chief concern is what is actually happening in this country—and in other countries where there is a direct impact here.

"That brings me to the next point. Earlier we spoke of chains of command and how only the man in charge sees the whole picture. The danger with that is, of course, the left hand not knowing what the right hand is doing. The chief of staff knows all that goes on. My own chief of staff knows all that goes on in case he has to take over at short notice. In theory I am responsible to the cabinet for the operation of the department but, in practice, I report directly to the Prime Minister. The deputy Prime Minister is kept advised of all I report. Sometimes I get involved with the Home Secretary and sometimes with the Foreign Secretary—sometimes with both.

"It can be complex at times but it is vital that only the Prime Minister sees the whole picture. This leads to some members of the cabinet getting upset and gives rise to the opinion that the department is staffed by incompetent idiots. They aren't seeing the *whole* picture. They are unaware of most of the operations we have been involved in over the years. I have my moments of sheer frustration—you follow me, Macdonald?"

"Yes, sir, and to be honest, I hadn't thought about these kinds of problems."

Sir Archibald dismissed the comment with a wave of his hand. "I'm telling you these things for future reference. From time to time, questions are raised regarding the necessity of maintaining the department at all. It is always the same old argument. We have the police, private security such as docks and railways, military and naval intelligence, the so-called Secret Service and a whole string of outfits with initials and numerals instead of names. Why the hell do we need the 'department'?"

The older man drank from his cup and then went on. "Every time it comes up, the debate goes back and forth but every time the Prime Minister exercises his prerogative and the department goes on. Sometimes he is backed strongly by his ministers, if it suits them! Sometimes not. Whichever, I'm always left with a bad taste in my mouth." Sir Archibald fixed his eyes on Macdonald and asked, "Why the hell do people like us do what we do? You, for example, earn more from your private income than from the department. I could accept elevation to the peerage tomorrow and I have more than enough money to last me for the rest of my life. I ask you again, Macdonald, why do we do it?"

He did not wait for an answer, but continued, "When we are young and in the field, we do it for the excitement. We are a special breed of men who need danger as part of our existence. We have to kill or be killed. We love intrigue, and we love to pit our wits against others. We like the devious challenge of undercover work. Fighting an enemy we may never see and yet who is better known to us than people we have been close to all our lives. We probe for his weaknesses and respect his strengths. One will win and the other will lose. There is no quarter given and none expected. There are no rules and the only real reward is winning. Rudyard Kipling called it 'the great game' and that's what it is. At all levels of the game it is personal. For each individual there is an opponent. Be it two men in the field face to face, guns drawn, or two men, thousands of miles apart, behind desks. It is always personal. When I say personal I mean just that. There are times in any assignment when we are so deeply involved in the duel that we forget the people we are working for—be it government, criminal organization, or whatever. We get so wrapped up in the assignment that it becomes our life." He jabbed the knife in Macdonald's direction, "You understand what I'm saying? It happens at *all* levels, not just in the field."

Macdonald nodded, "Yes. I have that feeling for the man behind Triad in this country."

"Good." Sir Archibald smiled, but it was bleak, without humor. "All you have to learn is how to fight him from behind your desk. As it happens, you are in a transitional stage, part field and part desk. You can get much closer to your opponent than I can." He placed the knife on the desk. "If you *really* think about it, the reason we do what we do is power. Money is only a means to an end. In all fields of human endeavor, power is the ultimate goal, and in the struggle for it, the strong are separated from the weak. The only result of the great game is that the victor has either increased the power of his side or destroyed the power of the other." He corrected himself, "Destroyed is too strong a word. Victory is seldom total. Let us say curtailed the power of the other side. That being so"—he leaned forward—"I ask you this: what power is Triad aspiring to in this country?"

Macdonald thought for a moment, then suggested tentatively, "I can only suggest political power."

"Right," Sir Archibald nodded approval. "My conclusion is the same and it has been accepted by the Prime Minister. At first I thought that flooding the United Kingdom with hard drugs could be a form of revenge for Britain flooding China with opium back in the heyday of the empire. But I dismissed that as a side issue. The drugs themselves could only be part of it. There is a great deal of money in drugs. What happens to that money? The answer lies in a fundamental truth: the means of controlling a country politically is to control its economy. A bit farfetched, Macdonald?"

"No, it is happening with Arab oil money. They have been buying into British companies and property." The younger man smiled, then added, "If you won't take me to task for stating an oversimplification, I would say the Arab-Israeli conflict has become more economic than conventional warfare. Jewish money, well established but devalued by inflation, versus almost unlimited Arab money. And in the end the wealthiest side is the one which is heard when a country—such as ours—has to choose sides."

Sir Archibald nodded vigorously, "That's the general idea. My problem was to figure out just where the Chinese money was going. I had to find an area where they could gain control. Nothing short of complete control would satisfy Triad. I had you and Maxwell plotting the extent of Chinese infiltration in the United Kingdom, but that was only part of it. You see what I mean about seeing the whole picture?"

"Yes," Macdonald said quietly, "I see a bit more clearly why forcing the situation was a mistake."

The older man shot him a look of appraisal, "I hope so. The thing that saved the day was your having the presence of mind to put Maxwell's body back close to the scene. I believe our involvement was not compromised because of that." He dismissed it with a wave of his hand. "Anyway, while you were doing your end,

I had another team checking out another angle. Do you have any idea what that was?" Macdonald shook his head. Sir Archibald smiled slightly, "I believe you are one of the few people who could have come up with the answer, given time. The answer is gambling. Make sense to you?"

"Yes, it does." Macdonald could see it quite clearly. The Chinese were notorious gamblers and they controlled all gambling in the Far East.

"I thought it might. You and I share a love for gambling. With us it is like our work. We love the challenge of it, but *we* control our gambling, it doesn't control us. Millions of people—hundreds of millions—aren't as fortunate as we. Gambling takes over their lives."

Sir Archibald passed a weary hand over his eyes, "As you know we were a wide-open gambling country until 1968, when the Gaming Act made gambling one of our most closely regulated and heavily taxed industries. There is no other country in the world where there are legal betting-shops, casinos, football pools, bingo, and a dozen other ways for a company to get into the gambling business legally. Obtaining licenses would be out of the question for the Chinese. The Gaming Board would very quickly put two and two together, as they did with the Mafia, and that would end the Chinese invasion into the field. However, the people we are dealing with are clever. They saw the Mafia lose out here and they learned a lesson from it. Instead, Triad is investing in established companies which are involved in gambling. They use dummy companies to buy up shares in every company they can—the promoters of football pools, the betting-shop chains, the fruit-machine operators, even the giants of the entertainment industry who own the gaming casinos. Every penny Triad makes on drugs goes into gambling enterprises."

Macdonald emmited a low whistle, "That must be one helluva lot of money."

"As you say, a helluva lot of money." Sir Archibald lightly tapped a manila folder on his desk. "I have a complete list of investments made in the industry since the Gaming Act of 1968. These are divided into two categories. One is the list of investors with nothing to hide. The other—by far the longer list—covers investors hidden by a screen. There are billions of pounds gambled in this country every year, and I can tell you that the profits—even after tax—are sweet. An ever-increasing percentage of these profits is finding its way to the gentlemen who control the companies on my second list." He pushed the manila folder to one side. "I will do something about it when the time is ripe. There are serious problems involved, and they will take time to sort out. However, I have a strategy. In any case, that is no concern of yours, and I would prefer that you don't speculate on the nature of it."

"If you say so, sir."

Sir Archibald studied Macdonald for a moment before going on. "Let us turn to matters that *do* concern you. As you know, the department keeps its fingers on the pulse of many diverse activities. The majority come to nothing, but prevention is better than cure. Occasionally we do come up with a good one. This came to our attention recently." He took a photograph from a drawer and handed it to Macdonald, "Recognize the face?"

Macdonald studied it carefully. He was vaguely aware of having seen the face before but was unable to place it. He handed the photo back, "Best I can say is I've seen this man—or a picture of him—somewhere. Can't go beyond that, I'm afraid."

Sir Archibald took the picture. "Would you recognize him if you meet him in the next week or two?"

"Certainly."

"Good. The man you have just seen is the member of Parliament for Suffolk East. His name is Clive Hunter and he is the original 'Mr. Clean.' "

"Oh, yes. I've seen his picture in the papers. He got in on a special election fairly recently."

"Exactly right. Our Mr. Hunter has an impeccable pedigree. Eton, Cambridge, the right clubs, he has a flat in London and a country place in Suffolk. Recently married and doing a good job in the House. Word is that he can go a long way in government." Sir

Archibald smiled grimly. "What do you think his special talent is?"

Macdonald shook his head, "Not the faintest idea."

"Our new M.P. is an expert on Chinese affairs. His knowledge covers all of the Far East and he speaks Chinese."

"Very interesting," Macdonald said.

"Something even more interesting is that he owns a company engaged in the import-export business between the U.K. and the Far East. It is called Far East Importation Company Limited—offices in London, Hong Kong, and Singapore."

"I'll be damned! That company is on my list, about the biggest of its kind in this country."

Sir Archibald smiled. "All of us in this business are damned, one way or the other. But, to proceed. Clive Hunter likes to gamble once in a while. I'm told he is very good at it." Sir Archibald smiled again, "Good in the sense that you and I are. He plays within a limit and, win or lose, enjoys playing. I am further told that he will be in Monte Carlo week after next. What I want you to do is meet him there. Have yourself a little holiday. Leave at the end of this week. Might be a good idea to take that very expensive car of yours and give it a run."

Macdonald grinned. Nothing escaped the Old Man's attention. The prospect of a holiday in the south of France wasn't to be sneezed at, especially if the department were to pick up the tab. He said, "You ask me to 'meet' Hunter. What does that mean?"

"It means you will effect an introduction. I want it to be casual and, if possible, I want a relationship to develop. Because Hunter is who he is, I don't want you jumping to any hasty conclusions. I want you to get to know him. It might be a blind alley, but there is nothing to be lost. I'm playing this one both ways. We have an M.P.—the Chinese tie-in—gambling. Could be that Hunter is not all he is supposed to be, but I'll decide on that. There could be a tie-in with gambling in the south of France, but I will arrange for somebody to keep an eye on Hunter's activities while he is on 'holiday.' Your job is simply to get to know him—understood?"

"Understood. I'll keep a low profile." Macdonald lit a fresh cigarette, "I'll leave on Friday, and I'll take the car."

Sir Archibald looked distastefully at the cigarette, "I want you to be clear on something else. The department will cover your expenses. If you decide to take a traveling companion, that is your expense. You can gamble as little—or as much—as you like, but it will be your money." Then he smiled and said, "You may keep anything you win."

25

About the time Macdonald was leaving Sir Archibald's office, a large truck swung slowly from a narrow waterfront street into the wider one leading to the gates at Glasgow's docks. The driver hated the streets at the quaysides. Cobbled, with single-track railway lines running down the center, they were laid in the days of horse-drawn vehicles. Modern trucks slid dangerously when rain mixed with oil to slick the surface. If the port had been thriving, the streets bordering the warehouses would have been paved, but since times were bad, the docks would close before resurfacing took place. "Bloody good thing, too!" The driver spoke aloud at the conclusion of his train of thought.

"What?" his mate, eyes closed and listening to a transistor radio, kept a hand moving in time with the music.

"Nothin'. You're gonna be stone deaf soon if you don't give up that bloody radio." The airbrakes hissed as the truck came to a halt at the gates to the docks.

A uniformed security man took a final drag at a cigarette and advanced to the cab of the truck. His practiced eye noted the registration number and he checked off the vehicle on a sheaf of papers on his clipboard. He held out his free hand to take the driver's papers. As he did so, he said, "Jesus Christ! I thought all you people had C.B. Sounds like a rock show in here!" As he examined the dockets, he addressed the driver, who was about his own age. "How can you stand that bloody noise?"

"I'm running out of patience." The driver scowled, "He's gonna get it wrapped around his ears before he gets much older."

"Good thing. But probably too late. Like the rest of them, he's likely stone deaf already." He handed the papers back to the driver.

The younger man opened his eyes, and said, "Couple of bloody squares! What do you want, bagpipes— or Vera Lynn singing 'White Cliffs of Dover'?" He laughed and closed his eyes again.

The security man winked at the driver, "He's a comedian as well, eh!" He walked around to the other side of the cab and opened the door. "How would you like a sore face, sonny?"

The young man's eyes opened quickly and his body snapped into a sitting position. It was the most alert he had been all day. He looked at the bulk of the security man and scanned the face. He didn't like what he saw. Forcing a grin, he turned the radio off, as he said, "Only a joke, pal."

"Joke, my arse!" The man's tone was quite friendly, but he had made his point. As he shut the door, he said, "And don't call me 'pal'!"

The driver laughed and let out the clutch. The truck gathered speed and moved out through the gates.

It took thirty minutes for the driver to negotiate the heavy traffic and reach an industrial park on the eastern outskirts. His mate, who hadn't spoken on the journey, located the unit they were to deliver their cargo to, and said, "That's it—over there!"

"Not much of a place. If they haven't got a forklift, they're gonna be out of luck!"

"Right, I'm not trying to move these cases."

"It would break your back!" The driver laughed as he switched off the engine, "You weren't built for it. Maybe your mommy should have bought you a guitar when you were a kid. You might have been a rock star today!"

The younger man scowled as he said, "You thinking about that fat bastard back at the docks? I could have taken him easy if it came to the bit."

"Aye, you and what rock group?" The driver laughed again, "Big John could eat you for breakfast and spit out your teeth." He gave the other man a friendly push, "Come on, let's see if there's anybody around this place. Maybe we'll get a cuppa tea."

The small warehouse was like a thousand others which had sprung up all over Scotland since the North Sea oil boom. A hastily erected sign hung over double doors said "Rig Suppliers & Fitters (North Sea) Ltd." The building was dilapidated, and the frseh coat of paint which had been applied did little to cover the cracked concrete and gouged woodwork. The windows were barred and weeds grew high along the sides of the building.

There was a small door set into one of the larger ones, and the driver kicked it to attract attention. After a few moments it opened and a man with Chinese features said, "Yeah—what can I do for you?"

That the Chinese spoke with an American accent did not surprise either of the Scotsmen. Americans came in all shapes and sizes, and since the discovery of oil in the North Sea, they had been arriving in droves. The driver held out the dockets which accompanied the delivery, "Got six crates for you. You have a fork-lift?"

The Chinese-American grinned, "This might look like a set from a horror movie, but we don't keep King Kong for shifting the gear." He took the dockets, "I'll bring the prongs—be with you in a minute." He closed the door.

The two men with the truck withdrew a few paces and waited. The younger man filed away "prongs" for future use. He liked the slang term, and henceforth all forklifts would be referred to as prongs as far as he was concerned. As the double doors swung open, the driver nudged his companion, "Let's get the truck open."

Ten minutes later, the crates were all on the floor of the warehouse and the double doors closed and bolted. The Chinese-American scribbled a signature on the top copy of the dockets and handed it to the driver. As he did so, the driver's mate asked, "Can I use your toilet?"

The Chinese-American grinned widely. "Use the

john in this dump? If you've any respect for your dick, you'll take it down the road to the pub!" He took a thin roll of bills from his hip pocket, peeled off two, and handed them to the driver, "While you're there, get yourselves a drink."

The driver took the money and shrugged, "Thanks a lot."

"You are entirely welcome." The American led the way to the door and saw them out.

When the sound of the truck's diesel engine had receded, the Chinese-American checked that all the locks on the doors were secure, then went to the back of the building and rapped sharply on the door marked "Private." It opened immediately and three Chinese followed him to the crates. Without a word the man who had accepted the delivery climbed aboard the forklift. He lifted one of the crates and moved the machine forward until the load was directly beneath a block and tackle suspended from the roof, then allowed the crate to settle on the floor.

The other three men moved forward swiftly, and in a matter of minutes they had removed the bolts securing the crate to its base. The man on the machine lifted the three sides of the crate off cleanly. Fiber tapes held the packing of waxed paper over padding which protected the machinery beneath. The fiber tapes were snipped and the sandwiches of protective packing material carefully removed. These were placed to one side and from the rear of the building identical fresh packing was brought to replace it. This was wrapped around the machinery expertly and fresh fiber bands were brought to secure it. The three sides of the crate were lowered on to the base and resecured by the original bolts.

In the course of the next hour the process was repeated until all six crates had been attended to. The packing material which had been removed was placed in an empty crate together with the fiber bands. A telephone call was placed, and a van arrived a short time later. The crate containing the packaging materials was loaded into the rear of the van and the vehicle left the industrial area. Once on the highway, the driver carefully kept the van moving at around sixty miles an hour—well within the speed limit. That evening he delivered the crate to a small factory in Birmingham. Early next morning a package weighing about one hundred pounds was delivered in Manchester. This contained the heroin which had been removed from the packaging.

The heroin had come into Europe via Rotterdam. It was part of a large consignment being held in Holland for gradual shipment to England. To have sent it in directly from Rotterdam would have meant the port of entry to the United Kingdom would be Tilbury on the Thames estuary. There the risks of customs officials finding it were high. For this reason the port of entry chosen was Glasgow, where any cargo associated with the development of oil and natural gas resources from the North Sea received priority. It was a constant race against the clock to get the oil ashore. Therefore it made good sense to move the heroin from Holland to Norway and ship it directly to Scotland.

VI
Monte Carlo

26

When Tony Macdonald considered who his companion would be for the two weeks' holiday in France, he knew it would be Avril. For just over a year she had been the only woman in his life, but he went through the motions of thinking about someone else anyway. It wouldn't be all that difficult to pick someone up in the ten days before he left. Avril would accept his story about having to go abroad on business, and he would have two weeks of fucking without any hang-ups. Good memories for cold winter nights of old age. He'd find something young and tasty. Someone fresh and exciting to experiment with at his leisure who would surprise him with her uninhibited lovemaking.

He laughed at his fantasy. What would really happen was she would have to be coaxed, and when she finally gave in, it wouldn't be worth it. She would be looking for a long-term relationship and after they got back, he would get tearful telephone calls and sad little notes every day. He was tired of those games. He telephoned Avril. She greeted the idea of having a holiday with enthusiasm. She told him she'd get things squared away at work and be ready to go in ten days. She left the traveling arrangements to him. She had a thousand details to attend to: clothes, hair, packing—and her Siamese cat.

Macdonald smiled as he thought of Avril. She was very feminine in some ways, but also methodical and efficient. Avril was all woman, and he liked it that way. That was what had intrigued him in the beginning. He had become sick and tired of the libbers with their constant references to equal rights and opportunities. He was old-fashioned enough to like his women feminine. He was all for equal opportunities for women and equal rewards for skills, but beyond that he wanted to open doors, light cigarettes, and make love without being accused of being sexist.

He and Avril met at a party. Macdonald was immediately attracted to her and when she was alone for a moment he drifted toward her to engage her in conversation. She was pleasant but did not respond to his charms. He knew she was aware of her beauty and also well aware that he was interested in her, but she had said nothing to encourage him. He had rushed things by suggesting she come to his place for dinner one night. It was stupid and he knew it, even as the words left his lips.

A shadow of disappointment appeared to cross her face. Then she appraised him coolly and said, "I prefer to eat *out* on early dates with men—it gives me a chance to get to know them. If we eventually eat *in*, it is at my place. That way *I* can cook and I get a decent meal before he tries to drag my knickers off!"

Angry at himself, Macdonald had replied, "Three things are wrong with that. One, I don't cook all that badly—two, if you wear knickers you are a helluva lot older than you look—and three, I haven't dragged panties off a girl in ten years!"

Unexpectedly, she laughed a soft pleasant laugh and said, "You must be terribly frustrated." Then she turned slowly and walked away from him.

The encounter left him feeling foolish. He retreated to the bar to nurse his pride with a drink. He could see her across the room and watched a steady flow of men approach her. She didn't appear to be interested in any of them. Then he did one of the smartest things in his life. Placing his drink down he walked over to where she was and said, "My name is Tony Macdonald. I behaved like a boor earlier and I apologize."

She smiled and held out a hand, "I'm sure you aren't really a boor. My name is Avril Wentworth."

Her hand was cool and soft to the touch, but he could feel a strength in it. There was an awkward pause. Then she said, "Yes, I will have dinner with you—but out."

He returned her smile, "Sometime soon, like tomorrow night?"

Their first date was a success, as were their subsequent ones. He learned she was a partner in an antiques business. She lived alone and was unattached. When he did eat at her apartment, he found it to be a treasure trove of choice pieces she had collected in the course of business. She said she was a lousy antique dealer because she fell in love with the best pieces and would not resell them. It wasn't true. She and her partner, an elderly lady, made a very good living. It was a month before he found out whether she wore knickers or panties.

Before Avril, Macdonald had thought himself incapable of love. Too many experiences had soured him. He was capable of the pursuit and possession of a woman, but it was all no more than a strategic campaign to get between her legs. Fucking and being fucked was all it was. And even when the sex was great it was never enough. One usually got tired of it before the other. Then came the hang-ups. The nature of Macdonald's work was such that marriage was impossible. He liked it that way; it always meant he could justify the end of a relationship. That was before Avril.

It had stolen up on him. Gradually he became aware of how eagerly he searched for her in a crowded room. That the sight of her—cool, beautiful and desirable—endowed him with a feeling of warmth and tenderness. And when they slept together, they made love. She hated the word "fucking" and said that it belonged in the vocabulary of animals. As their relationship developed, he discovered he could make love without fucking. Touching became important to him, but even more important, being touched. He was in love with her.

Admitting it to himself was something else. He concentrated on reasons why it couldn't work when he permitted himself to think about it. She was ten years younger than he. Her life had been sheltered from the *real* world. But he knew neither reason was valid. She wasn't really concerned about his age and, in any case, women mature earlier than men. As to the other reason, he never discussed the nature of his work with her and he had never told her of any of his experiences. It would have been pointless. Only a few knew of the twilight world of espionage and intelligence. *Hers* was the real world. He was the stranger. Yet she had gradually introduced him to her world. He rediscovered long-forgotten pleasures when he was with her.

Macdonald knew a decision would have to be made soon. They had discussed living together, and Avril was amenable to it. However, they both knew they were really talking about a situation that would lead to marriage. He was the one who always backed off, but he couldn't avoid the issue much longer.

Two days before they left, a knock developed in the engine of his car. Probably nothing serious but he called the dealer and demanded the engine be stripped as the car was still under warranty. He did not want to run the risk of something serious going wrong at a later date. Macdonald decided to fly to Paris and rent a car to drive south. His own car would be waiting when he got back to London.

They collected a Hertz car at the airport in Paris and drove to the Méridien Hotel. Double room in the name of Macdonald, a freshen-up, and dinner at the Lido. A late breakfast and they arrived at the Hotel Metropole in Monte Carlo early on Saturday evening. After dinner they went to the fabled casino. *Société des Bains de Mer et Cercle des Étrangers*—the Sea Bathing Society and Circle of Foreigners—was a curious title for the corporation set up by François Blanc to run the casino. It is accurate in that no Monégasque citizen is permitted to work or gamble in the casino. But it is certainly strange in that there was no beach in the principality at that time. Today there is a beach. Two popular misconceptions exist with regard to Monaco: the first, is that Princess Grace is the first American to share the throne and the second, that François Blanc founded the casino. In fact Alice Heine, born in New Orleans and a great beauty of her day, married Prince Albert of Monaco in 1889 and took her place beside her husband when he succeeded to the throne in 1890. As to François Blanc, he was the fifth person to hold the concession for casino operations in Monaco.

But it was Blanc, with his Society of Bathers, who put Monte Carlo on the map. The ruling dynasty of

Monaco, the Grimaldi family, lost four-fifths of the principality to France as part of the Turin Peace Treaty at the conclusion of the war between France and Austria in 1861. Blanc was a widely experienced casino operator. Born in France, he had made a fortune in Germany, and he very quickly made the Monte Carlo casino very profitable. Blanc saved the throne by agreeing to pay 50,000 francs per year plus 10 percent of the net profits in exchange for a fifty-year lease. By the time he died in 1877, Blanc left a fortune of 72 million francs and had married his daughter to Prince Constantin Radziwell—as well as making Monaco the most fashionable resort in the world.

When Alice Heine became Princess Alice in 1889, she brought culture to the tiny principality. Her shrewdness which was equal to her beauty led to a new lease being negotiated with the Blanc family. The Grimaldis used the increased revenue to bring in opera, ballet, and theater. All in all, life was pretty good for the new rulers—their happy subjects did not pay taxes and the high level of culture tempted the leading families of the world to their doorstep. These were the thoughts that ran through Macdonald's head as he approached the casino.

Once inside, his thoughts turned to the famous names associated with Monte Carlo. Bertie, the Prince of Wales, later Edward VII, indulged his enormous appetite for beautiful women at Monaco for some thirty years and was a frequent visitor under the name of Baron Renfrew. Other celebrated womanizers, such as Leopold II of Belgium, Emperor Franz Josef, Grand Duke Michael, and some of the Hapsburgs, were less discreet than their British counterpart. Royal bastards were legion and blackmailers ever on the lookout for claims that could lead to handsome settlements to avoid scandal. Prior to the Bolshevik Revolution, Russian royalty and wealthy merchants were the big spenders at the casino. They spent money as if there were no tomorrow—the royalty little dreaming what the morrow would bring and the merchants trying desperately to attract attention. After the revolution, the casino granted small monthly pensions to the former wealthy gamblers—at least to the few that survived.

Sarah Bernhardt, a compulsive gambler, lost her fantastic earnings at the tables as fast as she could collect them. Compulsion to gamble has ruined many famous people. André Citroën, the French automobile manufacturer, lost half a million dollars in one night. Gordon Selfridge of department-store fame was even more notorious for his gaming losses. It has been claimed that Citroën and Selfridge tried to make their losses appear as publicity stunts, but each finished up broke.

Charles Wells, immortalized in "The Man Who Broke the Bank at Monte Carlo," was a small-time confidence man who got just plain lucky. Despite all the talk of "systems," Wells admitted in later years that all his bets had been random. Breaking the bank was a ceremony that Blanc had devised to indicate that the cash reserve for that particular table had been exhausted. A black velvet mourning cloth was draped over the table until the bank was replenished from the strongroom. It was a brilliant publicity stunt for the casino. Wells did in fact break the bank twice in one day and topped his performance by breaking it for the third time the following day. That was in July 1891, and he returned in November of the same year to complete the most phenomenal run of luck in gambling history by breaking the bank for the fourth time.

The bulk of Wells's winnings was spent on high living back in London, but he returned to Monte Carlo in the winter of 1892. Lady Luck deserted the little cockney and he lost steadily. It later turned out that he had been gambling with money he had raised from gullible investors in one of his elaborate confidence schemes involving a fuel-saving invention for steamships. Wells was sentenced to eight years, and on his release resumed his career as a con man. However, he was never seen again at Monte Carlo.

The only "system" that has ever worked was developed by a Scotsman named Jaggars. He was an engineer and he calculated that because of friction in the mechanism controlling the roulette wheel, certain positions were favored more than others. He studied the wheel in operation and found that his theory was correct. By betting on the numbers close to these favored positions, he amassed a considerable fortune before the casino officials figured out how it was done. Roulette wheels were promptly changed daily, and the practice continues today.

Macdonald's reverie was interrupted by Avril. She tugged his sleeve, then repeated, "Are we going in, or did you just come to watch?"

"Sorry." He smiled down at her, "I always get a bit carried away when I come here."

"My first time, remember?"

He took her hand in his and drew her into the crowded room, saying, "This is the area known as 'the kitchen.' Mostly for amateurs and tourists. There are eleven gaming rooms in all but the ones where stakes are small are known collectively as 'the kitchen.'"

Puzzled, the girl asked, "Why 'kitchen'?"

"Who knows?" he shrugged. "Probably a holdover from the days when everyone knew their place. It is in the *salles privées* where the really big, big money is staked."

She giggled, "Have you brought a gun in case you lose and have to take the honorable course?"

He grinned down at her. She knew that he sometimes carried a gun and had accepted his brief explanation that he had to carry top-secret documents. "No gun. If I lose, you go to the white slave traders, simple as that."

"I believe you would," she nudged him playfully, "Too bad the goods are slightly worn. What you want is a nice juicy virgin."

"I always want a nice juicy virgin!" He drew her into the crowd. "Trouble is that virgins seldom are juicy and they have, in my experience, bad breath."

Her rich laughter drew looks from several men and, when she called him an egotistical bastard in a clear loud voice, a number of women looked their way. Macdonald put on a benign smile and moved forward.

A unique undercurrent of excitement prevailed in the casino where people are committed to the caprice of chance. Some played out systems with deliberation; others placed their stakes with an almost reckless abandon. The eyes of the women sparkled as the men followed the clicking roulette ball or studied the cards as they slithered across the green baize. Here, where stakes were relatively small, the element of fun lent gaiety to the atmosphere, and there was little real disappointment when the rakes of the croupiers settled after each loss. From experience, Macdonald knew that it would not be so in the *salles privées*. There the professionals—the dedicated and the obsessed—played with cold detachment. Attention would shift from players to croupiers when the ball settled or the spatula flicked cards face upward. The eyes of the women would be brittle if they were playing, and bored or fearful if watching. Those of the men would wander to the plaques of other players or seek out beautiful faces and interesting cleavages.

Macdonald enjoyed gambling and the atmosphere of casinos. He was grateful that compulsion played no part in his pleasure of the cards, wheel, or dice. He always placed a limit on what he was prepared to lose and always ceased to play when that limit was reached. To him, gambling was comparable to his profession. It was vital to assess the odds and wager accordingly. Each time the wheel on the roulette table was spun, and the ball flicked into it, the odds on any particular number were 35 to 1; on *cheval,* 17 to 1; *Transversale,* 11 to 1; *Sixaine,* 5 to 1; *Carré,* 8 to 1; *Douzaine* and *Colonne,* 2 to 1; *Odds, Evens, Red* or *Black,* even-money. The house has the advantage of *Zero* and takes the difference between correct and actual odds as their profit.

Dice combinations never vary: 7 can be made six ways; 6 & 8, five ways; 5 & 9, four ways; 4 & 10, three ways; 3 & 11, two ways; and just one way to throw 2 or 12. Odds of throwing a particular number can be figured on the basis that 12 and 2 are 35 to 1 with two dice. Craps in a casino demands that one backs the player to win or lose, and odds are carefully calculated to neutralize the apparent 4 to 1 advantage enjoyed by those "riding" on a player.

Study of possible card combinations fascinated Macdonald. He preferred poker to any other game and favored five-card draw. A royal flush can be made four ways but the odds are 649,740 to 1 against being dealt the right cards on any hand. A full house has odds of 694 to 1 against getting five cards to make up one of the 3,744 possible combinations. Thirteen ways to make four-of-a-kind, and the lowly pair with a two-to-one chance. After the first deal when one is "drawing" there are new odds to be remembered: 15 to 1 against getting a pair to complete a full house, for example, or 11 to 1 against getting the card required to make up a straight.

Macdonald found satisfaction in gambling. He could understand the urge of the housewife to play bingo as a form of release from everyday pressures just as he could appreciate the professional who staked high when the odds were favorable. He could accept the fact that most bingo players are amateurs—unaware that with 90 numbers there are 43,949,268 ways of making five-number combinations and that their odds of getting any particular combination are determined by this. He could *not* tolerate a professional who gambled against the odds when, by passing, he could stay in the game. A picture of Maxwell flashed across his mind and a feeling of chagrin flooded over him. It would be a long time before he could think of the man without painful regret.

The spell of the casino was broken for Macdonald, but he could see that Avril's eyes were shining with excitement as she watched the others play. Tonight would be her time to have fun in the kitchen and win or lose a modest sum before they strolled back to the hotel in the dawn light. They were on holiday and time was on his side. It was pleasant to watch her when she began to play and pleasant to bask in the knowledge that she would be in his arms when they went to bed. And then unhurried lovemaking as the sun came up and slowly drifting off to sleep when the normal waking world was getting into gear for another day. Reflecting that life was good, he strolled away from the table.

If Hunter was in the casino, Macdonald failed to locate him. He tried the restaurants and bars as well as the gaming area but no sign of the man. There was no urgency in making contact but it would have been reassuring to know the M.P. was around.

27

Macdonald and Avril spent the first week of their holiday in lazy relaxation. Happy in their own company, they didn't have much communication with other guests. If they took breakfast, it was in the dawn hours *before* going to bed. Brunch started the day for them, and they spent the afternoon sightseeing or just strolling around. Macdonald was familiar with the area, and he took great pleasure in Avril's delight. The only thing which marred the days was that Hunter had failed to appear. Macdonald tried to be patient, but he was getting edgy.

Although the casino opened each day at 10 A.M. it was mainly frequented by kitchen trade. The real gamblers seldom took their places until after dinner and, though he considered himself the equal of any in terms of skill, Macdonald did not have the kind of money to play regularly in the *salles privées*. He had decided to wait until the final days of the holiday and was content to escort Avril to the kitchen and let her play for fun. Some nights she lost, others she won. The sums involved were within the £50 limit he had insisted she set. She accepted the limit for each night's play but found methodical gambling a bore. Her temperament was more suited to random selection of numbers on the roulette table and the excitement of a large return on winning spins. But by the end of the week she had lost £100 and was pretty well disenchanted with the scene.

Macdonald had decided that the second Saturday would be the night when his modest bankroll would be placed at the tables in the *salles privées*. All day he experienced a mounting excitement at the prospect of handling the rectangular plaques; of hearing the riffle of cards in the dexterous hands of the croupiers; and the slap which settled the cards before they were dealt from the mouth of the aluminum baccarat shoe. Two thousand pounds was the sum he decided he could afford to lose—at current rate of exchange, 21,000 francs, twenty-one orange 1,000-franc plaques. He felt a moment of envy as he thought of the kind of money the other players would have at their disposal —the piles of pink, yellow, white, and green plaques that would confront him—pink being 2,000 francs; yellow, 5,000; white, 10,000; and green, 20,000.

However, he was cheered by the thought that Luck is a woman, and being female, enjoys an occasional brief encounter with his kind of man. His overtures would either meet with sharp rejection or gradual encouragement until her favors were his if he had the courage to take them. But he also needed the good sense to realize when she was tiring of him. Ever capricious, her favors could switch to any of her other suitors around the green baize. In that case, he would have to decide whether she was doing so from whim or outright dismissal.

He thought of Aristotle Onassis—the classic story of rebuff in the hundred years of Monte Carlo's history. The Greek millionaire had made his first million from tobacco and had served his country as a diplomat before ever owning an oil tanker. In 1951 he was on holiday in Monaco and he saw a building that he wanted to use for his worldwide business interests. Inquiries uncovered the information that the building was the former winter sporting palace and that it was owned by the casino. He approached the directors with an offer to rent the unused building and was refused. He then offered to buy it. That offer was also turned down and the directors refused to discuss their reasons. This cavalier treatment infuriated Onassis and he decided to teach the directors a sharp lesson in both business practice and manners.

He discovered that the casino corporation had issued some 1,000,000 shares of stock and that Prince Rainier's holdings were 200,000. Business had been bad for some time. It was a good time to buy, and Onassis did so until he had just over 300,000 shares. He then reached an agreement with Prince Rainier, and the Greek shipping magnate had controlling interest in the corporation. At the annual meeting in 1953 Onassis took over the corporation lock, stock, and barrel— what he got was the casino, a bathing beach, five hotels, and opera house and a ballet company. He rented the building he originally wanted to himself and appointed a general manager to run the corporation that he hadn't wanted in the first place! That was power. Macdonald was not in a position to take control of his own fate in the way Onassis could. But he did not really envy Onassis. He knew his limits and could live with them.

Tonight's gambling was to be solo. Macdonald wanted it that way and Avril understood. He arranged to draw the required £2,000 from the bank in francs. He had a separate £500 in francs for use at the roulette table in the kitchen, where he hoped to increase his capital for the big game. Win or lose, he would take his place in the *salles privées* at 9:00.

At dinner he restricted himself to fish dishes and a light white wine. Instead of a liqueur with his coffee, he settled for gin and tonic. He was well aware that these precautions might seem unnecessary to amateurs, but to Macdonald serious gambling required the same careful preparation as an assignment. It had the same draining effect on his stamina. To clamber over rooftops on a belly full of meat and red wine, his head clouded by whiskey or brandy, was an invitation to disaster. Diet is important when one's life depends on reflex, so with gambling, better a relaxed stomach and a clear head.

At the casino he had several more gins in the bar before going to the roulette table. There was still an hour until the baccarat session got under way, and Macdonald had decided to gamble his kitchen money in five bets. There was no point in fooling around with small bets if he were to increase his capital. He would take five chances at £100 each. His first play was simple, straight red. Black came up. He stayed on red and black came again. The third time red came up. Macdonald let it ride and red came twice more. He now had francs equivalent to £1,000. He passed on the next spin and red came up again. He passed again and it was black.

Now he was ready to gamble. He placed half of his capital on black and it came. He let it ride and red came. Back to square one. He put the remaining half on red and, when it came, let it ride, again red. He switched all of it to black and when it came he thankfully removed the pile from play. Luck had favored him and, as the ball settled in zero on the spin after he withdrew from play, he accepted this as a good sign. He tipped the croupier and turned in his chips for 1,000-franc notes. Lady Luck had smiled on him. He now had 42,000 francs cash to back up his original 21,000 for the baccarat table. Four thousand pounds ahead was a good time to quit and head back to the hotel, but the thought did not enter Macdonald's mind.

When Macdonald sat down at the baccarat table, all six places were filled on number-one tableau and one empty at his end. The six decks of cards were fanned out face upward, and the colored plaques neatly stacked in preparation. He glanced around at the other players but, as always, could tell little from their demeanor. It was only when play commenced that a pattern would emerge. When the stakes rose, weaknesses and strengths would reveal themselves to the banker. His job was simple: to make the session profitable for the casino. It would not be easy. The banker must be a human computer at the baccarat table. Playing against both tables, he must read the cards held by all the players and be aware of his chance of drawing the card necessary to beat them. The croupier's movements are swift when he deals, and players stand or draw quickly. The banker must act almost instantaneously. It is not surprising that many professional bankers are international bridge players.

The vacant chair was filled. Hunter and the banker nodded to the croupier to begin. The cards were turned face down and shuffled until there could be no doubt that the final six-deck slab was well mixed. The croupier offered the slab for cutting and then deftly slid it into the shoe. He announced that the game was open and that the first bank offered was 5,000 francs to each of the tableaux. The cards were dealt and, as stakes were small, each number one player matched that of the bank. So it continued around the tableaux, some won and some lost but nobody exercised their right to *suivi* after losing. Macdonald playing at number four, lost, but took heart.

The vacant chair had been occupied by the man he had come to meet.

It took almost an hour for the game to warm up and at the end of this time Macdonald was 20,000 francs down. There had been a number of occasions when the players "shared" to make up the banks offered and, as always, he had been irritated by this. If the sum involved was large, it was understandable, but not in this kind of company. He was encouraged when the bank was raised to 20,000 and both number ones accepted. The change in atmosphere was immediate. Both tableaux lost, and two and three at Macdonald's end refused. He nodded and said, *"Banco"* to the 40,000. Number one *suivied* at the other end. The cards were dealt, first to the other man, then to Macdonald, finally to the banker. With an almost triumphant flourish, the first man laid his cards face upward to reveal the king of hearts and nine of clubs—a natural. Macdonald had a pair of jacks. Ten and ten makes zero, and that was what he would have if he lost on this one. The croupier flipped a card in response to his request. It was a six of hearts. The spatula showed the bank to have an eight and a seven—total of five. He drew a queen and Macdonald felt the tingle of perspiration on the small of his back as his winning plaques were placed before him. Lady Luck was a queen.

He let the game pass until it was the turn of the man of his left. With francs equivalent to £8,000 Macdonald was in good shape, but he was only too aware that he could lose it in just one turn of the cards. The bank had lost to number two, and a fresh 20,000 was offered to number three. The man accepted, lost, *suivied*, and lost again. With the stake at 80,000, the player hesitated, then passed. Tableau one had also lost and now had a bank of 40,000. The player there *suivied* and, as he would get cards first, the bank would, in effect, be going for the larger stake at tableau two. Macdonald's mind absorbed the factors and he nodded, *"Banco."*

The player at tableau one had problems. He drew a card and got a black two. Since by the rules he had to stand on six or seven, he could not have better than seven in his hand. Macdonald had a red five and the ace of spades. He had to stand, but it wasn't good.

The spatula showed the bank to hold a black king and a three of clubs. A difficult decision for the bank, but there was no hesitation in his request for a card—it was a queen. She had come again for him and Macdonald paid homage as he watched the piles of plaques being pushed toward him. The man on his left smiled, "I made a pig's ass of that one!"

"It all depends on which of us the lady favors." Macdonald swung slightly to face him, "I would probably have played it your way, in your shoes."

The other man lit a cigarette, looked into Macdonald's eyes, then said, "Who knows?"

By 2:00 A.M. there had been no dramatic change in Macdonald's fortunes. He lost and won but had not risked on further heavy wagers. The pile of plaques was still equal to about £16,000. He had had lots of time to consider his situation and was still at the table. It was a healthy sum of money and one could do a lot with it. It could serve as a boost to his morale in that he had had his holiday and made a profit. It could serve as a nest egg if ever he had need of it. On the other hand, he had a long lease on the flat and all the furnishings were his. His car was paid for and should be waiting at home when he got back, good as gold after the engine overhaul. He had a credit balance in his bank a shade over £22,000, and there was nothing in the sales figures of Grand Clanranald to suggest that whiskey was going out of fashion. What it came down to was that £16,000 was a lot of money if one needed it. If one had financial problems it would be a beautiful windfall, and he would not hesitate to pick it up and walk away.

But he did not intend to stop. He would go on and try to double what he had. If he lost, it was because it wasn't his time to win. If he won, it would be because the fates decreed it. He would enjoy the challenge and excitement whichever way it went.

When the bank reached him again, his slate was clean. It was a new bank and he still had his money intact. The offer from the bank was for 20,000 and he accepted with a nod and clipped word. His cards totaled eight and it looked good but the bank had a natural nine. *Suive* and he got a red four and a black seven, total of one. He drew an ace and the bank, after drawing, had just three but it was enough. The moment of truth had arrived for him. He had lost two in a row and it would take all he had on the table to cover the next bet. He'd either double or lose all of the £16,000.

Macdonald was aware that the man on his left was watching him intently, interested to see what he would do. He nodded and said, *"Suive!"* A ripple of excitement ran around the table as he accepted and made his declaration. The excitement of the others meant nothing to Macdonald, but the slight nod of approval from the man on his left was important. There was a bond forming between them.

The stake for tableau one was lower than Macdonald's. The cards would go to the other end first, but the bank would be going all out to beat Macdonald. He did not look at his cards until the player at the other end was finished. He eased the two cards gently apart and saw that the bottom one was a dark partner for the smiling red queen on top. Mona Lisa with a friend telling him he held zero. The man at the other tableau had drawn a jack and it was obvious he held no better than four. Macdonald looked squarely across the table and asked for a card.

The two of clubs came over the green baize to rest before him. He could have sworn the queens exchanged a glance of mockery when the bank came up with another natural nine. The spatula removed the ladies from his view before his inner voice whispered, "To know all is to understand all." He was far from being downhearted. He had enjoyed the game and there was 3,000 francs left after the croupier's rake swept away his losses. He had also made contact with Hunter. To be sure, the contact was a poor one, but it could be developed either here or in London.

28

When he got up around noon, Macdonald had no regrets about his night at the tables. He had learned long ago that postmortems were a waste of time. His losses were just over £2,500 of his own money. The rest was money he had won earlier at the casino. It was over and done with. For the present, he had to find a means of getting closer to Clive Hunter.

Avril asked him how he did at the tables and accepted that he had lost but enjoyed the experience. Instinctively she knew she should not press for details. Macdonald's mood was good, and probing might result in his becoming irritated. It had been a very pleasant holiday and she had no intention of spoiling it.

After brunch they went to the bar. Both had excellent suntans and they had seen all the sights. This was the last full day before flying back to London, and they both felt lazy. It was inevitable that after two weeks together conversation flagged. The two of them sat in contented silence, knowing that in the evening they would have a sumptuous dinner and then retire for a night of lovemaking. Avril watched the people come and go, wrapped in her own thoughts.

Macdonald's mind was on Clive Hunter. Today was the last chance he would have to make a move. Perhaps he should have pursued the project more aggressively, but the opportunity had not presented itself. Several times during their stay he had seen Hunter, but never in the right situation for a casual meeting. When they came together it had to appear natural. To have made an approach directly would have been gauche. It wouldn't have fooled Hunter for a moment. Last night at the tables worked out very well, but now he had to follow up. He needed some kind of a break.

At that moment he saw Hunter cross the lounge. He must have been sitting at a table in the short leg of the L-shaped room. Without turning his head, Hunter disappeared through the doorway. Macdonald cursed inwardly. Hunter had been there all the time, and now he could have slipped away for good. He craned his neck to see if the woman who had been Hunter's companion for the past week was at a table.

Avril saw him and said, "Looking for someone?"

"No." He relaxed in his chair, "I saw a kite, or something, through the window."

"I've only seen you strain your neck that hard for women's bodies on the beach." She was whispering so that only he could hear, "We missed out last night because of your being at the tables. Would you like to go upstairs for a matinée?"

It was a tempting prospect. Lazy lovemaking and a refreshing nap afterward seemed a perfect way to spend the afternoon. If Hunter had gone off somewhere, there was no point in sitting around the cocktail lounge. Perhaps an opportunity would present itself in the evening—if not, he'd have to do something, gauche or otherwise. He smiled at Avril, looking very demure and proper after her suggestion, and was about to accept her proposal when Hunter reentered the room. He threaded his way through the tables and was about to pass theirs when he noticed Macdonald. He paused, then said, "Hello, there!"

Macdonald, who had been contemplating spilling his drink—anything, to catch Hunter's attention—stood up and held out his hand. "How are you today?"

Hunter shook his hand briefly as he said, "Not too bad, considering." Seeing the look on Macdonald's face, he went on, "I came a cropper on the same fence you did—after you had called it a day."

Macdonald smiled and said, "Perhaps we both learned a lesson, but I doubt it."

"You're so right." Hunter glanced at Avril, "Faint hearts and fair ladies—if you'll forgive my saying so."

Holding out his hand again, Macdonald said, "My name is Tony Macdonald." He indicated his companion, "This is Avril."

"I'm Hunter—Clive Hunter." He nodded to the girl, "How do you do?"

Macdonald gestured to a chair, "Will you join us for a drink?"

"Love to, but my wife is waiting. I've just been out to the telephone—damn thing follows one, even on holiday." He started to go but then turned back, "Would it be an imposition if I suggested you both join us for a drink?"

Macdonald glanced casually at Avril and when she smiled and nodded, he said, "We would be delighted."

"Fine!" Hunter led the way to a table at the other end of the room, which had been hidden from Macdonald's view by a pillar. When they arrived he made the introductions, "Darling, this is Avril—and Tony Macdonald—my wife, Diana." After everyone had murmured greetings and was seated, he signaled a waiter. While they were awaiting the drinks, he said, "Macdonald and I have our shirts at the same laundry."

His wife looked puzzled as Macdonald and Hunter laughed at his joke. Hunter said, "Don't look perplexed, darling. What I'm really saying is we both lost at the same table last night."

When the drinks arrived, conversation flowed easily. From Macdonald's standpoint, things were working out perfectly. It turned out that it was the Hunters' last day and Macdonald said, "I find traveling on a Sunday at the end of a holiday an anticlimax. Stealing the Monday adds the spice of wickedness."

"I agree," Hunter sipped at his drink. "I hate the sense of limitation 'two weeks' places on a holiday. Ten days always seems better—or, as you say, steal an extra day at the end of two weeks."

Macdonald was looking at Diana Hunter. He felt he had seen her before somewhere. It could be she was in one of the newspaper pictures he had seen of her husband, but he wasn't sure and he finally dismissed it from his mind.

Hunter showed he knew his gambling by telling some amusing anecdotes on poker hands. Macdonald came up with his favorite story of how he had once sat in on a game and lost a large pot with four-of-a-kind to a straight flush and how, later in the same game, he finished up with a royal flush and nobody went beyond the first raise. Time passed pleasantly and Macdonald was careful to avoid leading questions.

Let Hunter start the ball rolling. The two women were getting along famously.

Hunter asked, "What do you do, back in London?"

"Civil service."

"Oh, which branch?"

"Home Office," Macdonald's cover had been long established but he was always uneasy when confronted by questions relating to the nature of his work. He went on, "I do research work on highways, urban development, that kind of thing."

"You're an engineer then?"

Macdonald laughed. "No, I'm what's known as a professional civil servant. Governments come and go, but we go on forever. I do, of course, have teams of engineers, but I prepare estimates and schedules for government consideration."

Hunter seemed to sense Macdonald's reluctance to go further and said, "I'm sorry if I appear nosy. I am genuinely interested."

"Are you in engineering, then?"

Hunter laughed, "No. I, for my sins, am an M.P.— only recently so, but an M.P. nonetheless."

"Not a Socialist." Macdonald waved a hand to take in the room, "I should think Monte Carlo would spoil your image!"

Hunter chuckled as he replied, "Doesn't matter a whole lot these days. Everybody seems to go abroad for holidays. We all get paid the same, Conservative, Socialist, or whatever. All a question of one's private income, really." He chuckled again, "An M.P.'s salary certainly doesn't cover high living—at home or abroad."

Macdonald was silent for a moment, deciding it was best to keep it nice and natural and ask the obvious, "Which party are you? I wouldn't want to make a mistake. It's difficult to tell nowadays."

Hunter grinned and indicated his open-necked shirt, "No tie to give the game away, but I'm a Tory. I got in at the by-election for Suffolk East."

Macdonald wrinkled his forehead, "Yes, your face did look familiar. I remember now—must have seen it in the papers." He took a swallow of his drink and went on, "Funny how faces are so very tantalizing. One

173

sees a face which is vaguely familiar and can't remember whether it was school, army, or where. Can be very embarrassing at times."

Hunter nodded and lit a cigarette, "Perhaps we did meet at school. I was at Eton."

"No, wasn't there," Macdonald shook his head. "I was at Gordonstoun."

"Cambridge, perhaps?"

"No," Macdonald grinned, "I was at Oxford, but I hardly got my kit unpacked before it was time to leave for the service."

Hunter returned the grin and said, "It wasn't the army, then. I escaped that by a year or so."

Macdonald shrugged. "That means I have to be a bit older than you. I got caught for a two-year stint."

"Army?"

"Yes, I was in the Black Watch."

Hunter smiled as he said, "What else? I detect a Scottish accent coming through strongly at times." He glanced around in an exaggerated manner, "I have to admit I get confused. Is it Scottish, Scotch, or Scots when one refers to the accent?"

Macdonald toyed with the question for a couple of minutes. He was impressed by Hunter. The man had a way of interrogating without being obvious. The play-acting of the exaggerated glance and the friendly smiles and boyish grins were perfectly executed as he probed. The man was very shrewd. So far he had avoided mention of his own business interests. Time he was led in that direction. Macdonald put on one of his boyish grins, "I wouldn't lay claim to being an expert. I think that a 'Scots' accent is correct. Scottish perhaps, but never Scotch! That is the stuff one drinks." He did his bit of play-acting by broadening his Scots accent, "I hope ye drink it, ma mannie, because that's the business my family's in—and I need the money to enjoy holidays in places like this!"

Hunter laughed. "I can tell you I *do* drink scotch. I only hope I've been drinking the right one."

Macdonald grinned, "The answer to that is no scotch whiskey is 'bad.' Some are better than others, but none are undrinkable."

"Well put, but it doesn't answer the question." Hunter put just the slightest edge on his reply.

Macdonald sensed it but decided not to take issue. No point—this was supposed to be a casual meeting. Easier to be direct—*his* turn would come in just a minute or so. He said, "Grand Clanranald is our brand."

"Indeed!" Hunter appeared to be impressed but he wasn't finished probing. "What are you doing working for the civil service?"

It was Macdonald's turn and he relished it, "I'm the black sheep. They are glad to see me in a safe, reliable job." Then his tone altered just slightly, "What's your excuse for being an M.P.?"

The other man laughed delightedly as he exclaimed, "Touché!" At his outburst, the women stopped in midconversation and looked at him. Hunter looked at Avril and said, "I like your Tony! Not many of us individuals left in this world. You must both come down for a weekend in Suffolk." He waxed enthusiastic. "You'll love it. Plenty of space and fresh air. Horses and dogs all over the place. You and Diana can keep each other company while Tony and I match wits at the poker table."

Macdonald tried to appear casual as he sipped from his glass, "We accept your offer on one condition— that you and Diana have dinner with us tonight."

"Be delighted to!" Hunter smiled over the glass. "We accept your invitation to dinner. And now to answer your question, I'm in the import-export business. Stuff from the Far East. Mainly from Hong Kong and Malaya—sorry, Malaysia as it's now called. Food, ceramics, that kind of thing."

"I see." Macdonald felt he had won a small victory.

Then Hunter said, "I meant it about your coming down to Suffolk. Are you doing anything this coming weekend?"

"No." Macdonald turned to Avril, "Have you anything planned for next weekend?" She shook her head. "Good. We have been asked to the Hunters." He grinned in half-apology for not having consulted her, "We are all having dinner together tonight." Both women seemed delighted. Then, as Diana turned her head, Macdonald suddenly recalled where he had seen her previously. She was the woman Maxwell had tried to pick up in the casino that night in London! Feverishly, he tried to recall whether her husband had been around while he was trying to get Maxwell to leave. It came to him that the husband *had* returned. That was when things turned slightly nasty. Point was, did Hunter remember? Did it make all that difference, one way or the other?

29

Dinner and the evening that followed proved to be the highlight of the vacation. Before dinner Avril had told Macdonald that Diana was aware of their marital status and she had accepted it. Macdonald suspected the women would form an alliance to make a husband of him, but looking at Avril as she fussed in front of the mirror he concluded there were worse fates than being married to someone like her.

The meal was excellent and they took their time over it. With coffee they had several brandies and, at Avril's suggestion they started in on champagne around 11:00. They danced to the soft music of the orchestra until the leader increased the tempo and the place was swinging until well after 2:00.

All were somewhat hung over when they met for breakfast. After subdued greetings, they ate lightly in silence. Hunter suggested Pernod over ice with Vichy water as a cure for what ailed them. He proved to be right, and the congenial atmosphere was restored. By coincidence they were booked on the same flight from Paris to London. They decided to leave one of the hired cars at the hotel and drove to Paris together.

At the airport, they nibbled on sandwiches and had a few drinks. That the relationship had developed so quickly did not surprise Macdonald. Some of the more lasting friendships of his adult life had been founded on casual meetings. The spontaneous connection of kindred spirits was a phenomenon which defied logic. Macdonald accepted the pleasure of the moment knowing that if he and Hunter were to cross swords in the future, there would be time enough to adopt strategy. For the moment he would accept—watch carefully, but take things as they came.

The flight was uneventful and even London, shrouded in an early autumn mist, could not dampen their spirits. In fact, they were all glad to be home. The familiar landmarks were mute testimonials to the enduring qualities of England. To Macdonald it was home. Not the heather, mountains, and rivers he yearned for in sentimental moments, but home in that it was a return to familiar ways, familiar people, and a kind of stability.

The passengers were requested to remain seated until the plane came to a halt and reminded to take all hand baggage with them when they left the aircraft. They were thanked for choosing that particular airline and invited to do so again in the future. Wheels touched, then gripped, and the plane slowed on the runway. It taxied to a halt and Macdonald dismissed his sentimental thoughts of home when he noted the steady drizzle falling.

All four chose the green lanes at customs and they were not challenged. Hunter had a car and he insisted that Avril and Macdonald accept a lift to town. A porter trundled the luggage to the waiting Bentley and the uniformed chauffeur supervised as it was stowed in the trunk. That the chaffeur was Chinese did not surprise Macdonald. It was logical for a man in Hunter's business to have a servant who was bilingual.

The powerful car ate up the miles on the highway and when they glided to a halt outside the building where Macdonald had his flat, the chauffeur got their luggage from the trunk, then opened the car door. Farewells were exchanged and arrangements for the coming weekend confirmed. The Chinese stood respectfully apart until Macdonald and Avril had left the elegant car, then closed the door after them. Hunter waved a hand through the open window, then addressed the uniformed man, "Straight home, Tang."

Tang!

The car moved off. Macdonald had the presence of mind to smile and wave.

30

Avril was surprised when Macdonald said, "Wait here—I'll be right back." He disappeared into the apartment building and left her standing amidst the luggage. She was even more surprised when his car pulled up beside her a few minutes later. He bundled her inside and stowed her luggage in the trunk, then jumped in and swung the heavy car out from the curb. It shot across the street, took the turn into the main road at a tight angle, raced down the inside lane, then cut sharply to the outside lane. He shot across the intersection just as the light changed, causing a burst of irate honking from a car he cut off. The Mercedes finally settled to a reasonable speed and Avril, angry at his treatment of her, said, "What the *hell* are you doing?"

Macdonald placed a hand on one of her knees as he replied, "Sorry, love. There's something I must do at the office."

Avril brushed his hand away and said with heavy sarcasm, "It must be important. What am I supposed to do—sit outside and collect parking tickets while you do whatever it is?"

"Don't be difficult. It's something I have to do right away. I'll drop you off at your place first."

"Don't put yourself out!" Avril said angrily. "Just stop at the next corner and I'll hitchhike from there."

Macdonald turned his head toward her for an instant, then gave his attention to the road, "I haven't flipped my lid, but there are times when work comes first."

The set of his face jolted Avril out of her anger. She was curious about the work he did but had never questioned him about it. Instinctively she knew he wouldn't tell her the truth. She knew Macdonald better than any other man in her life, and she had become very aware of the incongruity between his position as a desk-bound civil servant and the man she knew. For example, his body was that of an athlete, and the scars did not go with the sedentary life of a civil servant. His reflexes were extremely sharp and a sudden movement by someone triggered an immediate response. At times his movements were so fast they suggested a background of rigorous training. He was even-tempered, but when pushed, his eyes could become deadly. She felt he could be lethal if attacked. He was a strange man, but he was the man she wanted. She leaned on the armrest and brushed his cheek with her lips, "I'm sorry, darling. I'm a bitch, but I love you."

He stroked her leg, "I love you and I know it is difficult for you at times but there is nothing I can explain."

They completed the trip to Avril's apartment in silence. She knew he loved her. The sexual aspect of their relationship was exciting and satisfying for her, and she knew Tony was fulfilled by her. When they made love it felt completely natural. They possessed each other but they did not just use each other. She was sure of this man. He was hers and she was his. There had been more attractive men in her life; Tony was too rugged to be called good-looking, but his major appeal was his character. He was self-possessed and confident without being arrogant. He was stubborn but considerate—a curious mixture of cynicism, puritanism, and compassion. She had seen him listening intently to elderly people as they spoke at length on subjects that bored other people, but he was capable of rudeness of anyone whom he considered to be a parasite. In private he spoke of sexual matters with freedom, but hated public display of nudity and disliked open sex in books or films. His comments could be scathing when someone offended his concept of decent behavior. He was capable of violence. She knew she loved him and that he loved her. She wanted them to be married, but he would have to ask. She hoped he would, but if he didn't, she wasn't about to try to trap him or beg.

Macdonald placed her luggage inside her front door and kissed her brow lightly. He ran a hand down her back and over the swell of her hips as he said, "I'll ring you later."

"For dinner?"

He was heading for the elevator, but called back, "I can't promise—but I hope so."

Macdonald swept into his office like a whirlwind. His secretary, not expecting him until the following day, accepted his brusque "Good afternoon" as he passed her desk and followed him into the inner office. She hovered for a few moments as he unlocked the safe and began pulling out a pile of manila folders, then asked, "Did you have a good holiday?"

"Great." Macdonald placed the files on his desk. "I want to see Sir Archibald as soon as possible." He glanced at his watch, "But give me fifteen minutes. I could use a cup of coffee and I want you to contact Steele, Crawford, and Parker. Get them here around 6:00." He sat at the desk and opened one of the folders.

The girl was very efficient and liked an efficient employer, but she did not like Macdonald. He was not her idea of an executive. Most of the work she did for him was routine, concerning estimates for roads, bridges, and other major construction projects. But when she had to ask him questions about these projects, it sometimes took him days to give her the answer. He did not appear to have the slightest interest in bridges or roads, but he demanded efficiency from her on other matters. Also, she got the mail *after* he had seen it. That rankled her. On one occasion she had taken it from the courier and neglected to lock it in the drawer of his desk. He had been furious and threatened to fire her if it happened again. To make sure it didn't he told the courier that mail was to be handed only to him. If he wasn't there it was to be held until he was available.

She didn't like Macdonald as a man either. At first she had found him attractive and was disappointed when he ignored her. To stimulate his interest, she began wearing her skirts just a shade shorter and allowed as much of her very good legs to show as she could without being obvious. Her final strategy was to discard her brassiere. Macdonald finally took notice, but his reaction was not what she hoped for. Having finished a session of dictation, she was walking to the door when he said to her, "Oh, by the way, if you have an uncontrollable compulsion to flaunt your tits and other assets, I have a friend who owns a couple of strip joints. I could recommend you to him. You would make a lot more money than you earn here and derive total job satisfaction from it." The next day her skirts were lowered and she was wearing her bra.

Now when she was in Macdonald's presence she was always conscious of her jutting breasts, and when she knew his eyes were on them she would blush. It was infuriating and she had considered asking for a transfer but could think of no justifiable reason. She poured the coffee, set up the appointment with Sir Archibald, and proceeded to contact the three men. They were always easy to reach, which surprised her, and she was equally surprised at the respect they had for Macdonald. Now *they* were men. Her body got appreciative appraisals from them when they visited the office, and she wouldn't find it easy to fight off the blond one—Steele—if he made a move. Maybe she should encourage him a little.

Macdonald found what he was looking for. The months of investigation had resulted in quite an accumulation of data, but what he wanted was right where it should be.

Hop Tang: Born Hong Kong January 16, 1931
Entered U.K.: September 8, 1965
Marital Status: Single
Occupation: Chauffeur, Houseman
Criminal Record: None
Hair: Black
Eyes: Brown
Height: 5 ft. 7 in.
Weight: 146 lbs.
Distinguishing Scars: None
Employer: Clive Hunter (Business: Importer-Exporter
   of Far Eastern products)
NOTE: Clive Hunter is incumbent Conservative M.P.
   for Suffolk East

Tang's address was given as the Hunter residences in London and Suffolk.

The bare facts conveyed absolutely nothing, and

Macdonald was angry with himself. He had seen this before and passed it over. The team had gathered the information and he had screened it before it was filed. But he had deliberately avoided doing any checking on Hunter or Far East Importation Ltd. after his briefing from Sir Archibald. As he thought about it, he knew where he had gone wrong. After losing Maxwell, he had lost his aggressive thrust. He had allowed Sir Archibald's conservatism to dominate his thinking. Everything was on the desk in front of him, and it had been there for weeks. What the hell had he been waiting for! A sign from heaven? God—in the guise of Sir Archibald Sanderson—to take him by the hand and show him the way? Shit! He flipped through the folders and there it was—notes on Clive Hunter. He flipped through again and found the notes on Far East Importation. Christ almighty!

Macdonald crushed out his cigarette and lit a fresh one. If he had paid a little more attention to his job and a little less to the possibility of incurring further anger from his boss, he'd be that much further ahead. Preoccupation with the wrong priorities and the routine of the desk had dulled his edge. High time he got it back! He should have cross-checked all of the items in the files properly. Had he honestly expected an obvious answer to emerge from the investigations? Someone in the Fu Manchu image—complete with skullcap and pigtail? Six-inch nails at the ends of the fingers and elevated sandals on the feet? What a dummy he had been. Maxwell had told him to find Tang. So he had looked for a Tang who was a person of standing in the community. Someone with an organization and freedom of movement, with wealth, and influence. His picture of Tang was as far from the truth as the Fu Manchu character.

He checked out the list of Tangs in the file. He had done it before, several times, but he hadn't approached it with an open mind. This time he found one other worth checking on. This one had six restaurants in Cardiff. He was Tang Tu Lee and, according to the files, the restaurant operation was successful but the owner a heavy gambler. It was unlikely that a senior member of Triad frequented the gambling clubs in

Cardiff, but that could be part of his cover. Perhaps even a tie-in with the theory of Triad taking over gambling in the U.K., well worth a second shot. Tang Tu Lee might just be clever enough to cultivate the image of being a fool. Throwing away the profits from his restaurants at gaming tables might just be the cover for a much bigger game.

The intercom on his desk buzzed. It was time to see his chief. He picked up the files, lit a fresh cigarette and headed for Sir Archibald. He hoped his attitude was as fresh as the cigarette.

VII
London

31

If Sir Archibald was impressed by Macdonald's suntan, he did not mention it. When Macdonald was seated, the head of department got straight to business by asking, "You made your contact?"

"Yes, everything went fine. We're invited down to Hunter's place this weekend."

"Mmm, I assue 'we' means that Miss Wentworth is included?"

Macdonald had to supress a grin. Obviously the man detailed to watch Hunter's movements had submitted a full report. Macdonald said, "Yes, we are both going. Did your man come up with anything of interest?"

Sir Archibald shook his head. "No, Hunter's vacation followed much the same pattern as yours. He and his wife enjoyed the sun and the beach. They shopped, toured, ate, drank and slept." He smiled slightly, then went on, "Mrs. Hunter apparently knows about as much about gambling as Miss Wentworth. Hunter, as you probably know better than I, appears to know about as much on the subject as you do. He lost a shade more than you." He smiled again but there was a wicked twist to it this time, "Of course I don't know how much of what you lost was actually yours." There was a pause as though he expected Macdonald to comment but, when he didn't, Sir Archibald went on, "Hunter assuredly made no contacts with anyone of consequence in the gambling world in France though we took all the steps we could to observe such contacts if they had been made. I think, consequently, we can assume that Hunter did nothing but enjoy a vacation in the sun."

"I feel the same way, but I don't mind admitting I had some nasty days when Hunter failed to show up."

Sir Archibald shrugged, "Just two nice British tourists taking in the places of interest. Nothing sinister in anything they did or in any of the people they met. Give me a rundown on what happened after you made contact."

Macdonald quickly did that but decided to delay speaking about Tang. When he had concluded Sir Archibald nodded approval. "All very harmless— Hunter appears to have accepted you." He paused, thinking. "Though there may be nothing in this procedure, I still want you to keep on with it. I have an intuition that we are following the right lines. Who knows? I may be right."

"Who knows indeed, sir?" Macdonald took a deep breath and told Sir Archibald about Tang and about the information he had found in the Triad files. He offered no excuses for having failed to tie together Tang, Hunter, and Far East Importation. Finally, he mentioned the second Tang in Wales.

When he had finished, the head of department sat for a time, then asked, "How do you intend to handle the situation?"

Macdonald's response was immediate. He had reached his decision prior to the interview and all he now required was approval. "I have my team coming in for a briefing this evening. I propose we take the initiative and check out the possibilities on our list. These are the Tang in Wales, the Tang who works for Hunter, Hunter himself, and Far East Importation." He then detailed exactly what he would have the team do.

Sir Archibald got up from behind his desk and paced slowly to the window. He looked out for a moment or two, retraced his steps to the desk and resumed his seat. Finally he said, "As you know, we have a split assignment with regard to Triad. Your end concerns confirmation of the existence of Triad, depth of infiltration, and drugs. Particularly drugs—quantities, distribution, and, if at all possible, how they get them into the U.K."

He shook his head slowly, "It is a devilish problem, and we need answers yesterday. For that reason I am in favor of your doing what you propose." But then he shook his head again and Macdonald suspected he wasn't about to get the approval he sought. He was about to press for it when Sir Archibald went on, "However, my strategy regarding the gambling aspect of Triad activity is at a tricky stage. All I can tell you about it is that I have come up with a solution. The details have to be worked out, and I'm going to have a tough job getting the people who matter in the government to accept it. Setting up the procedures, if and when I get acceptance, is going to take time. He shook his head again wearily, and said, "It isn't easy, Macdonald."

Then as though his last words were an admission of weakness the older man's shoulders straightened and the steel-blue eyes glinted as he spoke, "I have my problems and you have yours. I can handle mine and I have confidence that you can look after your end if I give you the go-ahead." He held up a hand before Macdonald could say anything. "You do what you have outlined, but impress on your men that they mustn't exceed their brief. God knows, we need some positive results on this Triad business. You and I will meet when they have finished and we will decide where to go from there. In the meantime, you and your ladyfriend go down to Suffolk. It's a fun weekend for you if nothing else.

"I will proceed with *my* plans. I just want to impress on you how delicate the Hunter situation could be if one of your bright lads fouls the deal up. I don't need an irate M.P. letting off steam at this stage—you follow me?"

"I follow you, sir." Macdonald was excited at the prospect of getting his teeth into something positive again.

"Good!" Sir Archibald indicated that the interview was over. "I'll see you when you have something to report."

Back behind his desk, Macdonald indulged in some soul-searching. He knew he was prejudging the outcome of events in regard to Hop Tang, and that could be dangerous. To offset this, he determined not to try to make the pieces fit until they arrived on his desk. Maxwell had been adamant that Triad would not use a non-Chinese in the organization itself. Macdonald believed this to be true. There was nothing to prove it, but Maxwell had had years of experience in the Far East. Accepting it meant that Hunter could not be knowingly involved. However, Hunter had the perfect legitimate setup, and Triad had undoubtedly seen the benefit of using it as a front. Macdonald decided to run another check on Hunter's background just in case, but something kept telling Macdonald that Tang was the key. Perhaps because of Maxwell and his promise to the dying man. . . .

At precisely 6:00, the three men filed in and sat in front of his desk. Different in size, features, and coloring, they had one thing in common: each pair of eyes were hard but they also mirrored sadness, disillusionment, and understanding of man's inhumanity to man. Macdonald could see himself in all of them and knew Sir Archibald could see *himself* in *him*. Theirs was a job where no Christmas office parties took place and no gossip over coffee about who was sleeping with whom. Nobody took up collections when a colleague "passed away." You passed and were forgotten.

Criticism of superiors or systems took place between the individual and his shaving mirror. An assignment was made and discussion was limited to the operative and his superior. It was recognized that individuals were expendable and inquiry was not encouraged. That each individual was aware of the identities of some of his colleagues was taken advantage of only in the event of emergency. Personal danger was not considered valid reason for exposing one's colleagues. Only danger to an assignment or a threat to collective security justified a distress call.

Macdonald studied each man closely. He took a cigarette from the box on the desk and offered them all one. When he had exhaled the first plume of smoke, he said, "The results of the legwork you have carried out on the Triad business shows promise. We now have a carefully catalogued dossier of activities which could be part of a national distribution network for hard drugs in the U.K. During the course of the investigation, I have issued instructions to check on a particular individual by the name of Tang. It is my belief that Tang is the man we want. He may or may not be the top man in the U.K. If he isn't, he is close to the top. We want to smash the whole setup, and, if we can, get the top man as a bonus. To get only the man and leave the organization intact would be a useless exercise.

"We have checked out all the Tangs in the country and we have two candidates. One is in Wales. Steele will handle that one. The man is a heavy gambler, but it could be part of his cover, and I want to be sure. I want his house and all six of his restaurants searched thoroughly—*our* way. No police and, above all, no sign of entry." His words brought a slight smile to Steele's lips but the man did not comment. The other two shifted in their seats, perhaps sensing that things were about to liven up after long weeks of boring routine. Macdonald did not disappoint them. "Crawford and Parker will each do two of the restaurants for you. Good as no doubt you are, seven break-ins in a week is tempting fate."

All smiled now and Macdonald looked at the other two. "When you get back from Wales, I have three more break-ins for you here. I want you to work them together. A London flat—an office and warehouse complex—and a country house. It is imperative that no sign of entry is detectable on any of these premises." He fixed his eyes on each in turn, "Do I make myself clear?" His smile was grim. "If you slip up and get caught, you will serve the full sentence—and pay stops until you get out."

Three heads nodded. Macdonald let his warning sink in. Then, after a pause, he briefed all three on what to look for and emphasized that nothing was to be removed from any of the places. He then assigned Steele to watch Tang Tu Lee after the break-in in Wales and dismissed him.

To Crawford and Parker he gave a rundown on Far East Importation Ltd., Hunter and Hop Tang. He stressed that their job was purely to search for evidence and shadow Tang when all three jobs had been done. The shadowing was to be carried out discreetly, and they were to stagger it between them to avoid detection. He made mental note to borrow four excellent men to shadow Hunter and Fotheringham. His own job would be to get as close to Hunter as possible socially and probe for openings.

The briefing over, he called it a day. A telephone call to Avril served to placate her and he became aware that he was very hungry, hungry for food and for her.

As he drove to her flat he thought about their relationship. He did love her, but would she really be able to accept his strange hours and refusal to offer explanations for his odd behavior? It was one thing for her to be his woman, but quite another to be his wife. As he thought of Avril as "his" woman, he had to smile. She was essentially her own woman. She might well become someone's wife, but she would never be anyone's possession. He possessed her when they made love, but he did not own her. Would he want to *own* her? No, but he sure as hell did not want any other man to possess her as he had. Theirs was the ultimate in fulfillment of sexual needs. Could they be equally compatible in other aspects of life? Time was running out, and if he didn't do something soon, it *would* run out. She loved him but she might get tired of waiting, or she might meet another man. God knows, he *wanted* her badly and often enough. Did he *need* her? Would she accept him as a husband who refused to offer explanations? As he parked the car, Macdonald made his decision. Get this damned Triad thing out of the way, and he would marry her. Until then he would continue to stall and hope time did *not* run out.

32

Clive Hunter had enjoyed his vacation in France. For two weeks he had been able to relax from the strains of being an M.P. and keeping watch on Far East Importation as well as coordinating his Triad activities. As with all successful leaders, he was quite capable of delegating authority to others. After a subordinate had proved worthy, Hunter was prepared to offer opportunities for advancement. In this way he had been able to build both his legitimate business interests and the scope of Triad operations. The Society made demands for expansion from time to time, and to meet these demands he had to be flexible himself and ensure that the cells throughout the United Kingdom were also flexible.

Manpower was not a problem. No shortage of "soldiers" to carry out simple instructions, and no dissidence in the ranks because all were well rewarded. Also, fear and iron discipline combined to ensure loyalty. Hunter's early difficulty had been selecting men capable of leadership. But once he had these men, his task of coordinating became progressively easier. It had been much the same with Far East Importation, but he had found the people to carry the load of management and when his priority was getting elected to Parliament, he had been able to devote himself to it with complete single-mindedness. Now he was established as an M.P., but to progress to a position of power in government, he would have to devote more time.

He knew that there were still two men in the United Kingdom who, like himself, were Caucasian members of Triad. He did not doubt that their pedigrees were established as soundly as his own. What he did not know was their identity. On the one occasion he had mentioned the subject, he had been discouraged by the Inner Circle. It was pointed out again that the Society must always take precedence over the individual. If something happened to him—the Leader in the United Kingdom—there had to be a replacement. What he did know was that the two were not presently active in Triad in the U.K. He was a member of the Inner Circle, entrusted with knowledge of Triad activity throughout the world, but he did not know everything. Although he knew there were two men in positions of power in the United States, he did not know anything about them.

Hunter did not question the wisdom of Triad policy. What happened in the United States was not his concern. The United Kingdom was his territory, and he was concerned about the growth of Triad in the years that he had been Leader. Activities had mushroomed to such a degree that he was bearing a very large bur-

190

den. Although he had Tang and the *Ahkungs,* he had nobody with whom to share the real responsibilities.

What he really needed was someone to take on one of his triple roles. But how could it be done? It was too late for him to pass on Far East Importation to someone else. There were only two Caucasian Triads, and he had no way of knowing if either of them was qualified, or even if the Inner Circle would agree. In retrospect, it would have been better if one of the other two Triads had been elected to Parliament in his stead. Too late for that—he was elected. The third possibility —the only option open—was for somebody to take over as coordinator of Triad activities in the U.K. In essence, it would mean his relinquishing being Leader. But Hunter did not really want to step down.

He had found himself forced to delegate more and more to others. At Far East Importation, Fotheringham was doing a good job, and there were young men coming up to share in the running of the legitimate business. Tang, apart from the unfortunate affair of the policeman from Hong Kong, had proved to be very capable. The *Ahkungs* were all good men, and Hunter had one of them selected as Tang's replacement if that ever became necessary. He had subordinates to replace the *Ahkungs* if *that* ever became necessary. All along the line the structure was safeguarded. The cells within the Triad structure were protected because members of any particular cell were ignorant of the identities of those in any other cell. Although any member of Triad could reveal himself to any other member, it was taboo to discuss rank or position within the Society. However, members were encouraged to exchange signs of recognition. This spread awareness of the extent of Triad influence and gave the lower orders a sense of security in an alien Caucasian world. Any Chinese in danger of attack could rely on swift aid from his fellows.

During his vacation, Hunter had reviewed all his activities and come to a decision about priorities. He would concentrate on his advancement in Parliament. The only threat to Triad at this point was that it was forced to use British citizens as fronts in setting up companies for the purchase of stocks and shares. In all instances, the people concerned were beholden to Triad, and if any of them presented a *real* threat, they would be disposed of. But a risk did exist, and Hunter wanted that business concluded as soon as possible. All the proceeds of ten years was tied up in it, and nothing must be allowed to get in the way of a successful conclusion.

On the social side, Hunter was fairly content. He and Diana enjoyed a satisfactory relationship. She seldom came up to London, and in his free time Hunter dined with parliamentary colleagues, usually at a club. It was important that his activities in politics included social contact away from the House. He had very little opportunity to become bored through the week. But on weekends he found time weighed heavily.

He had become bored with his circle of friends in Suffolk. It was for this reason he welcomed the meeting with Tony Macdonald in Monte Carlo. To Hunter the whole thing was casual—he could drop Macdonald and his girlfriend after the first weekend if things did not work out. As it happened, things had worked out extremely well. Diana and Avril got along splendidly, and Macdonald had proved to be excellent company, both at the card table and otherwise. He was just the type of chap Hunter wanted to socialize with. Someone who shared interests and had no axes to grind. A careful man, Hunter had Macdonald checked out after the first weekend, and he proved to be exactly what he had said he was: a civil servant of some standing, of independent means, and the black sheep of a very acceptable family.

33

It was two weeks before all the reports on the breakins were on Macdonald's desk. They were all negative. He was not disturbed by the reports on the chain of Welsh restaurants. That assignment was purely an exercise in elimination. But the negative responses on the London break-ins bothered him. His every instinct told him that Tang and Far East Importation were the key to smashing U.K. drug traffic.

The shadowing had produced nothing of value, but he decided to continue. If nothing else, he was building up behavior patterns on Tang, Hunter, and Fotheringham. Staff movements to and from Far East Importation were noted, but nothing unusual turned up. It was all happening there—he was sure of it. He had to get closer to what *actually* went on. Delivery trucks came and went and goods were received and dispatched in large quantities but, tempted as he was, he did not dare intercept any of the loads.

He arranged checks on cargo by Customs & Excise but these proved negative. All documentation was in perfect order and, short of searching every item on the manifest, there was nothing more to be done. Manpower was a big problem. It would take an army of operatives to cover the ground. The only alternative was to close down every wholesale and retail unit supplied by Far East Importation and deport all personnel. Macdonald knew he hadn't a prayer of getting official sanction for the move without positive proof. He regretted that the U.K. was not a totalitarian state.

He looked again at the report on the break-in at Far East Importation offices and warehouse. Nothing. The two men were experts and could find nothing that even remotely suggested there were two sets of ledgers and invoicing. Macdonald gathered all his papers together and had his secretary see if Sir Archibald were free. She came back to say, "In fifteen minutes." He spent the time having coffee and a cigarette. Finally he drained his cup, crushed out his cigarette, picked up the heap of manila folders, and made his way to the door. It would be all or nothing at the end of this meeting.

As always, Sir Archibald was neutral in greeting. It was only as the meeting progressed that his mood would manifest itself and, not for the first time, Macdonald wondered what his chief did in his spare time. Over the years he had met him several times at Twickenham and at the Oval or Lord's. On the rare occasion he bumped into him at a club, never once had it been suggested that they have a drink together. He knew that Sir Archibald enjoyed good food and wines. He also knew that he was a bachelor and lived in Chelsea. The "Sir" was in respect of his being awarded the Knights Grand Cross, The Most Distinguished Order of Saint Michael and Saint George. The initials G.C.M.G. did not appear on any correspondence and it was by checking that Macdonald had discovered which order his chief was listed on. Fourth in official order of precedence, after Garter, Thistle, and Bath, Saint Michael and Saint George is limited to a statutory maximum of one hundred G.C.M.G.s. It is nonmilitary and, in the instance of Sir Archibald Sanderson, was awarded for "having rendered extraordinary services to the Commonwealth beyond the seas." The citation was in keeping with the man's extraordinary life-style—his past was shrouded by a nebulous cloak. Nobody that Macdonald had ever spoken to could positively state that Sanderson had been involved in a particular activity or episode. People were aware that he had been "around" but doing what they had no idea. After chief of staff, Macdonald, as one of the four coordinators, was close to Sir Archibald but he knew nothing of his background. It rankled that the Old Man knew *his* to the very size of shoes, brands of spirits and cigarettes, and, without doubt, a catalog of his sexual involvements.

These thoughts flashed through Macdonald's mind as he settled in the chair facing Sir Archibald. He spread the files out on the desk, then said, "I propose to summarize the situation as it stands. I will have to cover ground that we have been over before—but I think it necessary." Sir Archibald merely raised his eyebrows. Macdonald tapped the first folder with a finger, took a deep breath and began. "This is the enitre list of businesses in the U.K. that are in any way connected with Chinese products or enterprises. This"—he tapped the second—"is a list of all persons in the U.K. who are Chinese, or are in any way connected with Chinese affairs. Everything and everyone in these files has been checked out. The only name that we have, so far, is Tang. All Tangs were subjected to special checks and just two fit the bill. One in Wales—and one here in London. I have concentrated on these two and, after full consideration, eliminated the Cardiff Tang. That leaves just the London Tang." His finger tapped the files, "In there we have thorough reports on businesses and people who, one way or the other, connect. We have come up with four names that could well constitute the Triad setup in the U.K." He held up four fingers. "Tang—Far East Importation Ltd.—Hunter—and Fotheringham!"

Sir Archibald raised his eyebrows again but did not comment. Macdonald opened one of the files. "This covers everything connected with the four names involved. I have checked as thoroughly as possible with the resources available and, after all that—including exceeding my authority to the extent of breaking and entering—we have nothing!"

"So?" Sir Archibald threw in the word in the silence that followed.

"I *know* that we are on the right track. Far East Importation is the only company big enough for the Triad operation. They cover wholesalers, retailers, and restaurants. They have connections in Hong Kong, Kowloon, Aberdeen, and a dozen other places out there. They ship in tons of goods every week from the Far East and, even more important, export to France and the United States. If the drugs coming in have to be refined they have the means of getting it to Marseilles —that is, if they haven't got a refinery here!"

"What proof have you?"

"None—not a scrap that would justify our taking action." Macdonald lit a cigarette. He indicated the files, "I am dropping Fotheringham from my list and concentrating on the other two."

"Why?"

"Not the type: lives in a very ordinary house. He has a company car and his wife has a Morris 1000. They go for two weeks' holiday to Eastbourne every August and a package tour in December. The sons are married, and there are three grandchildren. He drinks beer at his local and she does charity work. Fotheringham started out from pretty humble surroundings and got where he is by hard work and loyalty. He was a corporal in the army during WWII and last, but not least, is non-Chinese."

Sir Archibald considered, then asked, "What about Hunter?"

"I don't know." Macdonald had puzzled over this possibility and examined it from every angle. During the weekend visit he had studied the man and his surroundings closely, but had failed to find the slightest indication of a connection. It had been very much a "country" weekend and, apart from Oriental curios, the whole scene had been straight from the pages of *Country Life.* He spread his hands. "Hunter is as British as Cooper's marmalade. I have checked and rechecked everything. Parents were interned by the Japanese during the war. Father to one camp and mother and child to another. The parents died and the paternal grandparent traced the child. Family have been here since the Magna Carta and, though very little money, they have breeding and all that goes with it. The boy was accepted by Eton and was brilliant at Cambridge. He has a flair for anything Eastern—inherited from his father—and made a pile of money by getting in early on the import-export trade with Hong Kong. He was practically *forced* into becoming an M.P., and his wife comes from another family that was here to welcome Richard back from the Crusades."

"Nothing to suggest that he is something other than what he appears to be?"

"Not a thing!" Macdonald could not keep bitterness from his voice, "Charm, wit, looks, money, political connections, and every social grace in the book. Just about *too* good to be true, but a likable character and very much a man's man."

Sir Archibald looked at him shrewdly and his tone matched his eyes, "You like the man?"

"I do—I can't help myself."

"But you still include him on your list of suspects?"

"Yes," Macdonald chose his words with care. "It would be a perfect setup for the Chinese. A British M.P. who is destined to rise very rapidly in the government and is considered to be an authority on Far Eastern affairs. The Triad would have it made!"

Sir Archibald sat back in his chair and closed his eyes. Macdonald lit a fresh cigarette. The silence lasted a long time—the tick of the desk clock and muffled traffic noises were the only sounds Macdonald heard. He brushed ash from his trousers and waited.

At last the steel-blue eyes were again fixed on the dark ones opposite, and Sir Archibald said, "I can't buy it. Your proposal is a frightening one, and I pray to God that I am right and you are wrong. The possibilities offered by your suggestion are enormous but there is no evidence to back it up. Everything we know of the Triad organization points to your being wrong. Hunter is non-Chinese and, as such, is ineligible for membership. He would have to be at a very high level in the Triad structure to be entrusted with control of their activities in the United Kingdom, and to give a Caucasian that position would be unthinkable to them. Only Chinese are used by Triad." He waved a disparaging hand, "Sure, we have had many cases of British officials involved in graft and corruption. They got rich by turning a blind eye—the latter-day Nelsons. We know it is going on, but are almost powerless to stop it. But no non-Chinese has ever been involved in the *organization* of these activities." He glanced with distaste at the cigarette that Macdonald had just crushed in the ashtray, "No, I see Tang as our man. Chinese and in a position of trust with Hunter."

Macdonald nodded. He took a sheet of paper from one of the folders, and said, "I have to agree. Tang's background fits better than Hunter's. However, the report on Tang's activities would hardly support the view that he is a Triad boss. Two weeks surveillance and in that time he visited Far East Importation four times, bought a pair of new shoes, had a haircut and visited a restaurant in Soho. We believe he had one of the girls in the restaurant for dessert, but he might be a kinky *mah-jongg* player for all we know!"

"His cover is bound to be good." Sir Archibald took the paper and glanced at the notes, "He has been here a long time now and I have no doubt that the *Ahkungs* have been in business for years." He handed the report back, "We don't know for sure but, if Triad works on similar lines to the Mafia, these *Ahkungs* are in business for themselves. Tang is responsible for supplying them with drugs, but each *Ahkung* controls his particular territory. Tang, in turn, will be responsible to the man above him—probably in Hong Kong—for the whole of the British network. It's all conjecture, of course, but that is the kind of pattern I would envisage."

Again Macdonald nodded agreement, "If we act on the premise that Tang is the top man in the U.K., we have to assume that he must have tremendous sums of money going through his hands, yet his bank account is in credit to the tune of just over two thousand pounds. Search of his quarters at Hunter's place in London and in Suffolk has yielded nothing. The money probably finds its way to Switzerland via France, but one would think that there must be a scrap of incriminating evidence around somewhere."

Sir Archibald grimaced, "I think we can forget all formal evidence in this instance. Everything we want to know is in Tang's head. The trick is to get it out of there!"

Macdonald's tone was grim, "I want permission to move on Tang—get it out of him the hard way."

Sir Archibald got to his feet and began to pace slowly to and fro from the desk area to the windows. Finally he sat on the corner of the desk and said, "We have to crack the organization and once we drag Tang in, we are committed. The wall of silence, similar to the Mafia's *omerta,* is the problem. If we don't crack Tang, we are back to square one."

"I'll crack him." There was no mistaking the conviction in Macdonald's voice, "I'll crack the bastard the same way he cracked Maxwell. I'll take him apart piece by piece."

"Fine, but how will you know that what he tells you is the truth? How do we get corroboration? Don't you think they will have an alarm system? By the time you get names from Tang, the others will have gone to ground!"

Macdonald did not hesitate. "I propose to enlist Hunter's help. Tang had to build up the Triad organization in tandem with Hunter's building up Far East Imports. I don't suggest that Hunter can pinpoint the

Ahkungs, but he can narrow the field." He shrugged, "We may not get all the small fry, but we should get a fair chunk of the bigger ones. We can set up watch on the people Hunter names and, when Tang cracks, we move in fast."

Sir Archibald shook his head doubtfully, "I don't like it—goes against everything I have been preaching since the department was formed. We enjoy a position divorced from normal police, intelligence, and military institutions. We have access to the records of these institutions and, when necessary, can enlist their help." His head shook again, "But to bring in an M.P. —and one who was a suspect—"

"What's the alternative?" Macdonald interrupted brusquely. He didn't like the idea any better than his chief, but he had come to admire Hunter and he was sure the man would have something to offer. Besides, there seemed to be no other alternative.

"I don't know." Sir Archibald gave him an angry look. "I only know I don't like *your* idea. I appreciate why you have put it forward, and I appreciate that you are offering it because there *is* no alternative." The eyes were ice cold. "However, I'm going to let you have your head. We are being pressured to make a move against the Triad threat. The Prime Minister wants action, but he refuses to allow me to bring in Hunter until I have positive proof that he is involved. Frankly, I would be happier if we took Tang, Hunter, and Fotheringham. You—Macdonald—are about to take an extraordinary risk. It's comparable to the situation where you used Maxwell. I'm *using* you! If it works out that Hunter—not Tang—is the man we want, I'd rate your chances on par with Maxwell's. Do *you* appreciate that?"

"Yes," Macdonald's voice was even. "I will be on the chopping block but"—he shrugged—"I want to do it."

Sir Archibald cleared his throat noisily, the closest he would come to offering words of thanks. He slid from the edge of the desk and resumed his seat.

Macdonald gathered his folders into a neat pile, taking longer over the task than was necessary. When he spoke, his voice was still even, "I'm going down to Hunter's place again this weekend. I will tell him as much of the story as I consider necessary and, if he is the true-blue British M.P. he appears to be, he should fall over himself to help. If, on the other hand, I have figured the whole thing wrong, and he is Mr. Big of Triad, you will have to think again."

Sanderson nodded, "In *that* case, we lose any chance of ever breaking Triad over here. We gain little by arresting Hunter at a later date and he will have time to ring all the alarm bells for Triad to restructure without him."

"If it's Tang, we hit the jackpot."

Sir Archibald made no reply, but as Macdonald was about to leave, he said, "One point I think we should clear up. I don't want you to make any reference to the gambling aspect of this deal. Go ahead as planned, but we confine it to *your* end of things. If we are right and it is Tang, we lose nothing. If we are wrong—which, God willing, we aren't—I will still have room to maneuver. Triad investment is on such a massive scale that we have to get them out of the gambling industry in this country and burn their fingers so badly in the process that they will take years to recover."

Macdonald nodded, "Very good, sir. No mention of the gambling." As he walked back to his own office he reflected that the gamble he was about to take with Hunter was the biggest one he had ever taken.

VIII
Suffolk—London

34

Macdonald and Avril had thoroughly enjoyed their first weekend trip to the Hunters' house in Suffolk. Originally a pair of cottages, it had been extended at both ends to form three sides of a square in ranch-house style, with a paved patio in the center. The front had been redone with an eighteenth-century facade, but the interior was strictly twentieth-century. Another couple, one of Hunter's parliamentary colleagues and his wife, were also weekend guests, and a number of people had been invited for dinner on the Saturday evening. The men had played poker until the early hours of Sunday morning. Since the others had played together on several occasions, Macdonald had been the odd man out. He had lost just over £20, but he had formed assessments of the strength and weakness of the other players and was looking forward to another encounter with them.

He had decided to leave the Triad business until Sunday. It would give him all day Saturday to observe Tang and Hunter at close quarters and, for selfish reasons, he did not want to cast a shadow on the weekend. Friday evening was spent lounging with drinks in the company of the Hunters and the Fisher-Harveys who had also been guests the last time.

Saturday passed pleasantly. They went riding in the morning and, though the weather was cold, it was dry. The horses were frisky and eager for the exercise. Hunter led the party at a brisk pace and he was expert in horsemanship. They lunched at an old-fashioned inn and cheered by a blazing fire and several drinks, they finished up singing around a piano. It was all so jolly and innocent that, for a time, Triad and drugs seemed to belong in another world.

Dinner, too, was an occasion when everyone was

relaxed, and it was difficult for Macdonald to remember that Tang was very likely the cold-blooded animal who had reduced Maxwell to the condition in which Macdonald had last seen him. He appeared to be the loyal Chinese servant—courteous to his master's guests, attentive to his duties, and absent when his services were not required. The report from Crawford and Parker stated that his salary was deposited at his bank every month and a small sum transferred to his mother in Hong Kong. Macdonald almost laughed aloud at the thought of Tang's having a mother—a Chinese version of Ma Barker.

After the meal they repaired to the spacious lounge where a bar took up the entire length of the far wall. Hunter served the first round of drinks, the carpet in the center of the room was rolled back, music turned on, and dancing and conversation passed the time until the men left to play poker at 11:00. A civilized evening for civilized people.

Five sat down to play—one less than on the previous occasion. It took a little time for the game to warm up and the hands were poor, with matching pots. The two dinner guests, a local doctor and man called Jerome who owned a factory that produced kitchen furniture, were steady players who made no attempt to bluff but were prepared to back good cards. Fisher-Harvey tended to chicken out when stakes got high. Hunter was a shrewd bluffer. He knew how the others played and took risks that were calculated according to the opposition. Macdonald had decided to play it Hunter's way.

It was straightforward five-card draw. No wild cards, and hand values were according to the book: royal flush, straight flush, four-of-a-kind, full house, flush, straight, three-of-a-kind, two pair, pair, nothing less than jacks. Discard up to three cards; a 50p. ante and a £5 top-limit raise. A tight game where the incautious could lose a fairly substantial sum.

After an hour, Fisher-Harvey was ahead by about £50. He had held a full house against Hunter's flush and a straight when Dr. Mellon held three-of-a-kind. On each occasion he had called, which confirmed that he was nervous even with a winner. Hunter was also ahead, but only by bluffing on small pots. Macdonald was down about £10 and that left the other two down about £70 between them. It was Macdonald's deal, and he flipped out five cards to each of the others. Jerome opened and asked for three cards, obviously a high pair. Hunter took two—possible three-of-a-kind or trying to make up a flush or straight. The others took three cards each, indicating a pair or less.

Macdonald, ever the optimist, tidied the five cards in front of him and lifted them as one. King of hearts faced him. He eased it aside with his thumb to reveal the king of clubs. He slid the top card in place and gently eased the bottom card upward with his forefinger, king of spades. His pulse quickened, and he was aware of the others watching him with interest. Hunter's interest was mingled with amusement. Not that he was amused at Macdonald, he was amused *with* him. To the man who really enjoys cards, the elaborate examination of a hand gives much pleasure. A flicker of answering amusement twitched on Macdonald's mouth and he fanned out his cards to reveal jacks of diamonds and clubs—a full house.

He closed the cards and pretended to consider for a moment before saying, "Dealer stands."

"Bluffing?" Hunter took a final glance at his own hand and placed it confidently on the baize.

"Could be," Macdonald placed his hand down. "Care to try me, or will you fold?"

"I think I'll just go along for the ride," he turned to Jerome, "Up to you!"

Jerome threw a £1 chip in, "I'll open."

Hunter added his pound; Dr. Mellon folded; Macdonald went along and so did Fisher-Harvey. Jerome raised it to £2; Hunter made it £4; Macdonald went with him and Fisher-Harvey folded. Jerome took it to the limit of £5 but folded when both Hunter and Macdonald went along. Hunter put another £5 in and Macdonald matched it.

Just the two of them and £41.50p. in the pot. The atmosphere around the table had undergone a subtle change. It was the first time that Macdonald and Hunter had been in direct confrontation and, as often happens at the gaming table, a confrontation of this nature raises the level of the whole game. With the imposed limit of £5 raises, each man was restricted to unhurried addition to the pot until the table limit of £100 was reached. As Macdonald placed the chip that brought the total to £101.50 p., he had no option but to call. Hunter took his time over turning his cards face upward. The anticipation on the faces of the other turned to amazement. Four little fives. An extraordinary hand, but it happens.

From that point on, it became a game in which the highlights were when Macdonald and Hunter were left to battle it out on any particular hand. Both men were experienced, and one or the other would back down if only holding a bluffing hand. By 2:00 they had reached the table limit on three more occasions. Hunter won again by holding a full house against Macdonald's high flush, but on the next two Macdonald won with a straight flush that was higher than Hunter's and four-of-a-kind against a high flush. The dinner guests, Dr. Mellon and Mr. Jerome, decided to call it a night, and all of them left the table to rejoin the ladies. Macdonald and Hunter were reluctant to abandon the game at the point of stalemate and they prevailed on Fisher-Harvey to return until it was resolved one way or the other.

Fisher-Harvey played the role of dummy and he was content to go through the motions until the other two held cards they considered worth backing to the limit. On several occasions, either Hunter or Macdonald got a hand but in each instance his opponent had nothing. The end came on Hunter's deal. Fisher-Harvey opened and drew three cards to improve on a high pair, but Macdonald, with a show of slight reluctance, decided to stand on his original cards. Hunter picked his up and took a long time over examining them. He had three nines—hearts, clubs, and spades. The other two were useless—five of clubs and ten of hearts. He had to draw two, but he pretended to ponder before declaring his intention. He tucked the new cards at the back of his hand and slowly fanned all five out. First his three nines, then the ace of hearts. The last card was nine of diamonds. He smiled gently. It couldn't be more appropriate—the card known as the curse of Scotland.

Macdonald answered his smile, "You'll have to be good."

"Pretty good." Hunter squared his cards and laid them neatly on the table. "I have had a sign that this is the hand that will decide who is the better man."

"That being the case, the gods have been cruel to you. I feel I should warn you that you're in pretty rough company with what I have."

Hunter's eyes gleamed. It could be that Macdonald was bluffing but, at this stage in the game, he would not back bluffing cards past more than two or three raises. Four nines made a strong hand. It would take a better four, a straight flush, or a royal flush to beat them. Macdonald was playing a pat hand. It was unlikely that he had been dealt a straight or royal flush. More than likely he had a high flush or, at best, a full house. He could have four-of-a-kind but, since Hunter held the ace of hearts, it couldn't be aces. Fisher-Harvey had opened on a high pair—jacks or better—so Macdonald's four had to be either tens or one of the two court cards Fisher-Harvey had not used as openers. Three possibilities of four that could beat his nines. But he had to discard the ten of hearts, so that left just two possibilities that could beat him. It looked like a safe bet to back the nines. He turned to Fisher-Harvey and said, "You're the opener."

With the pot at just £4.50, Fisher-Harvey folded and Macdonald immediately raised to £5. Hunter matched the bet and they continued to pass chips to the center of the table until the £100 limit was reached. Both men were irritated by having to go through the motions but, at this stage, they preferred to observe the rules rather than simply put the chips in *en masse*. As Macdonald put in the bet that brought the pot to maximum, he called on Hunter to show his hand.

Hunter did not immediately do so. He took a long time to light a cigarette. "Sure you want me to?"

"Quite sure." Macdonald was emphatic but in no hurry to see the cards—half the enjoyment was in the byplay after the duel.

Hunter picked up his cards and fanned them out so that only he could see the faces. "They aren't wonderful, but I have a feeling that they are just a shade better than you've got."

"If they aren't wonderful, they aren't good enough."

"How about a side bet?" Hunter was convinced that the nines were going to do it.

Macdonald smiled. "I'm just that kind of a bastard." He took one card and turned it face up. It was the jack of spades. "What did you have in mind?"

Hunter considered, "How about a case of whiskey?"

"Sounds good." Macdonald's smile deepened, "Which particular brand?"

"Chivas Regal is a favorite of mine."

"There's a coincidence! I go for that myself." Macdonald sat back and drew on his cigarette, "I shall drink to your health every time I open a fresh bottle."

Hunter grinned. "Don't count your pink mice." He tossed the ace away and turned the others over, "Four little nines!"

Macdonald studied the four cards for a moment, then said quietly, "Those are very good, but—I'm afraid—not good enough." He left the jack on the table and picked up the other cards. Slowly, he placed them in order one by one—all spades, ten to the left of the jack and queen, king, and ace to the right.

"Jesus Christ!" Hunter's astonished exclamation held nothing but congratulation, and Fisher-Harvey echoed it.

Macdonald addressed Hunter, indicating the cards, "Do you mind if I keep them?"

"Certainly—of course you can." Hunter was still amazed at the other man's luck in being dealt the royal flush. "And don't feel badly about the whiskey—I would have done it to you."

A look of understanding passed between the two, and Macdonald added, "I know you would and—believe me—I didn't feel a thing."

As they were having a last drink before bed, Macdonald recalled something Hunter had said earlier and he asked, "The sign you mentioned during the last hand—was it the nine of diamonds?*

"Yes," Hunter nodded. "I must confess that I'm superstitious about things like that."

"So am I," said Macdonald and, later in bed, he remembered that in the same deal he had gotten the ace of spades.

35

Everyone rose late next morning, and the Fisher-Harveys left before lunch. Hunter had some business to attend to, so Macdonald decided to postpone the Triad business until the afternoon. He and Avril were returning to London in the evening, but there would be plenty of time for an uninterrupted talk away from the house in case Tang had the place bugged.

It was just Macdonald and the two women for lunch and, since they had an inexhaustible store of topics to discuss, Macdonald took the time to think over what he would divulge to Hunter. He would leave out Maxwell and the break-ins. It would hardly be appropriate to tell his host—an M.P.—that his home had been ransacked. He would remain vague about "the department" and not mention Sir Archibald. As an M.P., Hunter should be prepared to accept Macdonald's identity card, and a telephone call to the minister would verify his standing with government security. He would have to admit that a check had been made on Far East Imports and that Hunter's own background had received the fine-tooth-comb treatment. Again, if he was what he was supposed to be, Hunter could hardly object.

Having decided the broad outline of his approach, Macdonald pushed all thought of it from his mind. He

---

*When John Campbell, Earl of Breadalbane, instigated the massacre of the Macdonalds at Glencoe, in 1692, the Earl of Stair—John Dalrymple, then Secretary of State—wrote the instructions to the commander of the expedition on a playing card—the nine of diamonds.

concentrated on the two women as a diversion: Avril, with raven hair, deep brown eyes and dark complexion; Diana, blonde, blue-eyed and fair-skinned. Diana had the advantage in terms of background and formal education but, as is often the case, she lacked the common touch. She knew little of the realities of life and though she could converse fluently, her range of subjects was limited. She seldom offered an opinion with any feeling of originality; more often, it was a rehash of an opinion expressed by someone else. Her manner was animated, but he got the strong impression it was window dressing. Her eyes reminded him of windows in an empty house.

Macdonald could not deny that at this point in her life Diana was a very desirable woman. Her full breasts and slim legs that swelled gracefully into shapely hips exaggerated her slim waist. She would be a good bedmate but he suspected her breasts would sag in time and her legs thicken. Macdonald laughed inwardly at himself. What he was doing was boosting his own ego. He was a very lucky man to have someone like Avril, down-to-earth, intelligent, with an appreciation of the social graces, and a strong dislike for humbug.

His thoughts were interrupted by Diana's suggesting a walk in the fresh air. There was a good two hours of daylight left and it would fill in time before he had the opportunity of confronting Hunter.

When they returned, Hunter met them on the driveway. He was surprised when Macdonald placed a restraining hand on his arm as he was about to follow the ladies indoors. However, he allowed Macdonald to close the door and lead him away from the house toward the stables. Macdonald wasted no time in preliminaries. He offered the M.P. a cigarette, lit both, then said, "I need your help on a very delicate matter and I prefer, for reasons that will become clear, to speak to you away from the house."

"Oh?" Hunter was alert.

"Yes." Macdonald showed Hunter the yellow identity card, "Have you seen one of these before?"

Hunter looked closely at the piece of cardboard inside the clear plastic sleeve, then shook his head, "No. What is it?"

"A security clearance. When I told you that I worked for the Home Office, it was, in a sense, true. But I have nothing to do with bridges or roads. My department is concerned with security."

"What kind of security?"

"Shall we say matters that threaten the internal and external well-being of the nation."

"What does that mean?" Hunter drew impatiently on his cigarette, "Are you police, Secret Service, or what?"

"None of those. We are a separate body, concerned with special assignments." Macdonald looked him straight in the eyes, "Have you come across Triad in your Far East dealings?"

Hunter's face gave away nothing. Inwardly his mind was racing, but outwardly he maintained calm. He nodded, "Of course—a Chinese secret society. Everyone who travels in the East comes across it sooner or later." Macdonald wasn't sure what he had expected but, whatever it was, Hunter's reaction did not reveal surprise. He seemed interested and curious.

Macdonald put his card away and went on, "I have been assigned to investigate Triad activities in Britain. This has involved the checking of all companies and people concerned with the importation and distribution of Chinese goods—"

"So our meeting in Monte Carlo was no accident." Hunter's interruption was a harsh statement. Macdonald flipped his cigarette into the darkness, "Pure accident. I give you my word that I had no idea who you were."

"Bit of a long-shot coincidence, wasn't it?"

"Granted, but I made the connection when you told me you were engaged in trading with Hong Kong."

Hunter looked thoughtful for a moment, then asked, "So where does that leave us?"

Macdonald smiled without humor. "It leaves us with another coincidence."

"Oh, what's that?"

"Your man Tang. If I am right—and everything

points to my being so—Tang is the man behind the Triad organization in the U.K."

"Balls!" Hunter laughed with derision, then continued, "I've known Tang longer than I care to remember. He's a simple Chinese peasant!"

"Perhaps," Macdonald said calmly, "but surely that would be the impression a clever man would want to make." He eyed Hunter keenly, "How well do you actually know Tang?"

The question gave Hunter valuable time to take stock of the situation. His mind was racing, and he knew he had to be very careful. When he finally answered, it was accompanied by a shrug of his shoulders. "Who knows anybody? Tang has served me well over the years, but I must confess that his private life is a closed book to me. One doesn't probe into the activities of one's staff, does one?"

"No," Macdonald answered carefully, "but one does form a pretty good idea."

"Granted, but the most I can offer is that, to the best of my knowledge, Tang is content to do his job and, apart from the odd day off, keeps busy doing—" his voice seemed to trail off, and he finished lamely —"doing things."

"Exactly!" There was a note of triumph in Macdonald's voice. "But busy doing what?"

"Christ knows! I have always assumed he pottered around with cars. Or he read or something," Hunter made himself grin. "For all I know, he might be working his way through college with a correspondence course."

There was no answering note of humor in Macdonald's voice when he said, "I have reason to believe that our friend Tang has long since graduated from a college that writes diplomas in the blood of their unfortunate victims."

"Sorry." Hunter deliberately dropped his facetious overtone, "I can see that you are serious about this." He paused and then said, "Tell me, how did you get onto Tang?"

"A number of things." Macdonald was deliberately evasive. "We have been looking for Tang for some time. The day you dropped us at my flat, you called him by name. It shook me a bit, and I went immediately to the office to check. He fitted the bill beautifully."

"And you've been checking since?"

"Yes. We have covered every angle."

"And you can prove all this?"

"Not in a court of law, but certainly to my personal satisfaction!"

"Your satisfaction? Is that enough?" Hunter made his voice sound outraged. "I mean to say, you surely need more than that."

"Don't, for Christ's sake, go all British on me! We are dealing with a bunch of thugs that would cut your balls off with a hacksaw. Don't give me that crap about 'sticky wickets' or 'straight bats!' These bastards don't leave clues lying around in the best traditions of Sherlock Holmes!"

Hunter eyed him speculatively, "I suppose not, but you must admit it is all a bit cloak-and-daggerish. You show me a card that doesn't mean a bloody thing to me and tell me that my manservant is really a top man in a Chinese secret society. It's something that takes a bit of swallowing."

"I'll grant you that," Macdonald said. "I'll give you the telephone number of the appropriate minister, and you can check out my authority. In the meantime, I want you to listen to the whole story. After that—" he spread his hands—"you have to decide whether or not you want to help."

"Fine," Hunter nodded, "seems reasonable to me."

When Macdonald had finished telling his story, there was a long silence. Hunter was unpleasantly surprised at the thoroughness of the investigations and how close the conclusions were to the truth. All that had been said proved his belief that you could never underestimate the abilities of law-enforcement agencies. He now needed time to assess the situation and restructure his organization accordingly. In the meantime he had the advantage and, by playing along with Macdonald, could buy time. He broke the silence by saying, "The whole thing is staggering. I have, of course, heard of

211

the activities of various Chinese gangs but I never imagined that they were organized so much like the Mafia."

Macdonald's response was bitter, "It would come as a shock to the world at large if the activities of these people were generally known."

"And what do you propose? Assuming you are what you say you are, how do we proceed?"

Despite earlier misgivings, Macdonald was impressed. Hunter had reacted just as a person in his position could be expected to. Even now, having heard the full story, he implied that verification of Macdonald's identity was required. He had asked all the right questions at all the right times during the narrative and had in no way given rise to suspicion by accepting outlined situations. These situations would have required foreknowledge of events other than historical fact and only involvement in Triad activity could have provided that foreknowledge. On each occasion Hunter had asked for corroborative evidence. Not that he had the means to check sources quoted by Macdonald, but it showed that the man had a logical mind. Now Macdonald had to come up with means of using him in practical terms. He reflected on it, then said, "If you can get Tang out of the way here and in London, I would like to search through his gear."

"It wouldn't surprise me if you told me you had already done that!" was Hunter's dry response.

"Give me credit for possessing some ethics."

"Like the ones you used when you investigated my background and the way Far East Imports is run?"

"That was necessary," Macdonald smiled. "For all I knew it could have been you—not Tang—who ran the Triad."

Hunter's answering smile was guileless. "What was it that convinced you it wasn't me?"

"Eton, Cambridge—and the fact that you are non-Chinese."

"My being an M.P. had nothing to do with it?"

"Frankly, no. It would be an ideal setup for the Triad to have someone at Westminster on the payroll —and I wouldn't put it past them!"

Hunter frowned, "Nor would I. I must confess that
212

at times it has worried me how Western nations under-estimate the Chinese. I know them pretty well, and they don't miss a trick." Then he rubbed his hands together briskly and said, "Apart from getting Tang out of the way, what else is there?"

"We must consider the possibility that Tang set up the Triad network in conjunction with your building up Far East Imports. It would be the most logical way to organize things." Macdonald lit a fresh cigarette. "You could go through the stages of development with me. With a bit of luck, you should be able to provide valuable information."

"Bit of a long shot, isn't it?"

"I don't expect you to be right every time, but at least we can cover the likely ones." Macdonald's voice took on a grim note, "That way, when we get Tang to talk, we can catch the birds before they fly."

"You are sure that you can get Tang to talk? I thought it was death before dishonor and all that rubbish with these people."

"In principle, yes." Macdonald's face was set in hard lines. "The trick is to place death just out of their reach. That way they will tell you anything in return for being allowed to die."

Hunter had been watching the other man's face as he spoke. Now he said softly, "Very interesting theory, that. You have given me a lot to think about."

"Then we can count on you to help?" Macdonald wanted Hunter to declare himself formally.

Hunter's reply came without hesitation. "Certainly. I'll do everything I can." A faint smile hovered at the corners of his mouth, "I'm sure you will forgive me if I avail myself of your offer to telephone for confirmation of your standing with the government. As an M.P., I can't afford to get mixed up in something I haven't checked out. The whole thing is intriguing but it does smack of a story written by the chap who wrote these *Fu Manchu* things."

"Sax Rohmer?"

"The very man!" Hunter said with a smile. Then went on with a note of apology in his voice, "Don't misunderstand me. I know enough about the Chinese to realize that they can be very devious. Many of the qualities attributed to them by writers of fiction have a sound basis in fact."

Macdonald lit a cigarette, "Shouldn't we get back to the ladies? They are probably wondering what the hell we are talking about for this long."

"Yes, you're right." Hunter's tone was deliberately casual as he asked, "What do you suppose Triad does with all the money they make from drugs in this country?"

"Who knows?" Macdonald shrugged. "Probably to numbered accounts in Swiss banks and from there to the Far East." He made his voice as casual as the other man's as he said, "You know more about the Chinese than I. What do *you* think they do with it?" He watched Hunter carefully as he waited for his reply.

It was Hunter's turn to shrug. He thought for a moment, then said, "It could go to finance their operations in the Far East, but I doubt it. They have a firm grip on gambling, prostitution, and a dozen other rackets in the Orient and Asia. All of these are highly profitable fields that don't require a lot of capital. The only suggestion I can make—and it is pure speculation—is that the money goes to the Chinese government. You yourself said earlier there are close connections between Triad and the Communists. I have certainly heard such rumors in my travels—it wouldn't surprise *me* if there was an element of truth in it."

"Perhaps you're right." Macdonald drew hard on his cigarette, "But my major concern is to stop them so they can't make any more money, rather than figuring out what they do with what they have already made."

The two men returned to rejoin the ladies in silence. Each had a lot to think about.

36

Hunter lay awake most of the night. He waited until his wife was asleep and then examined the possibilities open to him. His acquaintance with Macdonald, though short, was sufficient to convince him that the man was no fool. That Macdonald had taken him into his confidence with regard to Triad was a stroke of unbelievable luck. He realized that Macdonald must have run a very tight check on his background and activities. That his cover had withstood the thorough investigations had nothing to do with luck. The years of careful planning had paid off. It was now a question of sacrificing part of the organization in order to save what could realistically be kept intact. It would be a severe blow, but he had to cut his losses with an eye toward the future. Macdonald's revelations had shaken him, and there was no doubt in his mind that he had been told only what Macdonald and his superiors deemed necessary.

How had they gotten so close? He recalled the Maxwell incident. Had he been connected with "the department," as Macdonald called it? Or had the organization itself been penetrated? Was *he* the guilty party through neglect? With so much of his attention directed at establishing himself in Westminster, there could have been a relaxation of general security. But he doubted that. There had been nothing in what Macdonald had said to suggest that they had any concept of the scope of Triad in Britain. That Macdonald had enlisted his aid suggested that their investigations were not leading anywhere. It had to be that investigations had proved abortive. It followed, therefore, that somebody—be it Macdonald or his chief—was out on a limb. Someone was committed to uncover Chinese drug activity, and they were so close that he had to act fast. But how much would he have to give them? Certainly Macdonald—if not his superiors—must be aware of the cell structure of Triad. Macdonald would not be satisfied with an individual—he had said as much. What they wanted was a leader and a recognizable structure. He would have to provide them with just that. Not too much and not too little.

Tang would have to go. No way around that. Simply a question of whether they got him alive or dead. Dead would never satisfy them. They would not feel that they had gotten enough of the organization. But there was also danger in giving them Tang alive. How effective would their torture be? That there would be torture was beyond question, and Macdonald's eyes had indicated extreme measures. But alive it would have to be. He would have to hope that they got nothing beyond what he wanted Tang to give them.

Tang did possess enough information to destroy just about everything he had built up. Fortunately, he could restructure very quickly. But could Tang stand enough torture not to reveal the most vital piece of information of all—Hunter himself. It was a gamble he would have to take. Far East Importation could be replaced and, without doubt, in time *he* could be replaced. But Triad would lose its foothold in Parliament, and it would become almost impossible to get another man there for a long time. The code of Triad demanded that he stay and accept what fate decreed. If he saved himself at the expense of Triad, then Triad would execute him. If, however, he survived and Far East Imports continued to function, they would have suffered a setback but nothing that could not be recovered in time. There existed no choice for him. His fate was in Tang's hands, and the fate of the organization depended on his skill in deciding what to save and what to sacrifice. He spent the rest of the night considering all the possibilities.

The next day he met Macdonald at Far East Imports. All his decisions had been taken, and the report was on its way to Hong Kong. Tang had been left in Suffolk. Going through the company books with Macdonald was an exercise in duplicity. There was nothing there for the government man to find, and it gave Hunter the opportunity to finalize which parts of the organization he would instruct Tang to reveal when the time came.

It took two weeks for Hunter to restructure, and it was therefore two weeks before Macdonald was in possession of a full list of suspects. Hunter made sure that the list of "suspects" included several wholesalers and restaurants that were in no way involved with Triad activity in order to cover himself and also to confuse the investigation. Knowing that Macdonald did not intend to arrest Tang until all other suspects had been placed under surveillance, he put off advising Tang of the situation until the new Triad structure was established. That way Tang had no knowledge of new locations and procedures that had been adopted.

When informed, Tang accepted the situation stoically. Hunter explained how the crisis had developed and told him of the names, locations, and relevant details that were to be divulged. Triad discipline was such that, whatever thoughts Tang may have had, he asked only questions concerning his instructions. Without change of expression, he accepted his fate when Hunter explained that he would be subjected to extreme torture and that death would be all that could relieve him. "Macdonald will show you no mercy. He will take you to pieces, and it will be very difficult for you to pace your disclosures. I know something of this man, and beneath his veneer there is a savage!"

"But a Westerner." A smile flickered on Tang's lips, "I have no fear of what he will do. The pain will be inflicted too swiftly and will insulate me against the greater pain to follow."

"And at the end?"

"We are taught that fortunate is the man who dies only once."

Hunter nodded, "That is so. Many have died a hundred deaths in your capable hands. It is unfortunate that you have to be sacrificed."

As though accepting a compliment Tang bowed, then said, "May I ask that you revenge me on this man?"

"You have my word." Hunter returned his bow, "He may die only once, but he will pay for your life with his."

Hunter meant what he said. He meant it more than anything in his life. Triad code demanded Macdonald pay with his life for Tang's and for his interference in Triad affairs. He was thrice-condemned because Hunter himself had been used by Macdonald. It was a personal insult to Hunter's intelligence, and the fact he had outwitted Macdonald did not compensate for the insult. As an adversary he respected Macdonald, but someone always had to win and someone lose.

Hunter was relieved about one thing that had emerged from the two weeks he had "assisted" Macdonald. Despite subtle questioning, he could find no

217

suggestion that the department—whatever it might consist of—knew anything of the investment of Triad funds in the gambling industry in Britain. The possibility existed that he was wrong, but Hunter didn't think so. In any event, he could only proceed on the assumption that he was right.

37

Macdonald should have been elated as a possible Triad structure emerged from the two weeks he and Hunter spent studying the lists of Chinese people and business premises in the U.K. The files at Far East Importation yielded all kinds of useful information, and Hunter was the key to it. He would take large sections home with him and spend hours poring over them. Each morning he would have another piece of the jigsaw for Macdonald. If only half of the people and locations proved part of the Triad setup, the department would pull off the biggest coup in years. Of course everything depended on Tang. When the time came to bring him in and he was forced to talk, Macdonald would know the true value of Hunter's efforts.

During the long hours the two men were together, Macdonald's respect for Hunter grew. The man's knowledge of the Far East was extensive, and he was able to explain a great deal of the historical background of the countries dominated by China. His grasp of the economics of Asia and China was demonstrated a hundred times as he guided Macdonald toward understanding how Triad had taken control. Hunter would jot down a few notes, summon his general manager or one of the younger executives, ask a few questions, and have the answers. After ten days, Hunter was able to trace a clear pattern of the way it would have been possible for Tang to create a Triad operation within the framework of Far East Importation. After study, Macdonald had to admit the feasibility of it. He also had to admit to himself that he couldn't have done it without Hunter.

Yet Macdonald was not completely happy. Too much depended on the say-so of one man. He was reminded of the old adage: *In the land of the blind, the one-eyed man is king.* Hunter was king of this particular castle, and his suggestions had to be accepted because there was no way to test the validity of them until Tang was interrogated. The die was cast and—rightly or wrongly—Macdonald was stuck with it.

The pattern brought out by Hunter had the United Kingdom divided into three main regions. In each region there existed a major company involved in the distribution of imports from the Far East. Each of the companies supplied a network of smaller companies. The setup was a normal, logical chain of distribution for imported goods. It could, however, serve equally well for the distribution of contraband drugs. Macdonald recalled Maxwell's insistence that there would be *Ahkungs* in the United Kingdom, each responsible to Triad for a region. If Hunter was right, the owners of these three major companies were the *Ahkungs*. The only course of action open to Macdonald was to put the three major companies under surveillance. It had to be done very cautiously because it would be years before law-enforcement agencies would have another chance at smashing the organization.

Sir Archibald had given Macdonald a complete free hand. What he did was assign each probable Triad region to Steele, Crawford, and Parker. Their job, when given the green light from Macdonald, was to conduct an all-out raid on all targets. The personal task of each commander was to bring in the suspected *Ahkung*. Macdonald gave himself the task of bringing in Tang.

The whole operation was fraught with risk and Macdonald found himself getting more and more on edge. They could not brief the police in advance in case of a leak. The best he could do was request that the chief constables issue instructions for men to be kept on standby. The manpower shortage made this request very unpopular, but Macdonald wasn't interested in *their* problems.

With regard to Customs & Excise, Macdonald could do nothing but have them on standby also. He found the senior people very cooperative, their attitude influenced no doubt at the prospect of getting their hands on a large haul of contraband drugs. Macdonald could sympathize with them. Their task in drug control was out of proportion to the manpower at their disposal. The abysmal record of drug seizure did not truly reflect their efficiency. He hoped for their sake, as well as his own, that Operation Swoop—as it had been designated—would prove to be a winner.

When the day came to pick up Tang, Macdonald used Steele and Parker as backup. As it turned out, the other two men proved to be unnecessary. Tang offered no resistance when Macdonald stuck a gun in his ribs. The resistance came when the questioning began. Tang's face, a block of stone, and his eyes, black and unfathomable, stared at Macdonald across the desk. There had been no question of his being taken into formal custody. He had not been advised of his rights, and all of his clothing was stripped from him when they arrived at the underground interrogation room. Now Tang, in a loose robe, was waiting to face whatever had to be faced. His body was relaxed and he had attuned his mind to respond only to matters he was to divulge.

Macdonald wasted no time on preliminaries. Tang would be missed, and he had to be made to confirm the structure of Triad. If he didn't talk in the next few hours, Operation Swoop would be in jeopardy. Macdonald sat for a time and studied Tang. He knew that the memory of Maxwell would affect how he would break the Chinese. Breaking Triad was the important thing, but his personal feelings could not be left out. He sipped from a cup of coffee and smoked, knowing it was having no effect on the prisoner. Carefully, he crushed his cigarette out in the heavy glass ashtray, then said to Steele and Parker, "I want our friend's hands, palms down, on the desk." When his order had been complied with, he picked up the ashtray and deliberately broke each of Tang's fingers. The men holding Tang's hands looked at Macdonald in shocked disbelief when he had finished. No strangers to violence, neither man had expected anything before at least one question was asked.

Tang had screamed loud and long. Now slumped in the chair, his hands were folded in his lap and he whimpered like a wounded animal. Macdonald poured fresh coffee into his cup, then sipped from it. When the cup was empty, he placed it on its saucer, then rose and walked around the desk to where Tang was. He grabbed the man by the hair and forced his head back so that his face and that of Tang were almost touching. Then he asked "You remember Maxwell?"

An unintelligible mutter came from the man's lips. Macdonald chopped him viciously across the bridge of his nose with the hardened edge of his free hand and heard the bone crack. Releasing Tang's head, he said, *"I* remember Maxwell—and I remember what *you* did to him." He went on, "You are going to die within the next few hours. The condition you are in when you meet your ancestors will depend on how cooperative you are. You will find me not unreasonable. I have an interpreter standing by, and if you don't understand my questions, I'll bring him in. But I want you to understand one thing clearly—I will break one of your bones each time you fail to answer me. If you have got that clear, tell me now."

Tang's head, blood streaming from his nostrils, came up slowly and nodded. His eyes blazed hatred. Macdonald nodded approvingly, "Say yes, so I'll know you understand English."

The word came out as a hiss, "Yes."

"Good, now we can get on." Macdonald took his time lighting a cigarette. "How would you like me to have your teeth removed, one at a time."

"No."

"You're getting the idea." Macdonald picked up the ashtray, leaned across the desk, and hit Tang across the mouth with it. Teeth splintered and broke, blood spurted from Tang's mouth, and he screamed. Macdonald resumed his seat and addressed Steele, "Give our friend some water. He sounds a little dry."

As the cool water splashed over his face, Tang hated Macdonald as he had never hated before. But he could also feel a fear of his tormentor being born. He had not expected to be treated this way. It wasn't consistent with the methods usually employed by Westerners. He knew the man on the other side of the desk *meant* it when he said he was going to die.

He had expected to. But what would happen before then? And could he withstand the pain to come? As Maxwell had done before him, Tang concentrated only on what he was prepared to reveal.

Over the next few hours, Tang, after persuasion, told everything he had been instructed to. The man's answers fitted with Macdonald's expectations. He had confirmed two of the *Ahkungs* suggested by Hunter but offered an unfamiliar name as the third. Nothing could change his mind until Macdonald offered the third name given by Hunter. Then Tang swore that *he* was the man. Of the smaller fry, Tang confirmed more than half of the names on the list and added some that weren't. Only when questioned on the investment in gambling did Tang deny all knowledge of it. He swore that Triad money was sent back to Hong Kong. Nothing Macdonald inflicted on him could change his story. Macdonald was not satisfied.

Tang's broken body was left for an hour, then strapped to a table by Steele and Parker. Electrodes were placed on his neck, and a charge of electric current passed through them. The body on the table stiffened and arched as if a grotesque rite of the supernatural were taking place. When the current was switched off, Tang's body slumped to the table. Macdonald advanced to the twitching wreck and began his questioning all over again. From time to time the current was applied, but the replies to Macdonald's questions remained the same.

When he had exhausted his line of questioning, Macdonald still wasn't satisfied. If Tang was the top man of Triad, he *had* to know about the investment in gambling. The electrode machine had done its work, yet he still had not confirmed Triad involvement in gambling. He had to do *something*. There was only one shot left, and if it didn't work out for him, things looked black. Tang—what was left of him—held the key.

He came to a decision not to use the interpreter, at least not at first. He did not want the man to see what had been done to Tang but—more crucial to success —he did not want his attention distracted when he did what had to be done. If Macdonald's plan was

222

successful, he was sure Tang would revert to his native tongue when he spoke his dying words.

First he carefully checked the tape recorder to make sure it was picking up Tang's words very clearly. Then he motioned to Steele and Parker to move away from Tang's body, and turned the electrode machine on. With the setting at "low," only a little current passed through Tang but it was enough to bring him to consciousness. The black eyes revealed that the mind was active and the lips twitched. Macdonald put his mouth close to Tang's right ear, "Would you like to die? Would you like me to release you from the pain?"

The eyes smoldered and the lips continued to move, but no sound came in answer to the questions. Macdonald's right hand rested on the control switch of the electrode machine. Slowly his fingers turned to increase the flow of current. Macdonald's voice was insistent as he said, "What happens to Triad money? How is it invested? What happens to the money?" His voice rose as his fingers caused the indicator on the machine to move remorselessly toward "high." Almost screaming the words, Macdonald demanded, "What happens to the money, you slant-eyed bastard? Who is the head of Triad? Who is it you report to? Do you want to die? Tell me—tell me! Tell me and I'll let you die."

The body arched as the flow of current increased and the mouth moved faster and faster as words, interspersed by screams poured from the lips. It was all in Chinese, but even Macdonald could understand the entreaty in his voice. As the pointer on the machine reached the highest point on the dial, Tang's systems reached the edge of endurance and he died. When the dying man's vocal cords gave out, the silence in the room was deafening.

Exhausted, Macdonald switched off the electrode machine. He took several deep breaths and then threw a blanket over the body. With unsteady fingers he made the necessary adjustments to the tape recorder, then said to Parker, "Get the interpreter in here."

When the man entered the room, he glanced briefly at the shape beneath the blanket before turning his attention to Macdonald. He was from Military Intelligence and it was his first job for the Home Office.

He was an experienced interrogator and he had expected to find the prisoner seated in a chair. He thought his role would be to translate questions and answers. Instead, two men, besides the one who had summoned him, stood by a recording machine on a moveable table. The oldest man of the trio said, flatly, "Listen to this. Listen carefully, then tell me what the Chinese was saying. If you want to hear it again after it's finished, just ask. I don't care how often you want to listen, but I don't want you to make any mistakes—understand?"

The army officer drew himself up to his full height —he wasn't accustomed to being spoken to like this. He said, "I understand perfectly. May we get on?"

Unprepared for what he was to hear, the man from Military Intelligence stood at attention. The switch was flicked and Tang's screams filled the room. The officer's face paled and his eyes darted from man to man. His eyes clearly revealed he considered them subhuman. When the sound abruptly ceased, the interpreter, visibly shaken, said, "I will have to hear it again."

In the silence which followed the second playback, the army officer mopped his brow with a handkerchief. Macdonald, hand on the machine, asked, "You want to hear it again?"

"No—I *don't* want to hear it again."

"What did he say?"

The interpreter said, "You understand it was a bit difficult to understand. It's been a long time since I've heard anything like *that*. Not since Korea—and that was a long time ago."

Macdonald's voice was sympathetic as he said, "I know it wasn't pleasant, but it is of vital importance that I know what he said."

The army man closed his eyes for a moment, then opened them. "It was a bit jumbled, but to the best of my knowledge, the man was repeating three things over and over again. One was a plea to be allowed to die. The other two things were answers to *your* questions." He addressed Macdonald directly to stress that he knew who had been asking the questions.

Macdonald nodded in unconscious acknowledgment, "Okay, okay, what were the answers?"

"That he reported to nobody and that the money was going into gambling—as far as I could make out. Something about it being legal investment. That's the best I could make of it. I could break the tape down and get you a clearer picture, if you like."

Macdonald shook his head. "No, that won't be necessary. You're sure that the gist of what he was saying was he reported to nobody—the money was going into gambling, and it was legal?"

"Quite sure."

"Thank you. I appreciate your efforts." Relieved, Macdonald walked toward the desk. "I think we could all use a stiff drink!"

38

Had a certificate been issued to mark the passing of Hop Tang, the time of death would have shown as 4:30 A.M. and the date October 14, 1976. By 6:30 A.M. the maps of the areas to be raided in Operation Swoop had been altered. The only major change was the headquarters of the *Ahkung* in the Midlands area, where Parker would be responsible for making the arrest. It was remarkable to the people in the department how accurate Clive Hunter had been in his predictions. Of the sixty-four locations, he had pinpointed, forty-one were correct. In all, Tang had betrayed eighty-five Triad cells. These covered wholesalers, retailers, and restaurants throughout the country. When the master map covering all of the United Kingdom had been plotted, the network established by Triad over the years was impressive.

Macdonald alerted the police and Customs & Excise that it would only be a matter of hours before Operation Swoop took place. Timing was crucial. It was imperative that everyone moved at the same time to prevent any alarm from being raised. Each unit was deployed to hit its target at precisely the same time. The police were responsible for the raids and would get full credit for them with the media. The last thing the department wanted was publicity of any kind. Senior police officers would lead each party, and only

225

the *Ahkungs* taken into custody by Steele, Parker, and Crawford would come to the department. All others would go to the local police stations to be charged and locked up, pending trial.

As soon as the lists of targets had been finalized, Macdonald sent Steele, Parker, and Crawford to deliver them to the chief constables. He fixed the time for Operation Swoop at 4:30 P.M. His only concern was that changing the lists to fit Tang's revelations might cause problems with the synchronization of the police units, but it was out of his hands.

Macdonald was at the side of chief of the Metropolitan Police Sir Peter Franks when Operation Swoop got under way. A section of the operations room at Scotland Yard had been specially set up for the project. The focal point of the room was a huge table with a map of the United Kingdom pinned to it. A battery of additional telephones had been installed with radio equipment set for a special frequency. At 4:14 P.M. a policewoman reported to Sir Peter that all staff were standing by. Macdonald surveyed the scene. At each telephone a policewoman sat patiently waiting for it to ring. She had only one call to take, pass the message along, and her job was done. Around the operations table were more policewomen, each holding a rake, like the croupier in a casino. Each wore headphones and as the messages were passed to them by the girls on the telephones, the rakes would move the markers on the map. Beyond the girls at the operations table were the radio operators. They would pass messages received from local units. Strolling around the scene were senior police officers who reminded Macdonald of pit bosses in a casino. This, however, was no game. Silence took the place of the excited chatter, click of plaques, and invitations to place bets. All the bets *had* been placed, and everyone was awaiting the outcome.

Sir Peter Franks and Macdonald did not converse while they waited for the action to start. They knew each other fairly well, but when they met socially, they would chat about the weather, mutual acquaintances, sporting activities, or the stock market. Never a suggestion that they shared a working interest. Now each was impatient for Operation Swoop to start.

At 4:38 P.M. the first radio message was received, relayed, and a rake moved one of the counters to the side of the operations table. After that, telephones shrilled and messages poured in. At 4:52 P.M. only one counter remained on the map. It indicated the headquarters of the London *Ahkung,* and Macdonald waited anxiously for it to be removed.

At 4:55 P.M. he said to Sir Peter, "What's happening?"

The chief of the Metropolitan Police beckoned to the senior supervisor and asked, "What's the problem?"

"A bit difficult, sir." The man was apologetic. "You know Soho. Seems the patrons of the strip joints thought it was a general raid on the district. They wanted to get the hell out of there in case they were arrested—you know, businessmen and the like."

"I know!" Sir Peter interrupted testily, "get on with it!"

"Well, sir, these people were pouring out of the strip clubs and our chaps were trying to get to the Chinese places." He swallowed, then said, "I'm afraid there's a mini-riot going on at the moment."

Macdonald could visualize the scene and at any other time he would have found the situation amusing. Now his concern was whether or not Steele had got his man. "Any word from my man, Steele?"

"No, I'm sorry, sir, nothing yet."

"Damn it to hell!" Sir Peter wasn't amused either, but for his own reasons. "What about the press or television—are they there?"

"No, sir." The supervisor was emphatic, "Nobody, as far as I know."

Relieved, Sir Peter said, "Get back over there and tell them to get the bloody thing sorted out."

At 5:12 P.M. the last counter was swept off the map. At 5:16 P.M. the supervisor advised Macdonald that Steele had reported all was well. Operation Swoop was a total success.

Back at the department, Macdonald took inventory

of the outcome of Swoop. A total of eighty-five raids had been carried out. Four hundred and twenty-seven persons arrested. Drugs worth a total of more than £4,000,000 sterling had been seized. Apart from the fiasco at Soho and a few skirmishes around the country, there had been very little resistance. Not one shot was fired and nobody seriously wounded in the scuffles. Operation Swoop *had* been a total success.

When the *Ahkungs* were interrogated, they yielded little information of value. After the interrogations they were disposed of in a manner that would have been considered highly irregular by anyone outside the department.

The smaller fry were duly tried for sundry offenses, found guilty, imprisoned, and then deported. Macdonald was grateful that Hunter did not ask too many questions regarding the outcome of Operation Swoop. Those he did ask Macdonald was able to answer fairly truthfully, even to the extent that Tang had died in custody. Hunter only commented that he could still hardly believe that Tang, who had served him so faithfully over the years, had been the head of Triad in the United Kingdom. Hunter also warned Macdonald that Triad would seek revenge for the death of Tang and the wrecking of their operations in the U.K. Macdonald assured him it was unlikely the Society had the slightest inkling of who he—Macdonald—really was.

Hunter had sacrificed a great deal to give Macdonald his coup. And as things stood, his involvement in Operation Swoop must have been brought to the attention of people who mattered in the cabinet. It could only be beneficial to his career as a member of Parliament.

39

It was a memorable Christmas for Macdonald. For the first time in his adult life, the festive season was more than just a holiday when people ate and drank too much. He had always disliked the commercial exploitation that overshadowed the significance of the occasion. New Year's he regarded as an excuse for a national drinking binge. The Scottish Hogmany, with its strict observation of pagan custom, had dignity when the rites were performed in native surroundings, but feeling was lost in London.

After Triad, Avril had moved into his flat in St. John's Wood, and the experiment was working—so much so that he was seriously considering legalizing the union. Sir Archibald had assigned him to a counterfeiting job that was proving to be interesting. Although he still would have preferred direct involvement rather than desk control, he was beginning to derive real satisfatcion from seeing the overall picture. An unexpected result of the Triad affair was that he and Hunter were to appear on the New Year Honors List. Macdonald had no real ambition to acquire a title, and so the stepping-stone award meant little to him. Avril, on the other hand, was delighted. Perhaps in time she saw herself as a Lady. It was the same with Diana Hunter. Clive Hunter agreed with Macdonald that the whole thing was humbug, but admitted frankly that it would help further his political career.

Macdonald and Avril spent all of the Christmas holiday with the Hunters in Suffolk. It was very festive —illuminated trees outdoors as well as in, wreaths of holly, sprigs of mistletoe and log fires, Christmas carol service at the village church and carol singers, complete with lanterns, serenading the houses. Festive fare at table with people enjoying themselves, but not working at it. Diana banned the playing of cards for the duration and anyone who introduced a subject not in keeping with Christmas paid a forfeit of having to entertain the other guests with a song, dance, or humorous recitation. To crown the occasion snow blanketed the countryside.

The snow lasted through New Year's Eve, and roads were becoming difficult. Macdonald had wanted the Hunters to spend New Year with Avril and himself in London, but because of lack of accommodation, it was impractical. Therefore they were going back to Suffolk. Macdonald had decided that New Year's Eve was the right time to ask Avril to marry him. But once he had decided to ask her, he began to worry that she might not accept. Perhaps she liked the situation as it stood. No hang-ups if she decided to move out one day. Perhaps *not* being married was attractive in that the female could be as independent as the male. He was certain of one thing: Avril would remain independent, married or not.

It was snowing heavily when they left London, but it wasn't until they were past Woodford that driving became really difficult. The trees of Epping Forest protected the road to a degree, but where there were open fields, the snow was drifting in banks. The rising wind drove a curtain of snow and the wipers fought to keep the windshield free. Comfortable in the car, the temperature outside was hovering at the freezing point. Macdonald kept the speed of the car down and eased into corners to avoid skidding. He was sorry now that they had not used the train, but the Mercedes was in excellent condition and he just had to be very careful. It took four hours to complete a trip that should have taken less than two.

The Hunters were concerned at their late arrival and, though the party was in full swing, everyone had been a little restrained due to fear that Avril and Macdonald had been involved in an accident. Now, with a large whiskey in his hand, Macdonald felt on top of the world—it was a great feeling to be among friends, especially tonight.

The liquor flowed and the music got louder as the party went on. Everyone threw aside restraint and drank more than usual—nobody falling about or being a nuisance, but conversation tended to be disjointed. For Macdonald's benefit, a number of Scottish dance records had been bought and there was much laughter at the hilarious contortions as couples collided trying to do the country steps. Sheer exhaustion brought it to a halt. At midnight everyone joined hands and sang "Auld Lang Syne," end of the old and beginning of the new.

To Macdonald, this was always an emotional moment, a time of regret and a time of resolution. Many times in the past his resolve had faded, but not this time. He kissed Avril lightly on the lips and said, "Happy New Year, darling. Will you marry me?"

Her eyes were misty when she smiled and said, "If

I don't get a better offer before Monday, you have just got yourself a deal." She returned his kiss, "Happy New Year to you, darling."

When the handshaking and exchange of greetings had been completed, Avril returned to Macdonald's side. She raised her glass to him in mocking salute and there was a wicked gleam in her eyes, "Shall I call for silence now and announce our engagement?"

"Not on your sweet life," he shook a fist at her, "not unless you want me to be a widower before I'm a bridegroom!"

New Year's Day everyone had a hangover. Macdonald had two large Pernods over ice for lunch and was glad to drag his tired body back to bed for a couple of hours. When he reappeared downstairs it was to find that he and Avril were the only remaining guests. The Hunters suggested they stay over for another night, but Macdonald felt sufficiently fit to drive. Diana then suggested they leave his car, go home by train, and get the car on the weekend.

Macdonald considered it, but it meant someone had to drive them to the station and, though there was a lot of snow on the ground, the weather had cleared up. Besides, he wanted to be alone with Avril.

Diana insisted he have some hot soup followed by sandwiches and coffee. Thus fortified, he and Avril said their farewells and set off. The car had been under cover overnight, and the snow that had accumulated the previous night had all melted away. The engine soon warmed up and, with automatic transmission, Macdonald had little to do but steer. Avril snuggled her body close to his and had her arm through his. He kept the window on the driving side down an inch or so to allow cold air to play on his forehead but otherwise the car was pleasantly warm.

The road was treacherous—powdery snow on top of hard-packed ice—but Macdonald knew that once they got onto the main road snowplows and salted grit would provide safe driving all the way to London. He kept his speed down and avoided swerving and breaking whenever possible. He was beginning to relax as the vehicle swung smoothly around a bend that led to a steep hill with a particularly nasty hairpin at the foot of it—the last real hazard before joining the main road. Avril was teasing him about the lack of interest he and Hunter had shown about their names appearing on the Honors List in the morning newspapers. As his lips were framing a reply, he felt the front wheels pull the steering wheel to his left. Automatically, he turned the wheel to correct the drift, but there was no response.

Danger signals went off in his head and he threw Avril's arm from his. Both hands gripped the rim of the wheel, but he could feel by the slackness of the steering column that there would be no response from the mechanism to correct their course. Gently, he pushed on the brake pedal to check the gathering speed of the heavy car. Nothing. It was then—with terrible clarity—that he knew the car had been expertly sabotaged. Steering and brakes had been tampered with to fail in sequence just as they reached this dangerous point in the road. An expert job that would leave no trace.

Carried forward by its own weight, the car gathered momentum and swerved from one side of the rutted road to the other. Seized by panic, Avril was holding his arm with both of her hands and she was shouting at him. He was conscious of shaking his arm to free it and yelling at her to control herself, but he was concentrating in a desperate attempt to get some response from the steering wheel or the handbrake. Within seconds the road curved sharply into the first part of the hairpin, but the car shot straight ahead, smashing through the wooden guard rails. Macdonald threw himself over Avril to protect her as the Mercedes plunged down toward the trees.

The heavy steel body ripped through the grove of young saplings with hardly any loss of speed, smashed into a low wall, and rolled over and over before coming to rest on its roof. One after the other the spinning wheels gradually slowed, then stopped.

When Macdonald regained consciousness all was silent. It was some time before he could collect his thoughts. The position of his body gave him a view of the carpeted floor above his head. He tried to move his arms but found the left one would not obey. His legs would not respond, and his face was entirely numb. He felt for—then grasped—something with which to pull himself free. Hauling and levering, he succeeded in raising himself sufficiently to turn his head.

Avril would never banter again. The position of the raven-dark hair framing horror-frozen features was so twisted in relationship to her body that Avril would never do anything again.

A vision of the royal flush in spades flashed across Macdonald's mind, ace of death with the black queen.

40

The consensus of medical opinion was that he should be dead, but hate kept him alive. The doctors used all their skill to restore flesh, sinew, bone, and muscle. Given little chance of survival, the patched body received the care of a nursing staff trained to act on the principle that where there is life there is hope. No visitors were allowed. On strict instructions, the patient had been removed to a private world and a telephone number given to the day and night nurses. The moment the patient regained consciousness, the person at that number was to be contacted.

Sir Archibald had personally checked with the doctors about Macdonald's injuries. He also sent an expert to check over the wreckage of the car. He did not make contact with the dead girl's family, but he had someone attend the funeral to check out the mourners. That Diana and Clive Hunter's names appeared on the list was no surprise to him, and he regarded telephone calls by the Hunters to the hospital as a natural concern by friends. The doctors' reports confirmed that there was nothing unusual with regard to Macdonald's injuries, and the expert found no trace of mechanical failure. Sir Archibald realized that the expert could not be positive because the car had been so badly wrecked. It was highly unlikely that those involved in counterfeiting could be responsible for the accident or indeed be aware of Macdonald's existence. A senior operative was brought in as temporary coordinator for the counterfeiting investigation, and Sir Archibald awaited a message from the hospital as to whether the patient had recovered consciousness or "failed to respond to treatment." Beyond doubt Hunter was the man responsible, but Sir Archibald was prepared to await the outcome of the hospital report. It was a concession he was making as a man. As head of department, he would strike the blow at Triad by setting in motion the plans to prevent their efforts to take over gambling in the U.K. Hunter could be left aside.

It was four days before Macdonald was coherent enough to tell his story to Sir Archibald. When the head of department commented that he would leave Hunter free for a few more weeks, Macdonald knew that he would have the opportunity to take his own revenge. Macdonald was not even aware of the indignity of having his bodily needs attended to by a nurse. From then on, he had to learn to put up with the necessity of requesting bedpans and urine bottles along with having his private parts washed by someone else. Requests for a mirror were politely ignored. The days passed in fitful periods of sleep and semiwakefulness. There was a good deal of pain, but it wasn't until he insisted that no more drugs be administered that he was capable of assessing his condition for himself. Both arms were in plaster, but only the left one was broken. His right leg was also broken, and the upper part of his body badly bruised. His face was completely numb, and he looked out at the ceiling through a plaster-cast. Food and drink were given through a hole in the mask and a thick collar was around his neck. The fact that Avril had not survived the accident was "broken gently" to him. Macdonald had long since relived the moment of seeing that beloved head twisted at an unnatural angle to her body. He had whispered good-bye within his plaster mask and, from that moment on, resolutely refused to let any thought of her interfere with his plans for revenge.

The chief of staff came from the department and he gave Macdonald his word that no other visitors would be allowed until Macdonald requested them. He was surprised when Macdonald asked that bulletins regarding his condition be exaggerated. The doctor had said Macdonald would not be released for at least three months and that further extensive surgery would be necessary to his face. The chief agreed with Macdonald's request even though he thought it quite strange. He was concerned about Macdonald's mental state. Certainly the man betrayed no interest in anything. He lay in silence and apart from making his two requests, only the smoldering eyes gave sign of life. The chief of staff left the cigarettes he had brought and went back to file an adverse report with regard to the likelihood of Macdonald's ever being fit to return to duty.

Each day the doctors looked in briefly and inquired as to his comfort but did not disturb the dressings. The patient forced himself to offer banal replies and waited impatiently for something positive to happen. After six weeks, the cast was removed from his right arm and his left leg freed from dressings. The following day he could use these limbs and, despite protests from the nursing staff, had resumed smoking. When the doctor who had performed the surgery on his face removed the cast to examine it, Macdonald again requested a mirror. The doctor smiled and shook his head. "All in good time. Don't rush things."

"Either you have one brought, or I get up and find one." There was something in Macdonald's voice that left no doubt that he meant what he said.

The doctor eyed him levelly, then said, "You won't like it, but—if you insist—I'll let you have a look."

"I insist."

The doctor nodded, "Nurse, a mirror!"

What Macdonald saw *could* be described as a face. The bone structure had been smashed and the doctor had reset it in rough proportion, but the nose was flat and the bruised flesh a web of ugly scars. Only the eyes belonged to the face Macdonald remembered as his. It was the face of a stranger and only the pain beneath the scarred surface was his. He handed the mirror back without a word, and the doctor felt compelled to say, "At the time I had an impossible task.

There was nothing much to work on and"—he shrugged apologetically—"frankly, there didn't seem to be much point. We hardly thought you'd survive."

The intensity of the smoldering eyes increased and the scarred lips said, "You did a good job."

"I *will* do a good job." There was conviction in his voice. "I'll rebuild it good as new."

Macdonald was disinterested, "May I shave?"

"Yes, but the dressings and mask will have to be replaced afterward."

There was no bitterness in his voice when Macdonald said, "Just as well—the mask looks a lot better than I do!"

That night, after the nurse had left, Macdonald dragged himself from the bed and attempted to walk. It took him a week to coordinate the movements required for him to be mobile. Aside from the pain, the main problem was to avoid cracking the cast. Not only would that be dangerous to the healing process, but more important to Macdonald, it would give away what he was doing. It had to be kept secret. When he was ready he asked the doctor for a walking cast. Good-humoredly, the doctor said, "All in good time. We have a long way to go before you start to walk again." With surprising agility Macdonald swung himself from the bed and stood on the floor. "I mean *now!*"

Anger overcame surprise and the doctor exclaimed, "Are you out of your mind? Don't you realize that your leg will just not take your weight? The plaster will go, and the bone will have no chance! Get back in that bed!"

From behind the mask, the muffled voice said, "Sorry, I just don't have the time." With an almost comical jerky motion, he walked to the end of the room, turned, and faced the other man. "I can do it, but I need your help!"

Astonished, the doctor pointed to the bed, "Back in there. I'll have the plaster removed and, if the X rays show that you haven't damaged the leg beyond repair, I'll see what can be done."

"Fair enough." Macdonald was confident. It *had* to be all right—everything depended on it.

The next day he requested a visitor.

Steele was placed in a very difficult position. There had been no directive issued with regard to Macdonald, and he knew he should report what took place to his new coordinator. He did not. Instead, he carried out Macdonald's instructions. To a man of his training and skill, smuggling a suitcase into a hospital presented little difficulty. He placed it in the cupboard in Macdonald's room, left, and then returned at normal visiting time.

Macdonald had checked the contents of the suitcase and then finalized the details of his plan. When Steele had closed the door and sat down, Macdonald wasted no time. "I've had a look in the suitcase, and everything is there. If I could have avoided dragging you into it I would, but, in the circumstances, I have no option."

"Forget it," the younger man grinned. "Twice, to date, you have saved my life—so I owe you!"

"You understand that there is no way I can hide the fact that you helped me?"

"Of course I do. The department will check with the hospital and pinpoint me immediately. The Old Man will have my guts and that—as they say—will be that!"

Macdonald shook Steele's hand, then said, "The hospital layout?"

"Simple." Steele took a sheet of paper from his pocket and passed it over. "You are on the ground floor here. Outside is a short corridor. If you turn left at the end of that, another short corridor leads to the kitchens. Through the kitchens—there shouldn't be anyone there at that time of night—and out through the doors used for deliveries." He placed a finger on the diagram. "The delivery door is metal with a small door set into it. You just turn the handle and walk out." Then Steele looked at Macdonald, "It's getting back that will be a problem. If you leave the catch on the lock someone is bound to find it and there is no way to jam it."

"Forget it," Macdonald was brusque, "I don't intend to come back."

"What?"

"It's part of my plan to be found close to the hospital. I want it to look as if I'm heading *away* from here. It won't fool the department, but it will throw the police right off the scent. The nurse will notice me missing, and I'll be conveniently found about as far away as a man in my condition could reasonably be expected to get under his own steam."

Steele remained silent for a moment. He had something to say, but wasn't sure how to say it. Finally, trying to sound casual, he said, "Talking about your condition, do you feel up to this?"

"Yes." Macdonald knew there was more, and he waited.

"I'll do it for you." Steele almost blurted the words out and then went on hurriedly, "I can do it so that there will be no suspicion that you or I were involved."

The dark eyes regarded the younger man through the mask and there was a change in Macdonald's voice when he said, "It isn't every day that someone offers to kill for you." His words were measured as he went on, "I appreciate your offer, but this is my baby. This is no reflection on you, but you have killed only one man—right?" When Steele nodded, he went on, "At a distance—right?" Again there was an answering nod. Macdonald's voice was flat as he went on, "I have accounted for several. Some of these were the way this one has to be—eyeball to eyeball. Take my word for it—it's different."

"I could do it."

"I don't doubt it. But this is the kind of thing a man does only when he is personally involved. It is—for want of a better explanation—a very private thing. One does it because one has no choice. When it happens to you, you will understand what I'm trying to say."

"Okay. I understand."

But Macdonald had not finished. "This bastard is mine. There is a justice that demands he die at *my* hands. Not only that, but time is short. Right now, I'd stake my life that he has a map just like this one. When he learns that I'm really going to recover, he will send someone to finish the job he bungled. He may already have the plan in motion, but has bided his time because he doesn't realize how far along I've come. For once he has underestimated the opposition."

41

Clive Hunter had underestimated the opposition on two counts. Sir Archibald Sanderson had risen to be head of the intelligence unit known as "the department" because he had been the most efficient, most ruthless, shrewdest, and greatest survivor in the business. The thing that had always motivated him was pitting *his* wits against the enemy. One guiding principle he followed with fanatical adherence was to always hedge his bets. He took nothing for granted. He would analyze a given set of factors and follow them to a logical conclusion, then put himself in the position of his adversary and figure out his logic. By playing both ends against the middle, Sir Archibald was in the best position. He always allowed himself maximum flexibility, and that gave him the edge, the difference between success and failure, life and death. Too often, in his experience, an opponent blinded by his objective, or convinced of his invulnerability, could be outmaneuvered.

So it was with Triad. Sir Archibald had examined the threat over and over again. He had considered the successes of the opposition and the failures of law-enforcement agencies to halt the growth of the Society. He fully appreciated the resources and powers of the opposition and the pathetic weapons available to law enforcement to combat what was a truly international criminal organization. The conclusion reached by Sir Archibald was that the war would not be won in his lifetime. Having come to this conclusion, he had formulated his private policy in dealing with Triad.

He was involved on two fronts. The first was the policies of Triad. Second was the network that had been established over the years to carry out the policies of Triad. Sir Archibald had gone along with Macdonald in setting up Operation Swoop and shared in the victory when Swoop had proved to be a resounding success. The Triad network had been crippled, but their main policy was still intact. Sir Archibald *knew* Triad had control of a formidable array of dummy companies holding millions of pounds worth of shares in the gambling industry in the United Kingdom. It would take very little to tip the scales, and Triad would own the *majority* holdings in British gambling. With so much power they could have a major impact on the economy of Britain. Sir Archibald was a realist. He was also human. He had seen the greatest empire in the history of the world outlive its usefulness. Crumble and die as, piece by piece, it fell apart. He had been aware of the unequal distribution of wealth all of his life and he had watched the trade unions serve the needs of the working man, then outlive *their* usefulness. Tails wagging dogs was the order of things in the world. But England itself was still proud, and Sir Archibald would fight. He had devised the strategy that would win this particular battle against Triad.

Successive Socialist governments had nationalized key industries in the United Kingdom. Since the end of World War II, the Labour party had fulfilled promises to the electorate—or, to be more precise, the trade unions—by nationalizing gas, electricity, coal, railroads, air transport, road transport, water transport, and steel. The post office came under government control, as did radio and television. Leyland Motor Corporation had been added to the list, and North Sea Oil was next. The post office, gas, electricity, coal, and airlines were showing a profit but, over all, the many industries under government control had amassed a colossal deficit. Gambling, on the other hand, brought in more revenue than any other source.

When the British government nationalized an industry, they paid compensation to the shareholders of the individual companies. It was all fair and square, and nobody lost out on the deal. Whether the policy of nationalization was good or bad for the country was open to debate, but nobody could deny that it was imposed by a duly elected government whose declared policy was to nationalize key industry.

It wasn't so in other parts of the world. In some of

the emerging nations, nationalization was an easy method of providing money for the government. They *declared* an industry to be nationalized and *stole* the companies involved from the shareholders.

It wasn't easy for Sir Archibald to convince the Prime Minister that the only way to beat Triad was to nationalize the gambling industry in the United Kingdom. The Prime Minister had had to consult the leaders of the other major political parties as well as his own cabinet. The trade unions had to be consulted, and the chairmen of the various companies which dominated gambling in Britain. There had been top-level meetings followed by top-level meetings before an agreeable package emerged. All shareholders would be compensated provided they were bona fide. Holding companies would have to submit a list of their directors and the credentials of the directors would be examined.

It wasn't perfect. Sir Archibald could envisage all kinds of loopholes in the scheme. Clever accountants and tax experts would devise ways of circumventing legislation but that wasn't *his* worry. He was more concerned with a possible leak before the declaration of nationalization. He had taken every precaution he could to ensure secrecy, but he doubted it *could* be kept secret indefinitely. It was important that a certain Conservative M.P. did not get wind of it.

Because he had hedged his bets, Sir Archibald was sure that Hunter did not have all that many days left. He could—if he wanted to—reduce that number of days himself, but he had a respect for a certain member of his staff, and he believed in justice.

42

Getting dressed took an incredibly long time. Handicapped by the plaster casts, he could use only one arm and one leg. Inability to turn his head further complicated his maneuvers, but there was no way he could release the fastenings of the collar. He was reluctant to do so anyway, because without it his body might be too weak to support his head. The shirt was easy, and he was able to hook his underpants over the stiff leg after several attempts. The trousers were a real problem. He put his good leg in first and found that there was just no way to get the stiff one in. He reversed the precedure and, by struggling for a long time, he eventually succeeded but he was exhausted from his efforts. He lay on the bed panting and cursing that he had not thought to have Steele help him.

The jacket was impossible. The cast would not fit in the sleeve and then with the good arm in one sleeve and the other side draped around his shoulder, he couldn't close the jacket. In sheer desperation he decided that the left sleeve would have to go. His problem was that tearing the sleeve from the garment demanded use of two hands and a strength that he just did not possess. In the end he stood on the sleeve with his good foot and pulled at the jacket with his good hand. He was weeping and sobbing with sheer frustration by the time he achieved his goal. The sock slid on easily, and he was grateful that he never wore other than slip-on shoes.

He placed the skeleton keys in the right-hand pocket of his jacket. He checked the gun then jammed it in the waistband of his trousers. He wanted a drink badly.

Walking around the private ward was one thing, but the hundred yards or so to the delivery doors in the kitchens was like as many miles. Then when the door closed behind him he was struck by the coldness of the air. Weeks in a controlled temperature had conditioned him to warmth, and now his tortured body was starting to shake from the cold. Resolutely he headed for the area where the car would be waiting. His sense of direction was very weak and if Steele hadn't come to meet him, he would not have made it.

Getting into the car was not easy and when he finally made it, he collapsed in the passenger seat. Despite the cold, he was sweating profusely and trembling with fatigue. He was exactly one hour behind schedule.

Steele had driven to the center of London before Macdonald recovered. In a weak voice, he asked if Steele had thought to bring along a drink. When he had sipped the burning liquid from the flask, his head swam and only a tremendous effort of will kept him from passing out. A curious weightlessness in his body and limbs told him that he would have to be very careful not to lose control in the action to come. He deliberately took another swallow from the flask and fought against the sense of drowsiness the whiskey produced. Then he instructed Steele to park in a side street, and the two men shared a long silence.

Macdonald was determined to continue, but Steele had grave doubts of his ability to do so. It was almost midnight when Macdonald finally felt rested enough to proceed. His voice was almost normal when he gave the order to proceed.

Clive Hunter was listening to Tschaikowsky's *1812*. Previously he had listened to Mozart's *Eine Kleine Nachtmusik* and Beethoven's *Symphony No. 2 in D*. A negligent hand kept time with the orchestra and the other nursed a balloon glass in which the rich color of old brandy reflected the leaping flames of the fire. He raised the glass to his lips and sipped appreciatively. His other hand increased its movement as the piece climaxed in a crescendo of cannon and church bells.

In the silence that followed, Hunter spoke softly, "Are you aware, my dear Macdonald, that an ancient Chinese sage—one Seu Ma-tsen, is credited with saying that 'Music is that which unifies'?" Macdonald would have sworn that Hunter had been totally unaware of his presence. Now he shuffled forward and stood so that the light showed him clearly.

A wicked smile flickered across Hunter's face and he said, "You are a mess, aren't you?" He moved to rise, "I would say I was lacking in hospitality if I failed to offer you at least one drink."

Macdonald allowed him to get to his feet but warned him, "Don't touch anything except the bottle and the glass."

Hunter ignored the remark and proceeded to pour the drinks. When he was finished he brought one to Macdonald and solicitously placed it between the fingers of the hand protruding from the plaster cast. He then retrieved his own glass and resumed his seat. Having sipped at his drink he said, "You understand that I'm not usually this vulnerable. Tonight, however, I have no one to ensure my safety."

The brandy was spreading warmth through Macdonald's aching body, and he could feel some of the strength returning that he had used up getting into the apartment. His brain was functioning better also. It *was* remarkable that Hunter was alone. Was it because he had felt secure in the knowledge that he had nothing to fear from a hospitalized wreck? He took a little more of the brandy, "I have thought of nothing but killing you since I regained consciousness in that car. Ridding the world of an abomination such as you is the reason I stayed alive."

Hunter smiled sadly, and replied, "I suspect that the paradoxical element of our situation escapes you. You are probably out of touch with events."

"In what way?"

Continuing to smile, Hunter said, "This seems to be my night for quotations." Then he recited, *"Quis custodiet ipsos custodes?"* When there was no response from the other man, he said, "Forgive me—I had forgotten you did not have the benefit of a classical education at Gordonstoun. The translation is: 'Who will guard the guards?'" When there was still no response from Macdonald, he said, "You were always careful not to mention the name of the man who is the head of your so-called 'department.' It's a pity because I would have enjoyed meeting him. He must be a very clever man."

"I don't know what the *hell* you are talking about." The brandy glass fell from his fingers and thudded on the thick carpet. Macdonald felt weariness coming over him as he said, "If you're stalling for time, forget it. I won't buy it."

Hunter drained his glass, then replied, "I'm not stalling for time at all. Because of you and your very clever boss, I have run out of time. You see, Tony, there was a very interesting item on the 11:00 news. Obviously you didn't hear it and, quite obviously, you hadn't been told about it by your clever boss. The news item, my dear chap, was to the effect that the British government is to nationalize the gambling industry. All trading of shares on the London Stock Exchange has been frozen in effect from opening time tomorrow." Hunter shook his head sadly. "You understand that this places me in a very awkward situation. You must have succeeded in getting the information about Triad involvement in gambling from the late Tang. Your chief—or whatever you call him—put together this little package and now, as they say, the fat is in the fire."

As first Macdonald found it difficult to comprehend what he had just been told. Gradually the meaning of it filtered through and he thought of Sir Archibald. Sly old fox—he had been playing his own game all along the line. He took a firmer grip on the automatic and said, "I begin to see it all now. Your Triad playmates *will* be upset with you."

Hunter asked politely, "Would you mind terribly if I had a cigarette?"

"Help yourself, but move slowly."

When he had taken the cigarette from the silver box on the table and had lit it, Hunter said, "I made a bad mistake with Tang. He was a good man, and you must have used very efficient methods to get him to talk about the gambling project."

"Maxwell was a good man, too." Macdonald's voice grated as he went on, "I enjoyed taking Tang apart."

"I'll just bet you did!" Hunter grinned crookedly. "Maxwell was that colonial chap, wasn't he? I never did meet him."

"You did, you know. That was something that always worried me. I thought you or Diana might recall it and tie me in with Maxwell."

It was Hunter's turn to look perplexed. "What had Diana to do with it? She's a lovely girl, but not too bright."

Macdonald could feel his strength ebbing fast and he knew he was slurring the words as he said, "Avril was a lovely girl, too. She was bright and I loved her." He shot Hunter squarely between the eyes.

Hampstead,
London,
England—March, 1977

Vernon Carstairs Q.C. sighed deeply and sat back in the leather chair at his desk. The brief he was working on was the most important he had handled in his career. It was important for two reasons: one, the colossal sums of money involved; and two, if he succeeded in winning the case, he would have justified the confidence of those who had entrusted it to him. He would not appear in the courts to argue the case, nor would anyone in the legal profession ever know that he had masterminded the strategy to be employed. Carstairs was not concerned about fame and fortune. He had both. The first earned in a brilliant career as a barrister, and the second inherited from his father, a national figure who had inherited the family wealth from *his* father.

Carstairs looked around the study and pondered. Fine points of law were the keys to opening cracks in the binding legislation drawn up to protect the government's nationalization of the gambling industry. He had unearthed several and could quote precedents which would ensure the admissibility of them, and yet he wasn't quite satisfied. It would take a good deal more research before he was ready to embark on the all-important test case.

The work was rewarding. But it was nothing next to the satisfaction he felt that he, at last, was Leader of Triad in the United Kingdom. The years of waiting were over.

ABOUT THE AUTHOR

ALISTAIR MCCOLL MACKAY was born in Niagara
Falls, New York, in 1931. He grew up in Scotland and was educated in Glasgow. He has been
writing for the past fifteen years and many of his
articles and short stories have appeared in European magazines. His first novel, *The Triad Conspiracy,* was inspired by personal encounters with
Triad operations while serving with the British
army in Malaysia during the conflict with Communist forces in that country. Much later, as a
freelance journalist in London, he became aware
of growing Triad influence in the West and followed up on leads that resulted in a book which,
though a work of fiction, has a solid foundation
of documented facts, as evidenced by recent head-
lines and reports in London newspapers. Alistair
McColl MacKay has traveled widely, but now lives
in California and spends part of the year in London and Scotland.

DON'T MISS
THESE CURRENT
Bantam Bestsellers

RELAX!
SIT DOWN
and Catch Up On Your Reading!

☐	10077	**TRINITY** by Leon Uris	—$2.75
☐	2300	**THE MONEYCHANGERS** by Arthur Hailey	—$1.95
☐	2424	**THE GREAT TRAIN ROBBERY** by Michael Crichton	—$1.95
☐	2500	**THE EAGLE HAS LANDED** by Jack Higgins	—$1.95
☐	2600	**RAGTIME** by E. L. Doctorow	—$2.25
☐	10360	**CONFLICT OF INTEREST** by Les Whitten	—$1.95
☐	10092	**THE SWISS ACCOUNT** by Leslie Waller	—$1.95
☐	2964	**THE ODESSA FILE** by Frederick Forsyth	—$1.95
☐	11770	**ONCE IS NOT ENOUGH** by Jacqueline Susann	—$2.25
☐	8500	**JAWS** by Peter Benchley	—$1.95
☐	8844	**TINKER, TAILOR, SOLDIER, SPY** by John Le Carre	—$1.95
☐	8884	**THE DOGS OF WAR** by Frederick Forsyth	—$1.95
☐	10090	**THE R DOCUMENT** by Irving Wallace	—$2.25
☐	10208	**MAVREEN** by Claire Lorrimer	—$1.95
☐	10357	**THE HARRAD EXPERIMENT** by Robert Rimmer	—$1.95
☐	10422	**THE DEEP** by Peter Benchley	—$2.25
☐	10500	**DOLORES** by Jacqueline Susann	—$1.95
☐	11601	**THE LOVE MACHINE** by Jacqueline Susann	—$2.25
☐	10600	**BURR** by Gore Vidal	—$2.25
☐	10857	**THE DAY OF THE JACKAL** by Frederick Forsyth	—$1.95
☐	10940	**BLACK SUNDAY** by Thomas Harris	—$2.25
☐	11057	**PROVINCETOWN** by Burt Hirschfield	—$1.95
☐	11330	**THE BEGGARS ARE COMING** by Mary Loos	—$1.95

Buy them at your local bookstore or use this handy coupon for ordering:

Bantam Books, Inc., Dept. FBB, 414 East Golf Road, Des Plaines, Ill. 60016

Please send me the books I have checked above. I am enclosing $_____
(please add 50¢ to cover postage and handling). Send check or money order
—no cash or C.O.D.'s please.

Mr/Mrs/Miss_____

Address_____

City_____State/Zip_____

FBB—1/78

Please allow four weeks for delivery. This offer expires 7/78.

Bantam Book Catalog

Here's your up-to-the-minute listing of every book currently available from Bantam.

This easy-to-use catalog is divided into categories and contains over 1400 titles by your favorite authors.

So don't delay—take advantage of this special opportunity to increase your reading pleasure.

Just send us your name and address and 25¢ (to help defray postage and handling costs).